Kiss Me FOREVER

CARRIE ANN RYAN

NEW YORK TIMES BESTSELLING AUTHOR

KISS ME FOREVER

Montgomery Ink Legacy
Book 10

CARRIE ANN RYAN

KISS ME FOREVER

Praise for Carrie Ann Ryan

"Count on Carrie Ann Ryan for emotional, sexy, character driven stories that capture your heart!" – Carly Phillips, NY Times bestselling author

"Carrie Ann Ryan's romances are my newest addiction! The emotion in her books captures me from the very beginning. The hope and healing hold me close until the end. These love stories will simply sweep you away." ~ NYT Bestselling Author Deveny Perry

"Carrie Ann Ryan writes the perfect balance of sweet and heat ensuring every story feeds the soul." - Audrey Carlan, #1 New York Times Bestselling Author

"Carrie Ann Ryan never fails to draw readers in with passion, raw sensuality, and characters that pop off the page. Any book by Carrie Ann is an absolute treat." – New York Times Bestselling Author J. Kenner

"Carrie Ann Ryan knows how to pull your heart-strings and make your pulse pound! Her wonderful Redwood Pack series will draw you in and keep you reading long into the night. I can't wait to see what comes next with the new generation, the Talons. Keep them coming, Carrie Ann!" –Lara Adrian, New York Times bestselling author of CRAVE THE NIGHT

"With snarky humor, sizzling love scenes, and brilliant, imaginative worldbuilding, The Dante's Circle series reads as if Carrie Ann Ryan peeked at my personal wish list!" – NYT Bestselling Author, Larissa Ione

"Carrie Ann Ryan writes sexy shifters in a world full of passionate happily-ever-afters." – *New York Times* Bestselling Author Vivian Arend

"Carrie Ann's books are sexy with characters you can't help but love from page one. They are heat and heart blended to perfection." *New York Times* Bestselling Author Jayne Rylon

Carrie Ann Ryan's books are wickedly funny and deliciously hot, with plenty of twists to keep you guessing. They'll keep you up all night!" USA Today Bestselling Author Cari Quinn

"Once again, Carrie Ann Ryan knocks the Dante's Circle series out of the park. The queen of hot, sexy, enthralling paranormal romance, Carrie Ann is an author not to miss!" *New York Times* bestselling Author Marie Harte

"With snarky humor, sizzling love scenes, and brilliant, imaginative worldbuilding, The Dante's Circle series reads as if Carrie Ann Ryan peeked at my personal wish list!" —NYT Bestselling Author Larissa Ione

"Carrie Ann Ryan writes sexy shifters in a world full of passion and happily ever afters." —*New York Times* Bestselling Author Vivian Arend

"Carrie Ann's books are sexy with characters you can't help but love from page one. These are books with heart and heat blended to perfection." —*New York Times* Bestselling Author Jayne Rylon

Carrie Ann Ryan's books are wickedly funny and deliciously hot, with plenty of twists to keep you guessing. They'll keep you up all night!" USA Today Bestselling Author Cari Quinn

"Once again, Carrie Ann Ryan knocks the Dante's Circle series out of the park. The queen of hot, sexy, enthralling paranormal romance, Carrie Ann is an author not to miss!" *New York Times* bestselling Author Marie Harte

To those who keep me going every day.
I wouldn't be here without you.

Kiss Me Forever
A Montgomery Ink Legacy Romance
By: Carrie Ann Ryan

Cover Art by Sweet N Spicy Designs
Images by Wander Aguiar Photography

All content warnings are listed on the book page for this book on my website.

To be loved is to be yours. Or something like that.

Everly Montgomery

Kiss Me Forever

Falling for your enemy is bad. Falling for the man you only call your enemy is worse.

Reece Fox is a decade older than me but I'm his boss. And if the man growls at me one more time, he's going to learn the true meaning of the Montgomery temper. Yet I can't stop thinking of him.

After losing my fiancé, I've sworn off men, but when Reece does the one thing I never thought he'd do —ask for help—I can't walk away.

Brooklyn Montgomery is too young for me. She's not only my boss, but my friend's family. The definition of forbidden. We both know this. But I can't keep my hands off of her. When we finally give into the heat between us, there's no going back.

Only when a little girl shows up to our work, she changes our world completely with one word:

Dad.

Kiss Me Forever is an age gap, workplace, surprise single dad contemporary romance

featuring Brooklyn and Reece. Each book can be read as a complete standalone. An HEA is guaranteed!

Prologue
BROOKLYN

"Why do I have so many freckles? I think I have more freckles than everybody in the family combined." I scrunched my nose, staring in the mirror. My freckles had been the bane of my existence for longer than I cared to admit. It wasn't that I truly hated them, but sometimes I wished there weren't so many. They covered most of my face, not just my cheeks and nose like my siblings. No, they were on my forehead, my chin, all down my chest. My dermatologist swore I was doing just fine, and it wasn't anything to be alarmed about. It was just genetics.

And yet, none of my cousins had this wide array of freckles. Not even my brothers. And yes, technically they were my half-brothers, as we didn't share the same father, but still.

Riley laughed softly at my side. "You do realize that it doesn't matter what kind of freckles we have genetically? Because although I love you with every ounce of my soul, we don't share quite the same genetics. Some, yes, but not all of them."

I frowned at my cousin, or perhaps first cousin once removed (I could never understand what that meant), then conceded the point. "Okay fine. But your siblings don't have any freckles. And you only have like three. Our dads are twins. You would think we'd look a little more alike."

Riley, the oldest of her siblings, just snorted. "My friend. My cousin, near love of my life. We do look alike. We have the same nose, the same chin. Your eyes just happen to look gray and silver underneath some lights. While mine are boring blue."

"Okay, we don't need to go and comment about who has boring eye color, do we?" Mercy said as she leaned back in her chair. She had her e-reader on her lap and was barely paying attention to us. Considering I knew for a fact that our cousin Lex had kept her up all night doing things I didn't want to think about, I was surprised she had any energy left to even join in the conversation.

"Okay sorry, I love my eyes. I love everything about us. And I love your freckles," Riley said pointedly. "And Duke loves your freckles."

I blushed, that bright pink shining radiantly underneath said freckles. "He does, doesn't he? Once he tried to count each one with kisses, and it took all night." I put my hand over my chest, warmth sliding through me. Then once again I looked down at my left hand, at the new ring twinkling beneath the lights.

"I'm getting married. *Married*. I can't believe it."

"I can't believe Uncle Storm let it happen," Riley said with a smile.

"You know, I grew up with you guys, at least in the periphery. And I know you guys say that your dads are all overprotective and growly, and yet, I don't think so. I think they're just marshmallows."

"Oh they are. Especially for their little girls. However," Riley continued, "you don't tell them that. Because if you tell them that, they get more overprotective just to annoy you. It's sort of how things work."

"Do you think Lex will be like that when he's older?" Mercy asked.

"Duh," Riley and I said at the same time. Then my cousin and I met each other's gazes and burst out laughing.

I loved my family. I loved the depth of it, the immense number of us. Even though we all saw each other often, we were also smaller units. Meaning many times the only family I had and got to see every day were my parents and two older brothers. And Nate and James had that twin thing going on. So sometimes it was just nice to be surrounded by women, the girls I had grown up with. Of all of my cousins, I supposed Riley and I were the closest. We were the same age, had gone through all the same classes, and of course, our dads were twins. And in a family where twins ran rampant, it meant many connections.

I was just sad that Riley hadn't decided to come work with me. Instead, she had gone to organize and practically run the Montgomery Gallery by herself. However, our other cousin Jamie, until recently, was making sure that Montgomery Construction didn't blow up.

I frowned, wondering what we were going to do now that Jamie didn't work here anymore. And it wasn't as if she had moved jobs close by—no, she'd moved to a different state.

"What's that frown about?" Mercy asked as she set her e-reader down once again.

"I miss Jamie. And Libby. Why does our family keep moving to Wyoming? What's so good up there?"

"Ranchers in tight jeans?" Riley asked.

"And on horses. Knowing what to do with their hands? And with that slight accent that doesn't make any sense because they're from Wyoming?" Mercy put in.

"Okay, fine, that's all true. But I don't need a cowboy. I have Duke. He's fantastic." I'd grown up surrounded by healthy and happy marriages. I knew love was real and I could scream from the rooftops that it was finally my turn.

"And you're getting married!" Riley said as she twirled around. Her dress, a handmade piece by one of her friends, flowed around her, and I couldn't help but take a quick photo with my phone. I wasn't the photographer in the family but could do decently well with a point and snap.

"So do you think Patrick's going to propose?" I asked, meeting Riley's gaze.

She and Patrick had been dating for a couple of years and really gelled. He was a nice guy who thought Riley walked on air. As long as Riley was happy, I'd be in Patrick's corner. The moment he broke her heart however—if that ever happened—I'd use one of my trusty shovels and show Riley my ditch digging skills from work.

That's what friends were for.

She shrugged. "Maybe. We're doing great right now though, so if it happens it happens. I don't want to put so much pressure on it that I'm not enjoying the moment. I love him. He loves me. And we've been through so much together. I'm just happy with the way things are."

Mercy stood up and wrapped her arms around both of our waists. "And I'm glad that you guys have adopted me. Being around you two just reminds me that I don't have to sit in my booth alone all day. Even though I might get behind on my deadline."

"Deadline schmeadline," I teased. "Do I look okay? Even with all these freckles?"

"Stop talking about your freckles. They're gorgeous. And I'm glad you're not covering them up."

"I'm just glad that I can find a decent coverage foundation that has sunscreen in it that's not actually full coverage." I shrugged. "I may lament my freckles, but they're me. And it did remind me that Duke loves them."

"Go meet your perfect fiancé, then tomorrow we start wedding planning. I know the moms are going to have fun with it."

"Duke's parents will probably want a say, outside of the Montgomery purview," I teased.

"Maybe, but we still win. We outnumber them," Riley added.

"You outnumber most small towns," Mercy said dryly.

I rolled my eyes and finished getting ready, adding a coat of lip gloss, as well as mascara, and grabbed my bag from Mercy's side table.

We had all piled into her room earlier that day, and I knew one day soon she would move next door, and this house would go up for rent. It was just one more change in the way that our family was growing.

I was ecstatic for Lexington and Mercy. As well as Riley and Patrick. And now I had the man of my dreams.

Before Duke, I'd been the person who dated the wrong guy. All through middle school and high school I dated the guy who wouldn't stand up for me—or even himself. I didn't mind being the strong one. The most vocal in the relationship. I didn't mind being the one to always voice my opinions and stand up for us. But just once it would have been nice if they'd stood up for me.

Duke did that.

I made my way downtown, parking behind my mom's bookshop, grateful for the space since there was no other parking around, and then I walked the two blocks to the restaurant. There were tons of other places closer to us, but Duke's favorite place happened to be a steakhouse by his work.

When I got there, the hostess quickly took me to where Duke was seated, and the love of my life stood up and wrapped his arm around my waist.

"There you are. I've been waiting for you." He brushed his lips against mine, and I sank into him.

I loved everything about this man. His kind eyes, the way they crinkled at the edges when he smiled because he laughed so much. I loved his blond hair, a running joke in our family since most of the men in my life were all dark headed, and apparently the favorite hot celebrities weren't usually blond.

However, mine always had been. I blamed Legolas from *Lord of the Rings* when I had been a kid. It just was what it was.

When Duke lifted my hand and brushed his lips along my ring finger, right underneath my engagement ring, I blushed.

"I'm really enjoying my new jewelry. Though my hand's quite heavy now."

Duke threw his head back and laughed. "That's what I like to hear. Come on, take a seat. I ordered us your favorite sparkling wine. But we can change it if you want."

"That sounds perfect." He knew what I liked and ordered ahead, but never in an overbearing way. I liked being able to just relax after a long day in the gardens.

"I did *not* order any appetizers, because I have no idea what you want when it comes to food. Wine? I'm your man. Not so much with the apps."

I fluttered my eyelashes. "Considering I change my mind every single time we come here, that makes sense."

"And they have specials. So who knows."

I settled into the booth next to him, leaning against his shoulder.

Things just felt good.

We had new bids at the worksite, and while my hands were covered in minor cuts, and no matter what I did, it felt like I always had dirt under my fingernails thanks to my job, I loved it though.

Everything was finally coming to fruition, all of our hard work, and all of my hopeful plans.

Life truly couldn't get better than this.

"Well there's a familiar face."

I looked up at that rough, growly voice and rolled my eyes "Hello Reece." My coworker who I got along with but sometimes couldn't stand because he was bossier than my dad and uncles stood there with his girlfriend, Anya. They looked like they'd walked off the runway. Okay, she did. He was a little too rugged and menacing for that.

"Reece, good to see you," Duke said as he stood up. "Thanks for your help on that one project by the way."

"It was no big deal. Haven't seen you in here in a while."

My fiancé hugged Reece and I slid out of the booth to hug Anya tightly. I knew Reece and Anya had been together for a little while, though I didn't know her well. It wasn't as if Reece brought her to work. And she rarely came to work parties as she had a full-time job that took her out of the country often.

"It's so good to see you and congratulations!" Anya said as she held up my hand. "You did good, Duke."

Duke shrugged, a small smile playing on his lips. "I'll have you know that I asked a Montgomery woman for help on this. I am not going to lie about that."

"That makes sense. We women know our jewelry," Anya teased.

Reece blinked at me, then down at my ring finger. "I didn't know. When did this happen?"

I couldn't help the bright smile on my face as I wiggled my fingers so the ring caught the light. "Yesterday. I'm surprised it didn't hit one of your group chats."

Reece raised a brow. "I'm only involved in one Montgomery family group chat, and every time I try to leave it, somebody adds me back in. And nobody mentioned it in that one, nor the work one."

I snorted. "We enjoy teasing you with family things. Just because you growl a lot. And I'm sorry we didn't tell you."

"Whatever. Congrats to you both. Seriously. But I have to ask. How many family group chats are there?" Reece asked.

"I'm afraid to know that answer, "Anya teased.

"Would you like to join us?" Duke asked, and I smiled. Because even though we were celebrating our engagement, Duke was never going to let friends walk away without knowing they were welcome.

"We already ate, but thank you," Reece said, meeting my gaze. "I'll be sure to check the group chat later," he added dryly.

"And just for that I'm adding you to another one. But I'm not going to tell you when. You'll be surprised." I beamed, and he grunted. And as we said our goodbyes, Reece wrapped his arm around Anya's waist, and the two walked away, looking just as in love as ever.

Reece was a few years older than me and had been in the business longer than most of the people on staff, and I was grateful that he was around. Mostly because it was fun to tease him and his taciturn ways, and because he never complained about the youths, as some other older people in our company often did.

"I hope it was okay that I invited them to dinner. I just know there're no more reservations for the night."

I leaned over and kissed Duke softly on the mouth. "I'm glad you did. I would've too honestly. This place has great food, and they're good people."

"You know, I was jealous of him when I first met him."

I nearly choked on the wine that the waiter had brought. "What? Why?"

"Because he's this ruggedly handsome guy who can

lift most anything at a construction site and is overprotective with everyone that he works with. I don't know, I just got jealous."

"I should feel flattered about that, right?" I asked, confused.

"Maybe. Or maybe I was just a little insecure when we first met."

"You have nothing to be insecure about. We're getting married. And I can't wait. Reece is…well, he's way older than me so I never thought of him that way. You know?" Not quite a lie. A girl could fantasize, but Reece wasn't in the age range I dated so it wasn't a problem. And the old man would never think of me that way. I held back a grin at calling him an old man and knew I'd have to do it in person later.

Duke leaned forward, kissing me again. "And I can't wait either."

By the end of the night, I was exhausted, wrung out by one of the best evenings of my life, and had slept through my alarm the next morning. Duke had left, leaving behind a little note on my pillow. Just a Post-it, a D with a heart next to it. I kissed the note softly and set it on my vanity next to his other sticky notes. He was always doing that, leaving me little notes. And one day I was going to collect them all and make some form of art project with them. More than likely I would ask Riley to help. She was far better at that than I was.

I sent him a quick text to tell him good morning and I loved him and got on my exercise bike to work off any extra energy.

Today my mom and the girls were coming over and we were going to start wedding planning. I would invite Duke's sister and mother for next time. Today though, was just Montgomerys. And I couldn't wait for Duke's family to be mine.

After my workout was finished, I showered and made my way to the kitchen to have an afternoon coffee and lunch. My timing was a little off for the day, and I was glad I didn't have to work. I had been out far too late with Duke, but it was the start of our new lives and I was so freaking blessed. My doorbell rang at that moment, and I skipped over to it, wondering if my mom was early.

"Chelsea, it's good to see you," I said as I wrapped my arms around Duke's sister. She didn't hug me back, but then again, I was a little more exuberant than her.

"I'm so excited about the engagement, aren't you? I mean, we're going to be sisters," I said, practically dancing on my toes.

That's when I finally noticed that Chelsea hadn't spoken. In fact, she hadn't said a single word.

Instead I looked at her puffy eyes, the way she stood there, her skin gray, and my smile fell.

"What's wrong, Chelsea? Is it your mom? Is it Duke?" I asked.

But if it was Duke, I would know. After all, I was his fiancée. Somebody would've called me if something was wrong. His sister wouldn't just be at my door. Maybe she didn't want the wedding to happen. Oh God. Was this going to be one of those times where Duke's family finally told me what they truly thought about me, and want me to break up with him?

My chest tightened, and I watched as Chelsea's lips thinned before she let out a breath.

"He's... He's gone, Brooklyn," Chelsea croaked.

I tilted my head, an odd buzzing sound filling my ears.

"What? Who's gone? Come in and sit down, Chelsea. You're scaring me. Let me get you some water."

But Chelsea flinched as I reached out to her, and I stopped moving.

"Chelsea? Who's gone?" I asked, the urgency in my tone frantic.

"Duke. He's dead, Brooklyn. Duke's dead."

And I have no idea what she said after that, or even

what I did. Because I stood there, the sun glinting off the diamond in my engagement ring, and I watched as the world fell around me.

This was supposed to be my happy ever after. This was supposed to be our everything.

Because there was no way the love of my life was dead.

And it wasn't until pain radiated up my knees, that I realized the screaming I heard was me.

And there would be no coming back from this.

Ever.

Chapter 1

BROOKLYN

I WAS A PROFESSIONAL WOMAN. An adult. And one who could control her urges.

I also wanted nothing to do with men, did not want to date, had no desire to be with anybody, and yet...

And yet Reece Fox kept wearing those damn jeans.

I knelt in the soil at the house next door to his current project, small shovel in hand, and did my best to continue to plant the hydrangeas that would be the focal point of the side of the house. As a landscape designer, I knew how to get dirty. I constantly had dirt under my fingernails, on my knees, and in my hair. I never looked quite put together unless I scrubbed every inch of myself and did an everything shower twice over. It had been a long time since I had done an *everything* shower. A year to be precise. Only I didn't want to think about those times. I couldn't.

I swallowed hard, ignoring the grief in my gut that wouldn't go away, and glared at the man next door.

Why did Reece have to look so good in denim? It

made zero sense. My cousins, brothers, and friends constantly wore jeans while working. We wore blue-collar clothes for a reason. Unless we were meeting with clients, we tended to wear jeans or cargos that could take dirt and scrapes and everything that had to do with remodeling or building homes and businesses from scratch. I had dirt covering me up to my chest at this point, because I had been digging holes for literal trees, so I wasn't looking my best. There was a tear at the knee of my jeans, one that hadn't been placed there strategically by the manufacturer. I didn't want to toss this particular pair because I had worn them in perfectly. I would probably just patch them up or ask my mom to do so. She was much better with a needle and thread than I was.

Reece Fox didn't have a single hole in his jeans. The fact I had noticed how well he filled them out told me that I was probably dehydrated and needed to drink something. I rolled my shoulders back and pulled off my ball cap, letting my hair fall past my shoulders. I'd had it up in a ponytail earlier and had lost the elastic. Now I was just using the back of the cap to create some form of ponytail that was way too loose, and that meant my hair kept sticking to the back of my neck.

I was the epitome of a gorgeous woman, a desirable one, that nobody could stay away from. I snorted at that, and once again pulled my gaze away from Reece's ass.

He bent over, looking at something, and I needed to stop focusing on the way he stretched that denim. His thick thighs tended to do that anyway, since he was all corded muscle and strength. Why did I notice that? Because I was in a self-imposed drought and I was nearly delirious from lack of water.

I stood up, dusted the dirt off my pants, and put my hat back on so I could fix my hair.

I bent over, pulled up my water bottle, and chugged as much as I could. Some of it dribbled down my chin onto my T-shirt, leaving wet spots, but it wasn't as if I cared about how I looked at this point. The clients weren't on the property today, thank God, and that meant I could get my hands truly dirty, and put in as many of the perennials as possible.

I was one of the family owners of Montgomery Construction.

As a Montgomery, I could have gone my own way, found a different career path. I didn't have to go into landscaping like my aunt, but I had loved it. From an early age I had strived in growing things. I would go with my Aunt Meghan to different job sites and learn the real names and common names of different plants, how to dig a hole, and what to do if something wasn't working.

I was usually one of the last people on the job site, because, well, because most people thought what I did was just the cosmetics. My family didn't agree. While my cousin Lex was the architect, and my other cousin Dash was our contractor and foreman, I was right alongside them, as a key element of this business.

And with my cousin Jamie moving to Wyoming to be with the new love of her life—a man I respected, liked, and kind of hated because he had taken my cousin from me—I was also the only woman in the office.

Yes, we employed over a dozen other women in various roles, but it was the three Montgomerys at the lead, and Reece and Cullen right beneath us. Cullen was our master plumber and journeyman—then there was Reece.

A former fireman turned restoration builder. He was the expert in deciding what could be salvageable, safe, and worked with the most delicate of things. He was brilliant when it came to working on buildings that had once dealt with fire, and had leaned into floods, weather damage, and countless other things.

He was an asset to Montgomery Construction, and I knew it. Honestly, he could have gone to work with any other company—including the two other Montgomery construction companies within the family. He could go anywhere in the U.S., with zero ties, and make top dollar.

We didn't know why he was working with the Montgomerys.

Maybe just to annoy me.

Because he was always so damned arrogant when I was around. Overprotective, overbearing, and just plain rude. It didn't matter that while I wasn't technically his boss, I was in a higher place of command. He should show me respect.

There wasn't that big of a difference in our ages. I wasn't some little girl who couldn't handle things. I was Brooklyn Montgomery. I knew what I was doing. And I was damn good at it.

"Miss. Miss."

At that voice, I did my best not to clench my jaw. I couldn't afford to break a tooth so I put on my best smile. How I wish I could only focus on the way Reece filled out his jeans, versus the person I now had to deal with.

"Hello, Mrs. Green. How are you today?"

"I would be better if you could follow a simple direction."

I tilted my head and tried not to react how I desperately wanted to. "I don't understand."

"No. You just don't listen to me."

"What is it that you think is wrong?" I asked as I

gestured towards the landscaping. "We're following the plans. Why don't you talk to me over here so we can discuss it?" I did not want to get yelled at in front of my employees. I had four people on my team right now, all sweating and working their asses off to make sure Mrs. Green was happy. However, based on the way this project had been going, I knew this woman would never be happy.

Ever.

She wore gray slacks and a white blouse with a soft pink bow of some sort on it. She'd pinned her hair back aggressively, and overlined her lips so they looked even larger than natural. And she had beautiful lips to begin with. She wore high heels but didn't step on the grass thankfully. We hadn't had to put down sod—something I refused to do during the high heat of summers—and we were taking our time to ensure that the grass that remained from the start was healthy. Having high heels aerate it probably wasn't the best.

"Look at that. It's a pile of sticks. I want fullness. I want color. I want lushness. And you don't seem to be taking any of my needs into account."

"Mrs. Green—"

"Don't Mrs. Green me, Ms. Montgomery. I need to speak to your supervisor."

"I am my own supervisor. I'm one of the owners of Montgomery Construction. And if you're unhappy with our work, we can discuss it. How about we meet at the office and we can go line by line?"

I didn't have to listen to her berate me. Sure, the customer was always right might be a slogan people leaned on, but not me. I wouldn't be put down in front of my team when I knew for a fact Mrs. Green only wanted to yell. She notoriously did her best to get free things—something I wasn't aware of until after we'd signed her on.

She narrowed her gaze at me. "Do you think I have time for this? I have to meet with the board, and I don't have time to deal with some little girl who thinks she knows what she's doing. It isn't just planting pansies. And if there's a single pansy in this yard, I will be irate. I will report you to the Better Business Bureau."

"Mrs. Green," I said, my voice firmer. She narrowed her gaze at me, her eyes turning to slits. "Everything that you see is in the middle of construction. As I've told you prior, you are welcome to visit in the middle of our project, but it won't look like how you need it to look until the end. Every *single* thing we are doing has been approved by you twice over. If you have a problem, come to me, but do so at the office where we can go through things list by list. I am one of the owners of Montgomery Construction. And I'm not a little girl."

"How dare you speak to me this way. I'm going to go speak to one of the men in charge."

So she was one of *those*. Why not lean into the patriarchy because the patriarchy clearly has aided her in some way. Who cares about a woman having a job or any type of autonomy when you could make sure that the man in charge knew what he was doing. I knew for a fact that the board she spoke of was for a charity. One that maybe held one gala a year to donate money. The rest were just so they could pat themselves on the back and do lunches.

It was the same board my former fiancé's mother was part of. Not that Mrs. Green knew that. In my dirty jeans, and dirtier hair, I did not look like the Brooklyn Montgomery who had once been on the arm of Duke. *Duke Rochester.* But I wasn't that girl anymore anyway. She died right along with Duke.

"Do we have a problem here?"

I nearly jumped at the sound of Reece's voice behind me. He didn't stand in front of me or even beside me. No, he hovered right at my shoulder, but a few inches behind. That way I was still the lead, but now a man could come protect me.

"Are you the one in charge? Are you the one who can control this?" Mrs. Green asked Reece.

"I'm working on the house next door, and I wanted to see how things were going with you and Brooklyn

Montgomery here. She's the owner of the business I work for."

"Hmmph." Mrs. Green mumbled. "We'll see what your boss has to say about this." And with that, Mrs. Green stomped in her high heels to her convertible, slid in the seat, and slammed the door.

I was surprised she had the top down, but then she put a fat pink bow thing that turned out to be a scarf around her head, tied it under her chin, put on large sunglasses, and sped out of the cul-de-sac.

If I didn't hate her, I would admire her fashion sense. Because that was kick ass.

"You okay?" Reece asked, that deep voice of his oddly soothing and annoying at the same time.

"I was handling it," I said as I turned towards him.

"Whatever you say, Freckles."

"Don't call me that."

"I can't help it. You have so many damn freckles. I lean into the name."

"Meaning they're so original? Thanks. I know I'm covered in freckles. Have been for most of my life. Now if you could go back to doing what you were doing, I'll go back to my job."

"I didn't come over here to take over." He didn't snarl the words, but it felt like he wanted to.

"Really? Sure felt like it."

"I came to remind you that we have a meeting

down in the office soon. We were only supposed to work a half day today."

I cursed under my breath and pulled out my phone. I had four texts and one missed call, but I didn't recognize the number for the call, so it was probably spam. Each text was from a family member, and I felt oddly disappointed that it wasn't Chelsea. She was supposed to text me back yesterday, but I knew Duke's sister was busy. She was always busy these days. I ignored the bile rising in my throat at the reasons why and put my phone back in my pocket.

"Thanks for the reminder. And I didn't need backup."

"No, you didn't. Just because you can handle it though, doesn't mean you have to do it on your own. Would you fight with your cousins if they stepped up?"

"Yes. But they know better than to try to act like I'm the little lady."

"We both know that's not what I did. We also know that they would one hundred percent show up to take care of that woman for you. Just like you would for them. It's not a man-woman thing. It's an adult thing. Get over it, Brooklyn." And with that, he turned away from me and sauntered towards his truck. Perhaps it wasn't a saunter, but he always moved with such purpose, that I couldn't help but wonder what was going through his head.

And just because he might be right in his insinuations, didn't mean I had to appreciate them.

With a sigh, I made sure my team knew what was going on, and to contact me if Mrs. Green came back.

My team member winked dramatically. "Don't worry about it, *Freckles*. We've dealt with her kind before."

I shook my head, annoyed with Reece all over again. Though I knew he wouldn't say the name again. "You shouldn't have to deal with it."

"True, but you deal with it for us. Thank you, boss."

I smiled then and headed towards my truck. Reece was already gone, and for that I was grateful. We didn't always work on the same project sites. In fact, we rarely worked together. But we had gotten the contract for two homes in this neighborhood that happened to be side-by-side. Meaning there were plenty of Montgomery workers on call at once, and soon I would be moving over to Reece's side. That is if I ever made Mrs. Green happy.

I drank the last of my water and thought about pulling in for coffee, then realized that maybe I needed to since Jamie was no longer there.

When we had built this subset of the company, Jamie asked to be our house manager. She worked for a few businesses, organizing us, keeping us on topic, and making sure we knew what the hell we were doing, and she was brilliant at it. She still organized us and did the admin for the company. She just did it from Wyoming. Much like she did for the other companies that she worked for.

Jamie also used to bring in coffee for us, knowing exactly what we wanted.

I missed my cousin something fierce. We would eat lunch together and plan shenanigans. We're more like sisters than cousins. And as someone with two older brothers, I liked having another woman in my life. But she was happy, thriving, and the move was good for her.

I quickly pulled into the next set of businesses and parked in front of Latte on the Rocks. It was owned by two women who had married into the Montgomerys and were technically my cousins now. The tattoo shop next door was owned and operated by a couple of cousins, as were the two end businesses—Montgomery Security and Montgomery Gallery. I only felt a little sad that our office wasn't in this area, but it didn't make sense to have a construction and architectural office in a strip mall section of the town. Not that this felt very strip mall. There were gorgeous trees everywhere, and with the backdrop of the Rocky Mountains, you couldn't go wrong.

I walked into the cafe and smiled as Raven stood at

the cash register. She had her dark and hot pink hair pulled back from her face and looked radiant.

"Hey, Brooklyn. I didn't know you were coming in today."

"We have a business meeting, and I figured I would pick up some coffees to go. What do you say, in the mood to make things pretty?"

"Of course. I'm just sad that Jamie's not here to pick them up. Not that I don't approve of her move. I just don't know if I like Montgomerys not living in Colorado."

I pressed my lips together, trying not to laugh. "I was just thinking that. I know it's one state away, but it feels so far."

Between her and Libby living so far away, it's just not fair.

One of our other cousins had married the brother of the man Jamie was with. I didn't know all of the family tree, but it was nice that everybody seemed so connected, and my two cousins weren't alone.

"So how many coffees can I get you?"

"It's way too hot outside, so I'm going to need an iced praline latte."

"Got you. What about for the boys?"

"Lex, Dash, and Cullen will be there for sure," I said, naming off their drinks. I knew they also liked different versions of iced coffees, so they would get what they got.

"Anyone else?"

I grit my teeth, annoyed that I was even annoyed. "And one hot black coffee for Reece."

Raven rolled her eyes. "He's had a latte in here before you know."

I tried not to perk up at that. I did not want Reece Fox. He was annoying. Too old for me, and a man. I did not want to be with anybody ever again.

"Brooklyn?" Raven asked, her voice soft.

"Then get him what you think he likes. I don't know."

"We have a good daily coffee, I'll make sure he gets that." She winked as she said it, and I felt bad. Reece had been nice to me all day, even if he called me Freckles and growled about it. I needed to get over whatever was going on.

I stood off to the side people watching as I waited for my coffees. Latte on the Rocks had grown in business over the years and even during the slower times, there were still countless people coming and going. Raven came forward, coffee carrier in hand, and I reached out to help her.

"Thank you. Seriously."

"It's my job. I also put in an iced praline latte for Reece, because I think he might like that too. Just in case. And a few Danishes because I'm me and I can't help it."

"I love you. Thank you."

"I love you too, boo." She hugged me tightly, and since my hands were full, I couldn't hug her back.

The Montgomerys all hugged and touched and loved one another. But this hug was different. I knew it, she knew it, but there were no words needed.

After all what did you say to a person who wasn't a widow, because they didn't have names for fiancées left behind? Duke hadn't even given me a name or a title before he had decided to end his life. I could be angry with him for that. And sad. And destitute. And every other word you wanted to use to talk about what you said to the person left behind.

Everybody walked on eggshells when it came to me, and I wasn't sure what I was supposed to say to get them to stop doing that. I set everything carefully in my truck, grateful that Raven had packaged it so tightly, and headed down the highway one exit to our office. I was probably running late, but they would just have to wait. After all, I was bringing coffee.

Reece opened the door for me as I walked in, and I smiled up at him, determined to be nicer. "Thank you. Sorry I'm late. I got us coffee."

"Looks like it. I think Lex got some too," he whispered.

I cursed. "I probably should have texted the group chat. We're a little off without Jamie."

"Let me help you," Reece said as he pulled everything from my hands without even bothering to let me answer. Typical Reece.

"Thank you," I bit out, and we made our way to the front desk.

Lexington smiled up at me and pointed to the coffees that he had also purchased. "You've got the better ones, so we can all be caffeinated. Thank you."

"I should say thank you. But did you just get me black coffee?" I shook my head, a smile playing on my face.

"Maybe. I was distracted."

Considering the hickey on his neck, I knew exactly who had distracted him, and I did not want to think about that too carefully. I ignored him and handed everyone their drinks.

When Reece looked down at the two with his name on it, he glared at me.

"I didn't know what you'd want. You seem like a black coffee kind of guy."

"Yes, but I'm going to have this praline iced latte just to annoy you."

"That sounds about right." I shook my head, sipped my delicious sugary drink, and stared at the men in front of me.

Two of them were family, two of them not, but we had all been working together for years at this point. They didn't treat me any different than one another, and for that I was grateful. I just needed to remember that.

"Ready to head to the conference room and get this over with?" I asked, wondering why they were all staring at me.

"Sounds good to me," Lex said. Before we could move though, the door opened, and two older people walked through, as another man in a dark suit followed them.

I frowned, looking down at my phone quickly to make sure that I hadn't missed an appointment.

"Hi, how can I help you?" Dash, ever the people person, strolled up to them, hand out. "I'm Dash Montgomery."

The man who looked like a lawyer, briefcase in hand, shook Dash's hand. "Hello. We're here to see Mr. Fox."

Reece stiffened at my side, and I set down my coffee, ready to do what I didn't know, but it felt like Reece might need someone.

That's when I noticed there was a little girl standing by the older couple, her dark hair wavy around her shoulders, and a glare on her face. But I saw the fear in those eyes, and what the hell was going on? The girl had to be what ten, twelve?

"I'm Reece Fox," Reece said as he took a step forward. That's when I realized Reece's gaze was on the girl as well, and it looked like his face had lost all color.

"So you're Reece Fox," the girl snapped.

The pause nearly broke me, and I wanted to open my mouth to say something, but Reece merely tilted his head, his face still pale. "That's me. And you are?"

"I'm Bella. I guess I'm your daughter."

Chapter 2
REECE

THERE WAS an odd screeching sound in my brain that I knew needed to shut the fuck up. And yet, I couldn't quite get it to do what I needed it to do.

This little girl looked just like my mother. Even if she hadn't said the words aloud, and acting like she wanted to be anywhere else but here, I knew there was something wrong.

The phrase "What the hell" kept repeating in my mind, and I stared at this child, and the three adults with her, wondering if I was truly having an out-of-body experience.

I pulled my gaze away from the little girl and stared at the older couple, trying to figure out if I even knew them. They looked completely unfamiliar, and I wanted to be anywhere but here.

But here I was a forty-one-year-old man, who had lived life. I wasn't a virgin by far, but I hadn't slept around to a ridiculous extent like many of my peers.

I'd dated, been married once, and had always

made sure I wore a fucking condom. These two were not my ex-wife's parents, meaning this girl had a different mother. Although it could all be a lie. Maybe this was one of my brother's kids, but I didn't think so. Not when it felt as though someone had kicked me in the gut, and it all sounded too true to be anything else.

"Why don't you guys take the back conference room, so you can have some privacy?" Brooklyn put her hand on my arm, startling me out of my thoughts, and I turned to her, wondering why that small touch felt so comforting.

I didn't dislike Brooklyn. In fact, parts of me liked her a little too much. We got along except for when we didn't, and that was just fine with me. She wasn't my boss. Dash Montgomery was. And she didn't treat me like shit like some of the other people I'd worked with. She might be a little overprotective and reactionary for some things but considering the hell she had been through in the past year, I didn't blame her. And every job I had been in were primarily male dominated fields, so I knew a little bit of what women had to go through in order to gain any respect. She had my respect. And she was so fucking hot that sometimes it was hard for me to breathe. But I wasn't going to go there. She was way too damn young, and fucking with any Montgomery was asking for trouble or commitment. And that wasn't something I wanted in any shape or form.

I pulled my arm away, ignoring the odd look on her face. It wasn't hurt. It couldn't be. "Yeah. Let's do that." I cleared my throat and looked over at the older couple who sneered at me. In their eyes, I was a deadbeat dad who had fucked their daughter and left her alone to raise a child. Or, this was all a lie, and I had no idea what the hell was going on. Part of me hoped it was the latter. Only the fear on the little girl's face caught my gaze, and it was another kick to the gut.

I found myself in the conference room, Bella's grandparents and their lawyer sitting in front of me. Brooklyn had taken Bella to our lounge to get a sparkling water and a snack, and for that I was grateful. I had a feeling that no little girl needed to hear what was about to be said. The grandparents didn't look like they wanted to part ways with her at all, but the lawyer had urged Bella to go with Brooklyn. It was just one more mark in the column of what I owed the Montgomerys, and I wasn't sure when I was going to be able to pay it. I hadn't said a word since our first interaction, and neither had Bella. What the hell was I supposed to do now?

"Mr. Fox," the lawyer began.

"Call me Reece." My father was Mr. Fox and frankly I needed a moment to catch up.

The older woman lifted her lip in a snarl but didn't say anything.

I stared at the lawyer. "Is what Bella said true? You think she's my kid?"

"You know damn well that's your daughter."

I turned to the older man, at the pure hatred on his face, and raised my brows. "I don't know a damn thing. This is the first time I'm hearing of it. Who is her mother?"

The older woman clutched her bag to her chest, grief etching lines into her face, and a sudden gross feeling slid over me. "You know who she is."

"I don't. If I knew I had a kid out there—which I'm not sure that I do—I would've done something about it." I turned to the lawyer. "Why don't you tell me what's going on?"

"Mr. Fox." A pause. "Reece. I am here on behalf of the Longs. Cassandra Long passed away last month, and after going through probate and her will, we thought it best to come to you directly."

My mind whirled as I tried to put pieces together. *Cassandra Long. Cassie*. I hadn't heard that name in years. Twelve years to be exact. We'd dated for a little while, though we'd mostly only slept together. She'd been going through things with her parents, and I had just left the station, unable to be a fireman anymore after hurting my back. I'd been in the middle of changing careers, and she had wanted a little fun. And we'd walked away without saying another word to each other, at peace. I would've thought so at least.

I reached for the water bottle that someone had left on the table for the meeting, unscrewed the cap, and drained a good third of it.

"Cassie," I rasped.

"Her name is Cassandra," Mrs. Long snapped. "She wouldn't be so lowbrow as to go by Cassie."

Now things were coming back to me, and it made sense. There were reasons why Cassie had wanted to be away from her parents, even though we had been adults. And it seemed they hadn't changed in all these years.

"Mr. Fox, we are here to stay on target," the lawyer stated again, and I didn't bother to correct him.

"What happened to Cassie?" I asked, ignoring her parents.

"After a long illness, she passed away last month. As we were going through the will, we realized that there were a few legalities to go through. You were named as father on the birth certificate." The lawyer continued to speak, but it felt like I was in a tunnel, trying to catch up to the words.

She put me on the birth certificate. And she hadn't had the decency to tell me? There was a bunch of legal mumbo jumbo, and I tried to pay attention, but nothing was making sense.

"Bella wanted to see you," Mr. Long said into the sudden quiet, and I turned to the older man. "We're going to allow that. And frankly, we're getting too old to deal with her. Our daughter wanted her with you, and that means we're done."

My heart raced, my mind whirling. The casual cruelty of his words couldn't have come from that old man's mouth but reality was far too fragile for them not to have. "I'm sorry. What?"

"You've been out of her life for its entirety. You didn't even bother to care about her. But we are going to listen to our granddaughter's wishes and let you deal with the consequences of your actions." I blinked, trying to catch up.

I didn't think that's how custody worked, but I wasn't a lawyer, and I'd never had a child before. I wasn't even sure if she was my kid—looks deceiving me or not. "You're...just giving up a child? To a stranger? That I don't even know is mine?"

"It's not quite like that." The lawyer cleared his throat, sweat beading on his forehead. "We will talk to your lawyer, have a DNA test done of course, but if things go as I believe, we can finish things up quite easily without any need for dramatics."

I held up my hand, rage now warring with confusion. "No. I'm not going to say a damn thing right now. I need to talk to my lawyer. My family." I turned to the Longs. "I didn't know about this kid. I can promise you that. Because if I had, I would've been in her life. I'm sorry about Cassandra, but you just can't come in here and direct how things are going to be. Because if that's my kid, I have rights." Rights that meant I would take responsibility and not have her be treated like an unwanted puppy kicked to the curb. If this was how they acted with me, how the hell did the act with her?

"You suddenly want a child?" Mrs. Long sneered. "Good. Because she's yours. And you *will* be an adult and finally take responsibility."

"Responsibility? You're telling me that I'm a father, but I never knew. I don't know what the hell I want, but it's not your decision, is it?"

Each of them paled as the lawyer clucked his tongue. "Now Mr. Fox, there are avenues—"

I held up my hand, cutting him off. "Let me talk to my lawyer." And with that, I stormed out of the conference room, my hands shaking. This couldn't be true, could it? I wasn't a father. And even if I was, how had I missed twelve years of her life? I wasn't a deadbeat dad.

The lounge was at the opposite end of the hall from the conference room, and as I moved towards it, I heard Brooklyn's laugh, and my shoulders eased ever so slightly. I wasn't alone in this, not with my family, not with the Montgomerys. The Montgomerys never let you do anything alone. But it felt like I was walking through molasses.

I stood at the doorway as Bella and Brooklyn looked over a tablet, both smiling. Were kids her age supposed to have tablets? What grade was she in? Did she have a favorite color? Who were her friends? Did she have any allergies? Did she play sports? Where had she been in her life? So many questions, and I hadn't even known she existed until this moment.

Brooklyn looked up at me then, as if sensing me, and Bella followed her gaze. I turned from Brooklyn to look at the little girl who might be mine, and I saw the fear there.

"Hello, Bella," I said, clearing my throat.

"Did they tell you that they don't want me anymore?" she asked. "I'm a problem."

Brooklyn tensed, and I moved forward, unsure of what to do. I didn't know the legalities behind this, or what was true, but I wasn't about to let this little girl get hurt.

"First, you're not a problem. Never let anyone tell you that. I don't know what's going on, Bella, and if I am your father, then I guess we'll figure things out. But I didn't know you existed, Bella. I can promise you that."

"Mom didn't mention you." She looked down at her hands, and I cursed Cassie and her family for doing this. To Bella. To me. To us.

"We're going to figure it out. It's on the adults to figure it out. Okay?"

She looked up at me with angry, watery eyes and in that moment, I *knew* she was mine, and I told myself that I'd do anything to protect this child.

"I don't know what's going to happen next, but I'm not going to let you get hurt."

"Whatever." She stood up then, and I realized that her grandparents and the lawyer had come in behind me.

"We will talk to you soon. Bella, come with us," Mrs. Long stated as she held out her hand.

Bella sighed dramatically. "I guess I'll see you soon. Or not."

I stared down at her, wondering if I should reach out, or say anything. Instead, I swallowed hard. "No matter what, I'll talk to you soon." How the hell was I supposed to let this kid go now? Her grandparents clearly didn't want her and yet they were taking her away. What the fuck was I supposed to do in this moment?

She met my gaze then, and I didn't know what she saw, but when her shoulders relaxed, I thought maybe I had said the right thing. The lawyer said a few other things to me and handed me his card, and somehow I found myself standing in the lounge with Brooklyn behind me, feeling more lost than I ever had in my life.

"Reece? Can I call someone for you?" Brooklyn put her hand on my shoulder, and I let out a deep breath. As if her touch pulled me back to reality.

"I need to call my lawyer. And I guess my family? We have to do a DNA test or some shit." A metallic taste settled over my tongue and I swallowed hard, trying to focus on what life is going to become.

"Could she be yours?" Brooklyn asked, her voice oh-so-careful. I looked down at her, and resisted the urge to count the freckles that I had always been so attuned to.

"She looks just like my mom, Freckles."

Her eyes widened, going glassy, and she squeezed my upper arm. "Okay. Whatever you need, we've got you."

Lexington cleared his throat as he moved into the room, Dash right behind him. "Seriously, take all the time you need. And well, I want to say congratulations, but that sounds wrong."

"What the fuck am I supposed to do?" I asked. No one had any answers. Of course.

"Did you know her mother then?" Lex asked.

I nodded. "Not well. I mean, we were seeing each

other for a bit, but it wasn't serious. Then we broke it off, and I hadn't heard from her since."

Dash cursed under his breath. "And she never told you?"

"I'm on the birth certificate. Which doesn't do anything if I don't fucking know."

"And I guess there's not an alert or something that lets you know when you're put on someone's birth certificate. Like a Google alert that emails you." Dash tried to make a joke of it, but I couldn't find any humor at this point.

"They…are giving her to me. Or rather…just… letting go? I need to talk to my lawyer because the way they speak about her makes my skin crawl. They don't want her. How could they not *want* her? I don't care if they've been in her life for all those twelve years, because if she's my kid, I'm not just going to walk away. I don't know, something sounds weird about this. It's so fucking fishy, and I'm so far out of my depth I'm drowning."

"You're not alone," Brooklyn said, squeezing my arm once again. "You've got us, and I know your family's supportive. Do you have a good lawyer? If not, we know people."

I snorted, liking her touch far too much. "I would make a joke that of course, the Montgomerys know people, but yes, I have a lawyer for something like this.

I think. Fuck. I thought we were just going to have a meeting about the project, and here I am, living a fucking soap opera."

"I kind of liked the fact that it's not a Montgomery this time," Lex said with a shrug, and that made my lips turn up.

"It does feel out of character that it's me and not you guys."

"Well, you're not alone no matter what," Dash said with a firm nod. "I suppose we should start calling you Daddy now."

Brooklyn tried to hold back laughter beside me, her shoulders shaking.

I glared down at her. "Don't you start."

"I promise I won't. But Reece?"

I raised a brow in answer.

"I think I know the Longs."

I froze. "Excuse me?"

She held up both hands as I whirled towards her. "I didn't know they had a grandkid. And honestly, I don't even know if I've met their daughter. But the Longs, well, they were in the same circles as Duke's family. I think I remember them from a gala or something. But it's been a while."

It felt like the floor caved in under me, and I let out a shaky breath. "Meaning they have money and connections, and if Bella is mine—"

"If you're on the birth certificate, you have rights," Dash said. "And they said they were giving her to you. Like she's a fucking sofa or something."

I rubbed my temples. "I could hate you for that comparison, but they were so damn cold about it. I don't know how any of this works. Why are none of you Montgomerys lawyers?" I asked, trying to put some humor in the situation.

"We'll make sure that next generation has a few lawyers," Brooklyn said, worry on her face. "Take the night off and figure something out. I'm so sorry. From the few moments I had with Bella, she's amazing. She's smart, funny, and she misses her mom something fierce. No matter what happens, no matter what you're feeling or what her grandparents are feeling, there's a scared little girl here. And I know you're going to take care of her. No matter what."

I wanted to soak in the fact that she trusted me, that she believed, but in that moment, I couldn't think.

Because I had a feeling my life had just irrevocably altered to the point of madness.

I was a forty-one-year-old man. Single by choice. And apparently a dad.

Chapter 3
REECE

TRYING to figure out the next steps of whatever the hell my life had become, while on zero sleep, in a slight panic, and wondering what the hell I was supposed to do, wasn't for the weak. In fact, I kept pinching myself wondering when I was going to wake up from this nightmare, and yet it was all too real.

After the lawyer and the Longs left—taking Bella with them—I had stood there, feeling as though I was finally wrapped within that quicksand everybody had been so afraid of in the '90s.

I really thought as a child that quicksand would've been more of an issue in my adult life, and yet perhaps all of that preparation, including a traumatic experience with a movie horse, was for this moment.

I hadn't told the Montgomerys to keep this to themselves, but I knew they wouldn't spread word over social media or outside of their family. But their family included far too many people for my liking sometimes. I wouldn't be surprised if I was the subject of more than one family group chat. And knowing them, they probably already had a plan to ensure that I was taken care of and not alone in my insanity. But this wasn't a Montgomery problem.

This was a Fox problem.

Brooklyn and Lexington had already explained to me that I could have as much time as I needed, although I was the lead on a major project, and there was an upcoming restoration that nobody but me could do. I would cost the family thousands of dollars if I took too much time off. Not to mention Dash was following me on the main project, learning his way around fire restoration because he didn't have any experience.

I had once been the person putting out fires, and now I was the one trying to put things together after the fact. And even though Dash was technically my boss, he was nearly two decades younger than me and wanted the experience. I had so much on my plate without the addition of quicksand, and yet I knew if I needed to lean on the Montgomerys, I could.

Brooklyn had even mentioned that the family had a full childcare system, and if I wanted to have it on property versus at one of the main homes, I could. Apparently in the previous generation of Montgomerys, there had been so many children within all of their blue collar businesses, that they created Montgomery Daycare in order to keep the family business a family. All employees were able to use the system, and it was free. Free childcare just because you happened to work for a family that was fucking insane. But it wasn't as if I was going to look a gift horse in the mouth. one of the best out there.

I ran my hand over my hair, and finally turned off my truck, realizing I had been idling in my parents' driveway for a good ten minutes.

I had spent most of the afternoon and evening the day before speaking with my lawyers, going through paperwork, and realizing that this was a reality.

And now I needed to tell my family.

I should have told them yesterday. I should have called them, in a panic, even though I was forty-fucking-one years old. I wanted to lean on my parents, and have my mommy tell me everything would be okay.

And now I was a dad. Bile crept up my throat. A father. As in, someone with a child.

I didn't even know what grade twelve-year-olds were in. Let alone how Bella did in school, or what friends she had. I didn't know her friends, and I didn't know if she had known about me. From the solemn look on her face the day before, I had a feeling if she did know anything about me, it hadn't been complimentary.

What the hell had Cassie been thinking?

I let out a deep sigh, knowing I couldn't do this alone.

The knock on the window nearly ripped a scream from my throat, and I let out a deep breath.

Denver stood at the window, brows raised, and I realized that maybe I had been sitting in my truck for longer than ten minutes. I gestured for him to move out of the way, and I finally opened the door.

My younger brother looked a lot like me. Dark hair, broad jaw, broad shoulders. All of us Foxes looked pretty much the same. My parents had a new kid every two years until Aiden had shown up, and they had said that that was enough. I had no idea how my mother dealt with four boys, but all of us had graduated, gotten jobs, and were functioning members of society. Of course, none of us had stayed married, or started families, so perhaps we were failures in Mom's eyes slightly.

But then again, apparently I had made her a grandmother over a decade ago and hadn't known. What the hell was I going to do?

"You sick?" Denver asked as he tilted his head, studying my face. "I thought you fell asleep in your truck out there. Mom was going to come out with some soup, or call 911 on you. You're lucky I'm the one that did."

"I'm here too!" Rowan called out, ever the middle child.

I was the oldest, then there was Denver. And while technically Denver was also an eldest child, and the middle child, Rowan loved perpetuating the stereotype. They were all in their thirties and maybe looking to settle down at some point. I had been married before and hadn't planned on doing it again. So I had resigned myself to the fact that I would never be a dad.

Dear God. *I was a dad.* I shook my head, wondering what the fuck I was supposed to do.

"Are Mom and Dad in there?" I asked, gesturing to their home. It was the same house we had grown up in, a rambling two-story surrounded by old trees, with plenty of space for the grandkids my mother had reconciled herself to never have.

Fuck.

"Yes. And dinner's almost ready. It's the Fox family dinnertime. I realize that you hang out with the Montgomerys now, and they do their family dinners often, but we still have a routine."

I rolled my eyes, closed my truck door, and headed towards the house, ignoring Rowan and Denver, who seemed to be bickering about some sports thing. I would usually join in. There was nothing like beating my brothers at fantasy football or hockey or any other thing. We were competitive as hell, and had played nearly every sport that we could through club or school, or even neighborhood planning. We'd had more broken bones than my mother probably could ever think about or want in a lifetime and had been an absolute menace.

When I had joined the fire department, I wasn't sure that my parents would ever forgive me. They had been proud of me, but so damn scared. Then all three of my brothers had followed my footsteps, and my mother had never quite forgiven me for that. My brothers were still firemen, firefighters, and I had taken a different route. One too many falls, one too many strains, so I decided to fix what had been broken after my first job was done.

Maybe my mother would forgive me since I've made her a grandmother, albeit a little late.

"What the hell's going on with you?" Rowan asked, studying my face.

"Are the parents drinking?" I asked instead of answering.

Denver blinked at me and gave Rowan a look. "There's some wine open. Are you okay? Are you sick?"

"I'm fine. I think. Fuck. I might need to get something harder for this."

"Whatever it is, we're here for you. I promise. We'll give you shit for it, because we love you, but you're not alone." Rowan squeezed my shoulder, and I let out a deep breath.

Of course my family would be with me no matter what. Of course they were already worried about me. I knew I wasn't in this alone. Between the Montgomerys and the Foxes, I would never be alone. But nothing felt right in this moment.

"Hey, you're late." Aiden handed over a beer. I took it willingly, and Rowan gave me another look before heading towards the liquor cabinet.

"It's the middle of the week, and we're over here drinking? Well, if we're going to have bourbon, might as well enjoy it," Aidan said as he followed Rowan.

Denver stood by me, tension radiating off of him. "Going to talk about it?

"Let's go talk with the family."

I shook my head, unsure how to start, but as I walked into the kitchen, everything felt like I was going back in time. They had remodeled the house more than once since I was a kid. My dad was a carpenter, and that's where I had learned many of my skills. Mom was an interior decorator, and damn good at her job.

The place looked like a show house and yet still lived in. I had toed off my shoes when I first walked in out of habit, because one did not scuff up these floors or dirty the carpet, but the house still had evidence of little boys who had once lived here. Nicks and scratches that could be buffed out but had stayed because of the memories.

My parents' backs were to me as they hovered over the kitchen island, working on dinner. They had such a routine, and a sense of movement that came with over forty years of being together. They loved each other, fought, made up, and had raised us knowing they were producing children who would grow up into adults and venture out into the real world. They had made a family.

And I hadn't been part of Bella's life. I had lost all of those years, and I didn't know what the fuck I was supposed to do.

"Mom, Dad, Reece has something to say."

I glared at my brother, as my parents whirled, worry on their faces.

"What's wrong?" my mom asked. She wiped her hands on her apron and moved forward. Then she cupped my face and studied my eyes. "Something happened. Talk to me, baby."

"Let the kid breathe," my dad said. Kid. As if I wasn't in my forties. Early forties, but still.

I cleared my throat, unsure how to start this. Maybe I should have done it in the group chat after all. "Maybe everybody should sit down."

"I poured bourbon, it seemed like that type of

announcement," Aiden said, as Rowan handed me a glass.

My parents gave each other a worried look, before my mom pulled me into her arms.

"Are you sick?"

I shook my head. "Why does everybody think I'm sick? Why is that the first thing that comes to mind?"

"Because you're an old man in your forties, and that's what we think?" Aiden said. Then he rubbed the back of his head, since Dad had smacked it like he should.

"Watch who you're calling old, boy."

Aiden rolled his eyes, but I still saw the worry there. I stared at my family, words failing me. Tomorrow I would sign paperwork to get temporary custody of Bella. And I would take her home. I would have a kid in my house, and it didn't make any fucking sense. Her DNA test had already come back positive, having taken less than a day since it had been rushed, thanks to the Longs' money.

I was a daddy, and I needed to say the words. "Something happened yesterday..." My voice trailed off, throat going tight.

Rowan leaned forward. "Just say it, we're here no matter what."

I took a step back, needing to breathe, and thankfully they all let me. I wanted to pace, throw something, or have someone else say the words. But there wasn't anything to do other than blurt it out.

"I have a daughter."

My parents blinked at me, as my brothers stared at me wide-eyed.

"What?" Aiden asked, his voice high-pitched.

"You knocked somebody up?" Rowan asked before ducking my dad's hand.

"Why don't you start at the beginning?" Denver mumbled, looking as pale as I was.

"You have a daughter? Why didn't you tell us? Oh, Reece. You're a daddy. Oh my God, I'm a grandma." Mom's eyes filled with tears, and she threw herself in my arms. She was so itty-bitty, her head fit underneath my chin. I hugged her close and met my dad's worried gaze over her.

"What happened, son?" my dad asked, and I swallowed hard.

"I found out yesterday at work. Her grandparents showed up with her and their lawyer."

My mom took a step back, a frown on her face. "You've met her? What is she like? How old is she? Wait, is she not a baby?"

"Mom," I said as I cupped her face. "Let me just tell you the entire story. Then we can go over everything together. Because I have no idea what the fuck I'm doing."

"Language," Aiden blurted.

"I think this is a good time to say fuck," Mom said as she looked at her youngest son.

That broke the tension, and we all laughed, and I let my shoulders drop. "Her name is Bella. And she's twelve. And I didn't know about her until yesterday."

I finally took a sip of the aged bourbon, before setting the glass down and explaining everything. The lawyers, the DNA test, the twelve-year-old who didn't look like she wanted to be there, and the Montgomerys who were already helpful.

"The entire Montgomery family knows and we didn't?" Dad asked, disappointment in his gaze.

"They happened to be there, and I needed a minute to figure things out before I told everybody here in person. I just got the results back, and I didn't want to worry you in case I wasn't her dad. But I am. And I don't know what the fuck I'm doing. What am I supposed to do with a little girl who is apparently my kid?"

"So they had her all this time and are just *giving* her to you?" Aiden asked.

"I didn't know Bella existed. How the hell was I supposed to be in her life if Cassie hid her from me all this time?"

"Why did she hide her?" Mom asked.

I rubbed the back of my neck, once again wondering

why she'd do such a thing. "I don't know. Cassie and I weren't together for long. We had fun. Then we didn't. And she left. I've been married since then. Divorced. *Lived a life*. I haven't given Cassie a second thought, but I would've stood up. I would've been a father."

"You are a father," my mom said as she patted my chest. "And we're going to help you."

My dad moved forward and hugged me tightly. I held on for a moment, needing that breath, and backed up. "We're going to be with you no matter what. You said you get her tomorrow?"

My throat suddenly went dry, and I nodded. "Her grandfather has his hip replacement surgery set in two days, and they're leaving me with her. Leaving her with me. As if I'm some fucking babysitter."

"That doesn't give us a lot of time to set up your house for a preteen girl," Rowan said as he ran his hand over his hair. "But we can make it work. Mom's a decorator, and we can all lift things. We've got this."

Aiden began to pace. "What does a twelve-year-old girl even want for her room?"

Mom clapped her hands and put on the face she always did when we had to make a plan and stick to it. "We'll figure all that out. We'll make lists, and we'll make sure that Bella has a welcoming home. And she's welcome here too. Because that's my granddaughter."

I nodded, my hands relaxing out of fists.

"You're not going to fight the will, then? You want to keep her?" Rowan asked.

I knew my brother was asking the hard questions because that's what family did, but I wanted to hit him in that moment. "Damn straight. You didn't meet the grandparents. I don't know if I want to leave her with them if they decide they want her back. I haven't even had a full night's sleep in order to come to terms with this. But I'm a dad. This is my daughter. And I'm going to figure out what the hell that means for the both of us."

"Good. Good. And we're going to do it right alongside you. And the Montgomerys apparently," my mom said dryly.

I rolled my eyes, grateful for the humor.

"No matter what, though, that little girl comes first," my mom said softly. "She lost her mom, Reece. And now she's probably scared, angry, and feels all alone. This is going to be hard, baby boy, but you're not alone. I promise."

I stood there in my family's kitchen, knowing that they thought they would be there for me to help with all of this, just like Brooklyn and the others did. But was that really the case? I wasn't sure.

"What does she look like?" my mom asked as she

gestured towards the food on the kitchen island. "Everybody eat. Let's not let this food go to waste."

I smiled softly, as my chest ached. "I wasn't even sure I needed the DNA test at first because she looks like you."

My mom's eyes filled, as I hugged her close and realized that everything was going to change. Somehow, after all these years, I was a single dad, and I didn't know a damn thing about my daughter. No wonder she had looked at me like she couldn't stand me. Now, after this, I would go home, prep my house, and be ready to have a kid I didn't know live under my roof who, I was pretty sure, didn't want to be there.

This wasn't going to go well.

Chapter 4

REECE

Today was the day. An entire day where my life would once again change. All was well and I totally wasn't panicking.

I was completely panicking.

If my mother had any say in it, she and my father would be here, and my brothers would've taken the day off work and filled my house with their rambunctiousness. They wouldn't have let me feel alone and would've welcomed Bella with open arms. I had put my foot down on that. I had a feeling Bella didn't want to do this at all. I said, what, six sentences to her? If that. No, this little girl who apparently had half of my DNA wanted nothing to do with me.

It wasn't like I knew her enough to know what to say or how to handle this. But I hadn't been completely deprived of being near children in my life. Though I wasn't an uncle, my cousins had kids, and so did many of my friends. Hell, most of the fire station had bred like bunnies before I left. The fact that none of the Fox brothers had any children was an anomaly.

I knew kids. Somewhat. I could figure this out.

And this lying to myself thing was really working for me.

We had spent most of the evening and all this morning getting Bella's room ready. I didn't know her favorite colors, her favorite foods, or if she had touch aversion to some materials. Aiden had sensory issues sometimes, which made for strange bedfellows on the job. So we made sure there were no microfiber towels or blankets anywhere near even if she didn't have an issue with them. We'd gone with sage green as her primary color, with soft yellow accents. My mother knew what she was doing and had chosen things. We hadn't painted the room, since I'd put on a fresh coat of paint a few months ago, but if Bella wanted to change it, we would. Maybe she would be like Rowan and go through a goth phase and end up wanting to paint it black. That had nearly broken my mother's will.

Dear God. If she went through a goth phase, what would I do? Was she dating yet? Had Cassie already had the talk with her? How the hell was I going to do this?

I quickly pushed all terrifying thoughts out of my mind as a late model luxury SUV pulled into my driveway. Bella's grandma got out of the passenger seat, lifted her chin, and glared at me. What the hell was I supposed to do about this? It wasn't as if this was my fault. I hadn't been the one to hide my daughter this entire time. And I didn't want to steal her away from them. But I didn't know how they were as grandparents or people. What if they were hurting her? My heart flooded, and I wondered if I needed to hire someone to check that out. My lawyer would know what to do, hell, my family would know what to do. But I had wanted to do this alone today.

"Mr. Fox," Bella's grandmother said, her voice devoid of emotion. I had expected Bella's grandfather to get out of the driver's seat, but that's when I realized he wasn't driving. Instead it was a man I didn't recognize, and I frowned.

"This is our driver, and I decided to sit in the front seat to give Bella some time."

"I hope the drive wasn't too long." I sucked at small talk.

She seemed to think so too, because she merely raised a brow. I waited for Bella to open her door, and when it didn't budge, I moved forward. Bella's grandmother put her hand on my arm, and I froze, wondering what the hell she was doing.

"Mr. Fox. We are following what Cassandra

wanted. You seem to be competent enough. And now you will have to deal with your consequences."

I wasn't sure what Bella could hear through the window, and due to the highly tinted glass, I couldn't even see her. So I did my best not to growl or frown at the older woman.

"Ma'am. Let's have our lawyers discuss that."

She didn't respond but the snarl on her face remained. This wasn't promising. I had no idea what my lawyer would do, or what would happen after the legalities were finished, but that didn't matter. Right now, I needed to get my daughter out of the car.

I opened the back door, oddly thankful it hadn't been locked. For some reason I had assumed she would keep it locked for me—and I wouldn't blame her considering everything she had been through. Bella sat in the seat closest to the door and stared at me. Her eyes were red-rimmed, and her cheeks swollen."

"Bella. It's good to see you."

"Reece."

I held back a wince. She didn't know me and calling me dad or father or anything like that would probably be too much. Both of us were just getting used to this after all.

"I've got your room all set up, if you want to get out and point me to where your things are."

"My room is at my mom's house. Not at yours, and

not at theirs." She'd lifted her chin to where her grandmother stood, and I realized it was going to be even harder than I thought.

"I get that," I said, and I did. I didn't like change either. "How about this… The room that was my guest room that is now going to be yours for as long as you want it, is prepped. I have no idea if you like the color green, but my mom thought you might. So, it is what it is. How about that?"

She raised her brows at me, looking surprised. Hell, I wasn't going to force her to do something she didn't want to do, except she needed to get out of the car. We were like fish out of water, and I didn't want to make it harder than it already was.

"Bella Long, get out of the car," her grandmother snapped.

I looked over at Cassie's mom. "I've got this."

Bella let out a sigh, unclicked her seatbelt, and gestured for me to move out of the way. I took a few steps, and she hopped out of the SUV. She didn't have far to go, as she was decently tall. I had looked up a few milestones for twelve-year-olds, and realized that some were five feet, some were a decent bit shorter. Considering I was well over six feet, I figured she had to be at about the five-foot range. She was slender and wore a double tank top with a light flannel shirt over it, and loose fitting jeans. I didn't know what style that was or what group or clique that meant she was part of, but I figured she would let me know. Probably with a sneer. After all, we only had a few short months until she was a teenager. I could feel the blood draining from my face even at that thought.

The trunk opened as the driver went to the back to get two large suitcases, and I tilted my chin up at Bella. "Why don't you say goodbye to your grandmother, and I'll get your stuff."

"Whatever." She huffed and moved towards her grandmother. I tried not to stare, to give them privacy, but it wasn't easy since we were in close quarters. Bella crossed her arms over her chest and lowered her head.

"Be respectful. And show the Foxes who the Longs are. You are my granddaughter, Bella. Remember that."

"I can't really not."

"Grammar," she snapped.

I took the two boxes next to the suitcases and nearly staggered at the weight. I didn't think this was everything she owned but I'd do my best to make sure she had access to all of her things. She could have whatever she needed to feel comfortable. We would probably have to go shopping multiple times to get her what she needed.

"Her room is second on the right," I said to the driver, and the other man nodded. I looked over at

Bella, who glared at her grandmother, before she turned and walked towards me.

"Welcome to my home." *Our home.* I didn't say that though as I knew she'd throw it back in my face.

"Okay."

Okay? How was that an answer to what I just said. I looked over at Bella's grandmother, who had already gotten into the car, waiting for the driver. When the man moved past us, bags already in Bella's room, he said a quick goodbye and closed the door behind him. The engine turned on and, in a blink, the SUV was gone. I was standing in my hallway, holding two boxes, alone with my daughter. She stood in her doorway, facing the room that I had tried to put together with my family.

"Do you like green?" I asked as I set down the boxes.

Good going, Reece. That wasn't the best way to break the ice.

She looked over at me and snorted, a small smile playing on her face. "Yes. At least you didn't go pink."

I should probably do something about the attitude, but then again, she deserved time to lean into resentment. She hadn't asked for this either. I rubbed the back of my neck, once again out of my depth. "My mom thought green would be soothing."

"Does she live here too?" Bella asked. She still hadn't gone into her room.

"No, but they live two neighborhoods over. Do you mind if I set these down in your room? What do you have in here, bricks?"

Her lips quirked and I counted that as a win. "Books. And pencils. Notebooks. Things like that. I was supposed to go to art camp this summer. Not anymore though."

My stomach plummeted. "Oh. I'm sorry. They didn't give me your itinerary, Bella, or hell... I guess I'm not supposed to say hell."

She moved out of the way but didn't go into the room. Baby steps first. "You can say whatever you want. You're the adult. I'm the kid who doesn't have a choice."

I sighed and set her boxes next to the suitcases. "I'm sorry, Bella. For all of this. I know you're not happy, but we have to figure this out, I guess. Right?"

"Whatever."

"Don't whatever me," I grumbled. "My parents always hated when I said whatever to them in answer."

"So your parents are still alive?"

I nodded and pulled out my phone to show her a photo of them that I had taken a couple of weeks prior. "These are your grandparents. Though I hear these days that people get to choose what they want to be called. I don't know if they're a nana and pop like the people now."

Bella's lips twitched, and I counted that as the biggest win of the day. "They look nice." She leaned forward and stared at my mother. "She looks like me. A little."

I swallowed hard, the emotions getting the best of me. "That's what I thought when I first saw you. Which is why I stared at you like a fish trying to breathe without water."

A small laugh escaped, and my shoulders relaxed marginally. "You did look kind of weird."

"I try my best. But what do you expect, I was just sitting there, enjoying my workday, and suddenly you show up, calling me Dad."

"Mom said you were dead."

The phone nearly dropped from my hand, and I tightened my grip, my throat feeling dry. "What?" I asked.

"She said you were dead, and that's why I never got to meet you. But then later she said that you left, and you didn't want us. But one time she said that you didn't even know I existed. It just depended on the day. Mom liked to lie a lot to annoy Grandma and Grandpa. But it doesn't matter. Mom's dead now, and she's not coming back. And now I get to stay with you until you decide you don't want me."

Anger roared through me, and I knew I had never been as pissed as I was in this moment. She said I was dead?

"That's not going to happen. I'm still here. And I didn't know about you, or I would've been in your life, Bella."

"Whatever." She went pale. "Sorry."

So maybe there was hope for both of us yet.

"You said you had camp? Is there a reason you can't still do it?"

"Grandma said that you didn't want me to, so she canceled it."

I closed my eyes, counted to five, and told myself that yelling wouldn't help anyone. And Bella didn't deserve it. "How about the two of us make a promise?"

She looked at me then, confusion etched on her face that looked so much like my family's.

"We don't lie to each other. Because I didn't know about your camp. Just like I didn't know about you. If your grandmother canceled it, I'm sorry. But I had no idea. It's been a stressful few days, and I'm just trying to catch up here. Maybe we can call the camp, and I can get you back in? Is it a daily thing? Overnight?"

"It was a day thing. They had a waiting list, so I already lost my spot. But it's okay. Whatever. It was just a few hours a day during the week anyway."

"What was the name? We can call them. These are unique circumstances."

"Grandma lied too?" Bella asked, her voice soft.

I reached out and gripped her shoulder, before letting my hand fall. She hadn't flinched, and that was good, but everything was still so damn awkward. "I don't know what your grandma said or did, but I did not know about camp. So we're going to start over. With our truths."

"It was the Montgomery Art Camp. The camp is on its second year and it has to do with their gallery or something. The whole family is like crazy talented, and I was going to learn to work on shadows and things."

Relief flooded me, and I had never been so grateful to be connected to the Montgomery clan.

"Did you notice the building that you walked into when you first met me?" I asked.

She scrunched her nose. "No. I was too busy trying not to throw up."

"Same here," I said with a snort. Bella's lips curled into a smile, and I continued. "I work for Montgomery Construction."

Her gaze shot up. "What?"

"I'm a contractor and fire restoration specialist with them. It means that I try to fix things that were once destroyed. And the Montgomerys own the business. Their cousins own the gallery. In fact I'm friends with a few of them. And knowing their group chat they probably already know about some of our situation. I can't promise you one hundred percent, but I can give you a high probability that I can get you back into that camp."

"Really?"

And for the first time, this was a Bella that I hadn't seen. Her face animated, she was practically dancing on her toes.

My daughter was an artist.

And she liked the color green.

"That would be amazing. I didn't know. You really know the Montgomerys? Have you seen Leif Montgomery's tattoos? I know I'm too young for them, but he's so dreamy."

I blinked at her, wondering what the hell I was supposed to do with that information. "Leif is a friend and married to my other friend." I shook my head, knowing that explaining to a kid that someone in his twenties was married with children was probably idiotic. But here I was, once again out of my depth.

"I don't want to marry him or anything, geez. But he's so good at sketches. And one day when I'm old enough and have the money I'm going to get a tattoo."

Since I was equally covered with tattoos, I couldn't really say anything, but still. I felt like I was going to throw up.

"Leif actually did this tattoo," I said, pointing to a grouping of trees on my arm.

"Really?"

I nodded. "Yes. You're right, they are the best. But maybe no tattoos until you're thirty."

Bella laughed. "Grandma said never, so I guess you're the easier one."

I shook my head. "Oh no, you don't get to pit me against them. I told you we would be truthful to each other, so that means no trying to get your way against your grandparents. Including my parents."

"Fine." She let out a dramatic sigh, and I smiled. There was a little more of the Bella that I wanted to know underneath the veneer of sullenness. "If I get into camp, that means I have a few hours a day with them, but then what am I going to do? You're not married right?"

My heart kicked, and I shook my head. "I used to be. But no, I'm not married. I used to be, but not anymore."

She didn't visibly react to that information. "No kids?"

"Just you," I said dryly. "My wife and I decided we were better as friends, and now she's married with two kids, and they live in Montana. I've been staying in the Denver area, working."

Bella walked around the room, touching everything

as she walked by, before she sat on the bed and began to play with the duvet. "So I don't have any brothers and sisters out there?"

I shook my head. "No. You don't. I would say I'm sorry about that, but I don't know what you want the answer to be."

She looked up at me then, her eyes sad. "I don't know either. Why do you work with fire things?"

This I could answer. "I used to be a firefighter. I liked it, and was good at it, but I got hurt one too many times and decided to go into construction. Your grandpa's a carpenter and taught me all he knew. Your uncles are still in the firefighting business."

Her eyes widened. "I have uncles?"

I cursed under my breath, and she laughed. We would get used to this whole father daughter thing. Maybe. "Yes. I have three younger brothers. And they all want to meet you, but I figured day one with so many Foxes in the house would be a little ridiculous."

"My middle name is Fox," Bella blurted.

My heart did that little kick thing that was so new to me with this kid. "I know. I'm glad she gave you part of me, even though I didn't know you."

"Did you ever save anyone? Or go into a burning building?" She clearly didn't want to get into that and I didn't blame her.

"It was part of the job, and I did."

"How did you get hurt?" The worry in her tone slapped at me, but I didn't know if it was for me, or the fact that she had lost her mother so recently. Poor kid.

"I fell a couple of times, floors giving out, or just the comings and goings of being the person that goes into burning buildings. I didn't need the adrenaline rush like my brothers did."

"Will I meet your brothers?"

"You're not going to have a choice," I said dryly. "They will want to come over and meet you soon. If they get to be too much, just let me know. Maybe we can have a signal."

Her smile brightened her whole face and I knew I'd do whatever I could to make her smile like that again. "Like waving my hands in the air rapidly?"

"We can do that. Or go more subtle. It's up to you." The doorbell rang before I could say anything else, and I sighed. "That is probably one of them now."

"Oh. Well, I guess it's okay to meet them."

Gone was the happy, slightly energetic daughter that I was just meeting, and back was the shy girl who was out of her sense of normal.

"Come on, let's go see who it is. We can get you unpacked and figure out what I missed. Because I have no idea what a preteen girl needs."

"You think I do?" she asked, sarcasm dripping from her.

I had a feeling I was going to like this kid.

When I opened the door however, it wasn't one of my family members. Instead it was the woman who sent the unwanted adrenaline through my system and made my mouth go dry.

Brooklyn Montgomery, with her hair flowing down her back, the sun shining on those freckles that I wanted to count one by one, stood there with a large basket in her hands and a smile on her face.

"Hey there. I know you have the day off, and I thought about just leaving this on the doorstep, but it has food in it, so it's probably not the best place for it." She smiled up at me and then looked down and behind me. Her eyes widened, and she winced. "Oh. I had the timing wrong. I thought I would be here before Bella showed up. I'm sorry. Hi Bella."

"Hi Brooklyn," Bella said softly.

I moved to the side and gestured for Brooklyn to come in even as I took the large basket from her. It weighed nearly as much as Bella's suitcase. "I didn't know you were coming by."

She winced, her teeth grazing those plump lips of hers. "Because I didn't tell you. I couldn't sleep last night because I was excited for Bella." Brooklyn winked at my daughter, and Bella smiled brightly at her. No reservations, no worries. Just a connection between the two of them that snapped into place. What had they talked about during those thirty minutes they had been together in the conference room? And why the hell did I resent the fact that they were so easygoing?

Then again, Brooklyn was a woman and not related to her. It was just a girl thing. I didn't need to be jealous.

"I'm going to drop this off and head out. I brought some of my favorite things when I was twelve." She smiled at Bella, but my daughter just rolled her eyes.

"It's been like one hundred years since then, right?" Bella asked sarcastically.

"Bella—" I began.

Brooklyn pressed her lips together, laughter still breaking through. "Yes. I am so old, and my bones are brittle, but your dad is older," Brooklyn said dryly.

"Excuse me," I bit out, and the girls just looked at each other before giggling.

What the hell was going on?

Brooklyn continued as if I wasn't standing there… being old and decrepit apparently. "I remember you said you like to draw, so I asked my cousin what pencils to get. I'm sure you already have them, but I didn't know if you could bring them here or whatever. So Oliver gave me these to give to you, and a notebook, and a couple of sparkly things because I like sparkle, so I'm going to force sparkle on everyone. Then I brought over a cinnamon raisin loaf and a regular sourdough loaf thanks to Jane Dough. And some fried chicken. As well as a few sides. I didn't know if you guys had any food planned, and I was craving chicken. Not that I'm going to have any. I just need to give things out when I'm stressed."

Brooklyn said all of that in practically one breath, and I blinked at her.

"Thank you. I was planning on either sandwiches or heading out for lunch. I hadn't actually gotten that far." I rubbed the back of my neck as Bella stared at Brooklyn.

Bella leaned forward, wide eyed. "Who's Jane Dough?"

"The name of my sourdough starter." That beautiful, freckled face blushed, and I told myself it was idiotic to not only be attracted to someone I worked with, but to be attracted to anyone in the presence of my daughter. I didn't have time for this.

Bella's entire face brightened though. "Oh, my friend Natalie's mom does sourdough too. She has a little micro bakery. I think that's what it's called."

"I have a couple of friends in my sourdough support group that have micro bakeries. I only bake when I'm stressed or for my friends. So I bake a lot. I have a lot of family and friends thanks to being a Montgomery."

"Oliver Montgomery is your cousin or your brother or something?" Bella asked.

"He is. You know him?" Brooklyn asked, giving me an odd look.

I cleared my throat. "Bella here likes to draw—as you apparently know," I said dryly. I could tell Brooklyn held back a wince at that. I wasn't mad at her for knowing things I didn't, but I already felt two weeks behind. "And there was an issue with summer camp. I was going to call him or Riley to see if they can fix it."

"Oh, what's wrong?"

"Grandma pulled me out of summer camp and blamed it on Reece."

Brooklyn's face fell. "What? Wait, our camp? Not that it's my camp, but it has my name on it."

I nodded. "That's the one. Do you think I should call Riley, or who's running it?"

"Riley runs it, but I can do that. Why don't you guys get settled with the lunch that I'm forcing on you, and I'll handle it?"

"Stay," I blurted, needing support. Because I didn't know what I was doing, and Bella finally seemed relaxed.

Brooklyn gave me an odd look before a smile spread over her face. "I would love to. Because that chicken smells amazing and I was going to steal a piece on my way out."

Bella nodded. "It does smell good."

"Oh thank God, I was really worried you were going to be a vegetarian," I said, only partially kidding.

Bella scrunched her nose. "Steak is my favorite meal. But it has to be medium rare."

I put my hand over my heart and sighed. "It's true. You really are my daughter."

Thankfully, Bella laughed with Brooklyn joining in, and I felt as if maybe we had turned a corner. Maybe we could do this.

As long as Brooklyn was here, apparently. The woman I couldn't stop thinking about. The woman I couldn't have. But the woman who made my daughter laugh. I would just have to deal with all of that. Later.

For now we had fried chicken, sourdough, and the start of whatever the hell life was about to throw at us. I had a feeling it was only the beginning.

Chapter 5
BROOKLYN

"WHY? Why do they even make these things? Why does this even exist?" I gagged, once again washing my hands and trying not to throw up.

The sticky residue had formed a filth on my hands, and no amount of soap and hot water would remove it without scrubbing off a layer of my skin.

"It's not worth it. I just need to throw them away."

But I wouldn't throw them away because they were new, and I had just bought them accidentally.

I glared at the beeswax bowl covers for my sourdough, and rued the day that I clicked the wrong button for add to cart when I was replacing my old covers.

I had tried moving a different direction, using Saran wrap, a towel, and even a regular lid. But because I lived in Denver, the Mile High City, elevation baking meant I needed to be a little more calculated. My sourdough didn't like any of the alternatives. They liked a cover. And I missed the cloth ones my grandmother had made. I know if I asked, she would make more. Or rather, she would teach me how to make some of my own. But after I had worn out my other ones, I thought I could just buy some more and get through the day. After all, I had four bowls on my counter that would bulk ferment for the day while I was at work, and I would come home, shape, add inclusions, and stick them in the fridge overnight. Then, I would bake in the morning.

I needed extra things because I enjoyed baking when I was stressed, and one of my cousins needed three loaves for an event. They hated baking, so I was there for them. They could go to one of my aunt's shops and buy a loaf of bread, or even the grocery store, but I loved giving them things that I made by hand. And they liked my bread.

But beeswax anything? Worst invention ever. Who thought about making beeswax bowl covers? Now they were making beeswax bags to carry the bread in and keep it fresh apparently. That sounded like my personal nightmare.

I didn't usually have sensory issues, but apparently, I'd found my weak spot. After all, I usually had my hands in dirt, rather than dough, but apparently this was my last thread.

I washed my hands once again, grateful that I could finally feel my skin rather than the wax, and went to clean up. I was a decently clean baker, but there was always a handprint of flour somewhere when you were baking and dealing with your starter. I fed Jane Dough, marked my line to see how she would do during the day, set her up by the window so she could get some heat, and went to get ready for the day. I had to work on some paperwork that I wasn't in the mood for, and I wanted to check out a new plant shop that had opened recently. I liked working with three local ones, but I couldn't always get what I wanted for this area. I preferred going native with plants, and each one of the original nurseries that I had used since we'd opened the business had changed ownership. Things weren't the same, and it was grating. It didn't help that all three were owned by men who looked down on me for being the owner rather than someone who should just be playing with cut flowers.

I heard this nursery was owned by a woman, and I was going to lean into women power at this point, because being called little lady was the final straw for me.

I showered, blew out my hair, and quickly added a little bit of makeup, but not much really. Mostly just tinted moisturizer with sunscreen, and mascara. I would be digging in dirt for most of the afternoon, and I wasn't going to look fantastic by the end of the day.

Of course, nothing was going to cover those dark

circles under my eyes. I hadn't slept well the night before, and who could blame me?

I had no idea what had pushed me to drive all the way to Reece's house and barge in as if I had a right to be there. We were barely friends, and he annoyed me to no end most days—just like my cousins did—but he was a good man who looked scared as hell about becoming a father overnight. Especially to a nearly teenage girl.

I liked Bella. She had an attitude, but who didn't at twelve. I knew that her words and actions were more of a shield to protect herself, and I hoped Reece did too. She was scared. She had lost her mother, and I wasn't even sure if she had fully grieved or begun her grieving. I didn't know what would happen when it came to Reece, but I had seen the way he looked at his daughter as if she were a breath of fresh air, and the most magical thing in the world. In that moment, everything had clicked for him, and I knew he would burn down the world to protect her. Even if he had no idea how to talk to her or what to do with her. It was kind of nice seeing the sure and growly Reece who always knew what he was doing—even if he told me what to do at the same time—look out of his depth. Maybe it was wrong for me to get any satisfaction out of that, but maybe Reece deserved it too.

I knew I would be seeing Reece today at the project

site, though I didn't know if Bella would be coming with him, or if she would be at the Montgomery daycare. She wasn't old enough to be alone, and honestly, I didn't think it would be good for her to be alone at Reece's house when he was at work. While we had offered for him to take as much time as he needed, he was the only person who could work on this particular project. Stepping back now would derail everything, and we would lose tons of money. Frankly, I knew my cousins and I didn't care about that. We'd find a way to make it work, but Reece wouldn't let us flounder. So we weren't going to let him do so with Bella.

And why was I spending my morning thinking about Reece?

Or the way that he always crowded around me? Or the way that I couldn't stop thinking about him at the most inopportune times?

I put my hand over my heart and let out a deep breath. I didn't need to think about him. I had to think about Duke. And the fact that he had left me. He'd left us all. I looked down at my vanity and opened the small box next to my jewelry. He used to leave little sticky notes around the house. Reminders of where we were going, little moments of thinking of me. He had been so sweet with notes like that. That he hadn't left a note when he had decided that it was all too much.

And Chelsea hadn't gotten back to me yet. His sister and I hadn't been close, but we had always spoken to one another. We'd always answered each other's emails and phone calls and texts. And it wasn't as if I was trying to bother her. I had a serious question about the upcoming gala, but she didn't want to talk to me.

I couldn't blame her. Duke was gone. And I wasn't part of the Rochesters anymore.

And here I was, fussing and turning all night thinking about another man. I slammed the box shut and picked up my phone.

"Time to go to work."

I checked on my sourdough one more time, grateful that my stretching and folding was done. I would deal with it when I came back. As my house was decently cool, it would take a long time to ferment.

My phone buzzed as I got in the car, and I looked down at the screen.

DASH

I will meet you at The Plant Nook.

I scowled and called him rather than text since I needed to drive.

"Hey there, Brooklyn."

"Dash. Why are you going to The Plant Nook? I can handle an introduction to a new nursery on my own."

"I'm sure you can. But Jake said the owner was hot, and well, I can't just leave you alone with a hot woman."

"Are you fucking kidding me right now?"

"Of course I am," Dash said with a laugh. "I have no idea if she's hot or not. I don't even know her name. But I want to check out the new nursery before we head to the project site. You'll do all the talking, I'll just be there. I promise, I won't step on your toes. But the place looks nice. And frankly, I don't want you to go to a new place alone."

I sighed, wondering how my dumbass cousin could be so sweet and so stupid at the same time. "I'm going to be fine. We're not going to Landry's Nursery again."

"Because the new owner touched you," Dash growled.

"The new owner tried to kiss me, and he put his hand on my side. He also got a knee to the balls. I handled it on my own."

"You shouldn't have had to."

"And there's my overprotective cousin. You do realize that I have two older brothers, right? The twins are just as pushy as you are. I don't need any more older brothers."

"Technically, you're older than me."

"Therefore I don't need a pushy younger brother."

"I'm going, and you can't stop me."

I sighed, knowing it was true. And I hated the little part of me that was glad he was going to be there. I could take care of myself and I did so often. But the weirdness of what had happened at Landry's Nursery had been a shock to all of us. I hadn't pressed charges, because there really wasn't anything to do about that, but we had closed all of our contracts with them. I just had to hope that The Plant Nook had what we need.

I pulled into the nursery, which seemed to be hopping even though it'd only been open for twenty minutes. A smile played on my face as I looked at all the plants behind the gated area and through the glass of the green houses.

"Beautiful," I whispered. I loved plants. I loved trees and flowers and everything about growing something new. I wasn't fully into Cottagecore, but between sourdough, the numerous amounts of plants and landscaping I had, and learning how to knit, I was leaning into it just a little bit. I got out of my truck and walked towards the office. I wanted to meet with the owner and give her my card before I took a look around. If I liked what I saw, maybe we could talk about a contract. Or at least a connection.

"Brooklyn, wait up."

I rolled my eyes but waited for Dash as he came towards me. He had pushed his dark hair out of his face, and his beard was getting a little long.

I smiled up at him, and hip checked him. "Intruder."

"What? You're stuck with me. Lex would be here too, but he was waylaid by Mercy." He raised a brow, and I snickered.

"Those two tend to be waylaid in the mornings daily."

"I don't want to think about it," Dash said tightly.

Lexington and Mercy were still new in their relationship but had known each other since they were kids. And the number of times I had walked in on them around the office, his house, and even my house once, with their hands all over each other, was a little ridiculous.

We made our way into the office, and Dash went off to the side to check out plants or something, and I went to speak with the woman in an apron. She had light eyes and beautiful red hair that she piled on the top of her head. A redhead with an affinity for plants would probably bring out all my cousin's desire to discuss Poison Ivy and the Batman universe, but for now, I couldn't help but wipe the sweat off my palms and introduce myself. I was always nervous when it came to things like this. Especially with family around. They might not be judging me, but I wanted to prove that I could do this on my own.

"Hello, I'm Brooklyn Montgomery from Montgomery Construction. I was hoping I could talk with the owner or somebody in charge."

"Hi. I'm Aly, and I'm the owner of the Plant Nook. I've heard about the infamous Montgomerys." She winked as she said it, and I didn't know if I should be nervous or not.

"Oh. Well, it's good that I'm talking to you then."

"Don't worry. I've only heard good things. And I'm going to try to lure you to use my business."

My shoulders relaxed, and I laughed.

"You and I are going to become fast friends then, because I am in need of a new nursery."

"From what I hear, Montgomery Construction works with the big three around here."

"Is there a plant nursery underground chat system I don't know about?"

"We know all and keep our secrets."

"I'm working with two of them, I'm no longer working with the other."

"Please tell me you're no longer working with Landry." She cursed under her breath, and winced. "Sorry. I shouldn't talk about my competition like that. Not that he's competition," she bit out.

"No we're no longer working with Landry. And I have a feeling there's a story there on your side."

Aly shrugged, but I saw something in her gaze.

"Maybe once we get to know each other, we can trade stories over a drink."

"That sounds like a plan."

"Well, let me show you around, and we can talk. I know you guys work on new businesses and restorations, and I would love to work with you."

"We're Montgomery Construction, not Montgomery Inc. or Montgomery Builders. Though I will always pass your information along."

"Oh, I know about you guys. Don't worry, our secret organization of plant people have paperwork for that."

"What's so funny?" Dash asked as he came over to the front counter and leaned against it.

"Hello there," he practically purred, and I rolled my eyes. "I'm Dash Montgomery."

"Aly." She held out her hand, and he shook it. He didn't lean down and leer, instead he was the perfect businessman. Like I said, my cousin could be annoying at times, but he protected our family business no matter what.

"Do you work in landscaping as well?"

"No, I'm in full contracting, but I'm here to annoy my cousin."

"I hear there are a lot of Montgomerys." She gave me a look, and I laughed.

"You don't even know the half of it. But don't worry, I'll protect you from Dash."

"Hey. I haven't done anything wrong."

"You haven't. Yet," Aly said with a snort.

"Well, I see the two of you are in cahoots. I'm going to go look around before I head to the project site. See you there?" Dash said.

I nodded. "Thank you."

"Anytime, cuz." He sauntered off, and I watched Aly watch him walk away. Interesting.

"I have a feeling he was here to make sure that you're safe from certain people I met," Aly whispered.

I stiffened but finally nodded.

"We'll talk about that incident over that drink. But Dash is good people. I promise. He didn't want me to be alone for our first meeting."

"It's sweet of him. I hate that you even had to think about it though."

"Funny thing is I didn't think about it. He did."

Aly looked to where Dash had walked away, an odd expression on her face, before she gestured towards the other door.

"Let me introduce you to my favorite plants."

"You are speaking my love language."

By the time I pulled into the project site next to Reece's truck, I was energized and had already marked a few plants for my own home, let alone an upcoming project site. I needed to finish the landscaping today for this project, and then I wouldn't have to deal with this owner again. Then I would move over to Reece's, and I'd be by his side. Daily. Making things work.

I moved to the side of the house, ready to talk to one of my team members, and nearly bumped into Reece.

He looked down at me and gripped my arms so neither one of us would fall. I had my hands on his chest, and I sucked in a breath and licked my lips. His gaze went to the action, or at least I told myself it did.

"I see you're finally here." His words were low and growly as usual. Yet nothing was usual.

Teeth gritted, I took a step back. We lowered our hands, and I ignored the odd feeling of sadness when he wasn't touching me anymore. "I was checking out the new nursery. I found us a good one."

"Better than that asshole?"

Of course Reece knew what had happened. He was best friends with my cousins who never stopped gossiping about me.

"Yes. We're no longer working with Landry's. But I'm going to love working with The Plant Nook. I know it."

"That's good." He ran his hand along the back of his neck and then gestured behind me. I turned, confused, until I saw Bella moving forward. She had on a hat, her hair pulled back in a ponytail, and looked a little out of place, yet freaking adorable. "I had to bring Bella here because, well, I don't know what to do."

My heart ached for this little girl and the father she'd just met. The same man who'd always turned me into knots—even though I hadn't known what those reactions meant at the time. "When does art camp start?"

He named the date and I nodded, relieved Bella would have an outlet. "She wanted to come to the site and frankly, I won't be here that long. I just wanted to show her what I do, I guess. And I don't know, I didn't want to leave her at the child care in the first week. I'm losing my mind."

I reached out and put my hand on his arm. I regretted it the moment our skin touched, but I didn't back away. "I'm glad you're showing her part of your life, but you don't have to work today either."

"I don't know what the fuck I was thinking."

Bella came up to us before he could say anything else. I reached out and tapped my finger along the brim of her cap. "I love the Montgomery hat."

"I'm part of the team now," Bella said with a roll

of her eyes. She turned to her father, not meeting his eyes, her chin raised. "Reece, do you think I can sit in your truck? I just want to draw or something."

He studied her face. "Sure. We can make that happen. Or we can go somewhere. We don't have to stay here." He sounded so lost, that I couldn't help but step in.

I was probably making a mistake, but I wasn't going to let my friend flounder. "How about this, do you want to volunteer to help me work on a few of the flower beds? We're almost done over here, and I can show you a little bit about planting. And I say volunteer, because of, you know, the whole child labor law thing."

Bella's eyes brightened, and she looked over at Reece for a moment before glancing back at me. "Really? That sounds fun. Mom and I used to plant posies sometimes. But she would always kill things, and I don't know what I'm doing."

"I can totally teach you. If that's okay with your dad." I paused. "I mean, Reece."

Reece cleared his throat, before reaching out and squeezing my shoulder slightly. I ignored the burn of his touch, and the fact that he was touching me at all. "Give me about an hour to finish this up, and then I'll come out with you. Maybe Brooklyn can show me a thing or two about planting. I'm not great at it."

"But you have flowers in front of your house," Bella said, confusion on her face.

My ears heated, and I knew they were bright red. "I planted them. His front lawn looked so sad, so one day I just came by and did it without asking. I'm a terrible friend."

Bella began to laugh, and Reece let out a sigh. "Yes, the nighttime gardener. You never know when flowers will just pop up in your yard without permission." He snarled at me, though his eyes were dancing.

It had been at the beginning of spring after the last frost, and I knew he only let me do it because I had still been wallowing in my own grief. I was better now, I didn't think about Duke every moment. The fact that I had even looked at the notes today was a surprise to me. I wasn't the broken, shattered person I had been before. And it was because of small things—like Reece letting me attack his yard without permission.

We met each other's gazes, and I had no idea what was in those beautiful eyes of his, until finally Bella touched my arm. "Brooklyn? Are you okay?"

I blinked, tearing my gaze away from Reece, wondering what the hell was wrong with me. His daughter was right next to us for fuck's sake.

Not that anything was happening. It was just so not the time.

"Oh, I'm fine. I just need to get my hat because I'm a little overheated."

Reece grunted something, and I ignored him. It was best to do so.

"See you in an hour?" I asked Reece.

"If you're sure..."

"I really don't mind, Reece. I like Brooklyn," Bella answered.

I didn't know why that made me so happy, and I couldn't read Reece's to see what he felt about that.

"That's good. Today's a weird day, Bella. I promise I won't leave you to walk around a job site like this again. We're just figuring things out."

"I know. And you guys got me back into camp." She brightened up, and I couldn't help but see Reece in her.

"I'm glad it all worked out," I said.

"Thank you. Seriously." Bella wrapped her arms around me, and I let out a shocked gasp before I hugged her back. It was a quick hug. One moment she was there, the next she was gone, looking a little embarrassed. But I had to blink back tears. I risked a look at Reece, and once again I couldn't read the expression on his face. Was he happy that Bella and I were bonding? Or did he resent it? Or maybe I was thinking too hard.

"We'll be right around the front, don't worry. I'll keep her safe."

"I know you will, Brooklyn." He cleared his throat at that announcement that nearly sent me over the edge—of what I didn't know—and turned to his daughter.

"Listen to Brooklyn. And stay within her eyesight of her at all times. I know you were doing so with me already, and I'm grateful. But please, be safe. From now on, I won't take you to a place where you can get hurt. Okay? Not that you can get hurt here. Hell."

He was so cute when he rambled. And that was enough of that line of thought.

"It's fine, Reece. I like seeing where you work."

I think Bella was surprised at that admission, as was Reece. And instead of letting them wallow in their discomfort, I moved forward and held out my hand.

"Come on, Bella. Let me show you the wonderful world of flowers. Of course, you had to miss the day where I had to dig a trench and plant trees, but maybe next time. I could use those muscles of yours."

"You planted trees? But you're so small."

"She's stronger than she looks," Reece said, and I nearly tripped over my feet.

We waved goodbye to Reece and walked towards the front of the house. I had no idea what to do about Reece Fox. I had a feeling anything I did was probably the wrong thing. No matter what, the only thing that mattered was the little girl at my side. The little girl who was nearly my height to be honest. She was hurting, scared, lost, everything I felt a year ago. Like me, she wasn't alone. We weren't going to let her feel that way. She had Reece, his family, and she had the Montgomerys. As long as I remembered that there was another person in our lives who could be hurt as well. And I wouldn't think about Reece in any way again.

Chapter 6
BROOKLYN

HEAT BLASTED my face as I opened the oven, annoyed with myself for not putting in my contacts before I'd started my day. I quickly took out my two loaves, set them on the oven top, closed the oven door, and finished my process. They would cool on the wire racks while I got ready for the day, and I would bring them in to work. I hadn't slept well the night before, or the night prior to that. So my stress breaking had reached an all new level. I knew Lexington was annoyed with me for bringing so many carbs into the office, but between our teams, and people who came in for meetings, everything was eaten, and it meant my cousin didn't need to indulge himself.

Today was a jalapeno cheddar loaf and an apple spice brown sugar loaf. The apple one was ridiculously large because of all the excess liquid, but I was calling it a win.

Jamie would've loved this one. I ran my hand over my heart, annoyed that I was upset that my cousin and one of my best friends was gone. She wasn't gone, gone. She was happy and getting married and living in Wyoming along with our other cousin, Libby. They had their whole lives ahead of them, and I was proud of them. But I hated that they had left me behind.

I frowned, because that wasn't a good thing to harp on. They had found their happy ever afters and were living their lives accordingly. I'd thought I'd done that myself already. After all, I thought I'd found the love of my life, what more did I need?

I just hadn't realized we hadn't been on the same page.

I shook my head and pushed those thoughts out of my mind. No, I wasn't going to think about Duke today. I couldn't. Not if I wanted to focus.

I grieved him. I missed him. But I knew it was time for me to move on. And baking every other evening wasn't the way to cope.

I quickly showered before doing my hair. I had a couple of meetings and also needed to head out to one of the newer contracts we had. And since I would be meeting the committee that had worked on the historical preservations campaign, I needed to look a little nicer than usual. I added product to my hair, diffused it, and pulled it back in a loose braid. I'd be able to undo the braid and let it fall in waves around my face later. I didn't bother covering up my freckles, but I added sunscreen, some tinted moisturizer, and a little extra mascara and eye shadow. I wouldn't be working outside for too long, so that meant I wouldn't sweat it off, and I would still look nice for the committee.

Not for a certain coworker that I would be seeing today.

I blew out a breath, annoyed with myself for letting my thoughts go down that path once again. I didn't know why I suddenly couldn't stop thinking about Reece. Maybe it was because he was going through his own set of changes. That had to be it. I was worried about him and Bella, and how they were making do, and nothing else. It was totally not anything else.

I packaged up my bread loaves and got in my truck. I needed to head to the office first and go through a few pieces of paperwork, so dropping off the bread would be easy. Now it was time to schmooze.

Honestly, Dash was the best at schmoozing. It wasn't that he was insincere about it, but he was good at reading other people. And he can make anybody in his circle feel welcome. That was probably why I needed to keep him and Aly apart.

I snorted at that, knowing it was probably true. I liked Aly. A lot. We'd already had one quick coffee, and I had a feeling that I'd just found a new friend. But I had also seen the way Dash had smiled at her, and that meant I couldn't let my cousin ruin a good thing for me.

Not that he would do it on purpose. Dash didn't want forever right now, and while that was all good and well, I kind of wanted to keep one friend that wasn't married into the Montgomerys. A totally selfish thing to think, but maybe it was okay to be selfish today.

I grabbed my things as I pulled into the parking lot and checked my phone. Still no answer.

It was fine. It had to be fine. Duke's family no longer needed to be connected to me. They were grieving, and had lost their son, brother, cousin, and grandson. They didn't need to worry about the girl he'd left behind. I wasn't family. I was nothing. And the sooner I remembered that, the sooner I would be able to move on. No matter what move on meant in this case.

"Here, I got the door," a deep voice said from behind me. I nearly tripped over my feet, and a blush covered my cheeks. I hadn't even sensed him approach. I was off my game.

I looked over my shoulder, trying for a smile that conveyed that I hadn't been up far too late for the past two nights dreaming of him.

"Oh. Hi, Reece. You're early today."

He raised his brows at me and gestured for me to walk past him. I did so, cringing. What the hell was wrong with me? I could usually speak around Reece just fine. Okay, that was a lie. I'd always been a little off when it came to him. Probably because I was usually so nervous. He was an attractive man. And he didn't see me as anything but a co-worker. One he growled at when he thought I wasn't doing something right. There. That's what I needed to remember. He was usually an asshole to me. And that helped me get through whatever I was thinking of in that moment.

"Was there some form of bake sale that I missed?" Reece asked. Without saying another word, he took both loaves from me, as well as the muffins, bagels, and garlic knots I had made. I really didn't get much sleep these days.

"What? No. I just felt like baking. And you guys get to reap my rewards."

"You're lucky that I burn so many calories on the job," he said dryly. He shook his head, glaring at the bread, and I tried to reach out and take the bags from him.

"If you're going to be mean, you don't get any."

"The bread you brought a couple nights ago was good. Really good. And the fried chicken. I should probably learn how to do something like that."

Shocked he'd even mentioned me coming over without asking, I pressed my lips together and went into the break room. Without words, he helped me take everything out of the bags and set it on the table.

"I'm glad you guys liked it. Well, you liked it. Did Bella?"

"Of course she did. You're a damn good cook, Brooklyn. And baker. Whatever you want to call yourself."

"I'm a gardener who likes to plant trees. I just happen to have a sourdough starter."

"Thanks though. For everything. I'm not good at this you know. Saying thank you… or having to rely on other people."

"Oh. You don't really have to thank me for that. And you're doing great. Bella's at art camp today, right?"

It was the first day and my cousins were all excited for it. They had started the camp a few years ago, even before the gallery had opened, and now had a full on waitlist. I might've felt bad about using my family connection to get Bella back on the list after her grandparents had summarily kicked her off, but I didn't really. She deserved a little bit of happiness and sameness from before, and I would do whatever I could to make it happen.

"Well, I hope she has fun. And you didn't have to waive the fees. You guys pay me pretty well." He rubbed the back of his neck, and I forced myself not to look at the way that his biceps bulged as he did so.

I cleared my throat, knowing my face was bright red.

"Seriously, don't worry about it. It's our Father's Day gift to you."

I had blurted the words, and he stared at me, eyes widening. Then that small smile crept over his face, and I tried not to look like I was ready to pass out at the sight of it. I was losing my damn mind.

"Thank you. I don't know what I'm doing most days, but I appreciate it."

"It's been over a week now. Do you guys have a routine?"

"Maybe? She doesn't scowl at me every time we're in the same room together, so I'm counting that as a win."

"She's been through so much, and I know you both feel out of your depth, so if you need anything, you just let me know. Okay?"

"You've done a lot already."

I shrugged, lowering my gaze.

"I don't mind. Bella's a sweet girl, and it feels like she always wants to learn things."

"You helped her that first day on the job, making sure she wasn't alone. And yes, I could have taken the day off, and I probably should have, but she was doing so well with you, and frankly, I think we both needed something to do out of the house."

"I get it. And don't worry. All of us are here if you need it. How's it going with your family? Are they excited?"

"Yeah," he said, clearing his throat. "I think my parents are over the moon that they can finally call themselves grandparents."

"Mine are waiting grandparents as well, but they're out of luck."

"Your brothers haven't decided to go out there and have all the kids?"

I laughed. "Oh no. Not yet. James though, maybe. He and his wife have been talking about it, but I don't know if Nate ever wants to settle down," I said dryly. My brothers were twins, and each had gone through different versions of hell on their own. James had been married for over six years. He'd married his high school girlfriend, Sarah right out of college. James and Sarah worked for the school for the deaf, as James had been born deaf. My entire family knew sign language and did our best not to get rusty. I didn't know when James and Sarah would be ready to have kids, but my parents would be ecstatic.

"I've met James. He's nice. So is his wife."

An awkwardness settled in, and I realized that the two of us didn't spend much time alone. Nor did we talk about our families. But perhaps Bella had changed all of that. Or I was reading too much into this uncomfortable conversation over bread.

"Did you ever think you'd want kids of your own?" Reece asked.

He froze as soon as he said the words, and I had a feeling he was just as surprised they'd left his mouth as I was. I swallowed hard, trying to come up with an answer.

Because the thing was, I wanted kids. I grew up in a decently large family, and if you added all of my extended family, we were loud and boisterous. Some of my cousins had five or more siblings. I had two older brothers that I loved with every ounce of my soul. We didn't share the same father, but you wouldn't know that with the way the Montgomerys had pulled all of us in.

"You don't have to answer that. I'm sorry." He cursed under his breath. "I keep fucking up when it comes to you."

I looked at him then, amazed he had even said the words. Who was this man? This wasn't the Reece that I knew. Or maybe it was the Reece that I had always pushed away.

"Maybe one day. Duke and I had thought about it. Had talked about it even. But finding time was a little difficult at first. We were going to wait. Then he didn't." I shrugged before Reece could say anything. And then my world changed yet again. "One day I'm sure James will be the practical son that he is."

"Honestly, I thought one of my brothers would have kids first."

"They were never on your radar then?"

He shook his head, and an odd sadness filled me. "Not that I didn't want them. She didn't want kids, and I was fine with how we were. Until she wasn't fine and we divorced."

It was like a kick to the gut. I had forgotten he'd been married once. But then again, he was forty-one. He had lived a whole life so far, and had so much more to give. And he would do that for Bella. "You're going to be a great dad. You're a great dad already."

He snorted. "I'm not. Seriously. I have no idea what I'm doing."

"My dad had no idea what he was doing when he came into my brothers' lives. Well, I guess he was always there." I smiled at the memory. "Actually, my dad was there when the boys were born."

His eyes widened. "I didn't know that. I knew you guys had different fathers, but I didn't know that your dad had always been there for your brothers."

I swallowed hard, wondering how detailed I should get into the family lore. "My brothers' birth father passed away before they were born, and my dad was friends with him. So he sort of came into my mom's life to take care of her, and it turned into something more a little bit later. My dad didn't know how to be a dad, but he'd already been living that life without knowing it." I winced. "Of course, it turns out that Nathan and James' dad had a secret family and so there's even more siblings on that side, but in the end, my dad is the best dad I know. And he takes care of all of us. Including my brothers' half siblings that I just call siblings because it gets confusing if we don't."

Reece's eyes widened comically. "I did not know that family story. I know you Montgomerys have your issues, but hell."

"I know, right? But it doesn't matter. Not really. We're all one big happy family. And I'm somehow the youngest who doesn't get to walk out of the house without big brothers watching over me."

"That's what brothers are supposed to do. My three younger brothers had to deal with me as it is."

"And now Bella has a bunch of uncles who will love her no matter what. She's blessed. Even if this isn't exactly how life was supposed to go. You've got all of us behind you. No matter what."

"Excuse me, I didn't realize I was interrupting."

My hand dropped as if I was scalded, and I

whirled to see Chelsea standing in the doorway, notebook in hand, her chin raised. The hurt in her gaze blinked away before disdain was all that remained.

What the hell was Duke's sister doing here? I searched my mind for who we were supposed to meet, and I swallowed hard, nearly choking.

"Hello there. You're not interrupting anything. We're discussing bread. Are you here with the Restoration Institute?" Reece said, giving me time to figure out what the hell was going on.

What was Chelsea thinking? With me touching Reece's arm like that. It was such a betrayal, that I nearly let the tears fall. But no, that was wrong. Duke was gone. He had been the one to leave. He left all of us. And it wasn't as if I was moving on. Especially not with Reece. And yet I couldn't help but let the sense of dishonor wrap its spindly claws around my throat.

"Yes. I seem to be the first one here."

I moved forward and rolled my shoulders back. "Chelsea. It's good to see you."

"Is it? For somebody who continues to text me even though you haven't gotten the hint, you seem to be moving on quite quickly."

I staggered back as if struck, but before I could say anything at the viciousness of her tone, Reece was in front of me, and I resented him for it.

"The meeting room is across the hall, let me take you there. Ms. Montgomery here was just setting out some of the things she brought from home."

"I don't care. If this is how this business is run, I'm not sure the Restoration Institute needs to work with you."

"Chelsea," I gasped. "What's wrong with you?"

"What's wrong with me? You continually text us as if we want to hear you. And yet here you are, touching another man? You constantly try to hook yourself into our lives when you're not wanted. You seem to have moved on in a blink of an eye."

"Okay, that's enough. If you don't want to work with the Montgomerys, fine. We have a waiting list. However, I remember your name from the documents, and you're at the bottom of the ladder from what I see. You don't have the right to make these decisions. Do you?"

"I don't know who you think you are, but we're not having this discussion. I wasn't talking to you."

"And you don't get to talk to her like that."

"Reece. It's fine."

"Reece, is it? Well, how long have you been seeing him? Were you fucking him when my brother was alive? Maybe that's why he did it."

I hadn't realized I had even stepped toward her, until I was in her face, shaking.

"Don't. Don't dishonor his memory like that."

"You're doing it enough for me."

"And that's enough of that," Reece said, as he slid between us, pushing me out of the way. He didn't touch Chelsea, and for that I was grateful. She was just the type to sue if anyone ever dare crinkle her precious suit.

"Go. Your business is done here."

"Like we would ever work with some blue collar Montgomery."

"Is something wrong here?" Dash asked as he moved forward, the glare on his face so deep that I knew he'd heard enough.

I tried to hold back tears, but as a single one fell, I knew it wouldn't be the last.

I had no idea what I'd ever done to make Chelsea lash out like this, but I wanted to throw up. Or scream. Or do anything but fight back. Because how was I supposed to fight back to the lies she'd just spewed? My stomach whirled, but Chelsea just glared.

"I think I've seen enough here. We'll be using another company."

"No. You won't. You signed a contract, and from what I know, you don't have the authority to cancel it. However, your boss does. So why don't we talk with them? Reece?" Dash asked, and I had no idea what it meant, but Reece just gave him a tight nod, before

Dash, Lex, and a few others in suits practically pulled Chelsea away.

I had no idea what was being said, but my hands shook, and I looked at Reece's back, wondering what the hell I was supposed to say.

"I didn't— I don't— I'm sorry."

"Come with me," he snapped, and I took a step forward without thinking. Then I froze, realizing that I couldn't go with him.

"I need to fix this. I can't have this encounter hurt the contract."

"Fuck the contract. I was right when I said we don't need them. Dash was just making sure he put her in her place."

"I don't know what just happened," I said, shaking my head.

"Come with me," he ordered again. He pulled me by my arm and practically dragged me out the back door. Thankfully, no one else was around to see. Then I was outside, the sun on my face, and I bent over, hands on my knees as I tried not to throw up.

"Breathe," he ordered. And then he handed me a bottle of water that I hadn't even known he had.

"I'm fine. I promise."

"You're not fine. And you shouldn't be. Was that Duke's sister then?" he asked.

I flinched at the sound of Duke's name but nodded.

"Yes. She hasn't texted back in over a month, but I thought she was just busy. I didn't realize she hated me. Or blamed me for her brother killing himself."

As soon as I said the words, I stood, my hand over my mouth. I'd never said those words out loud. It wasn't fair to anyone. Suicide was a terrible thing. To the person who took their own life, just the thought of it was unbearable. Because it was something within them that couldn't fight back. But to the rest of the people left behind, there were countless emotions that thrived. Loss, anger, confusion. And now blame. There wasn't one right way to deal with this loss, or to deal with what happened after. I didn't blame myself. I had enough therapy and strength within me to not do so.

But Chelsea blamed me.

And I didn't know what I was supposed to do with that.

"Fuck her. It wasn't your fault. Do you understand me?" Reece pinched my chin and forced me to face him.

"I know it's not my fault. But why does she blame me?"

"Because she's hurting, and it's easier for her to lash out at you than actually feel something. But fuck her. She's a bitch, and I don't care what she's feeling right now. She can go to hell for all I care. She doesn't get to hurt you just because she's hurting. Duke hurt you enough."

"I didn't even know he was in pain."

"People hide things so damn well, Brooklyn. We both know this." The awkward silence settled between us, and I swallowed hard. But his hand had moved to cup my cheek, and I stood there, letting him. "We'll never know why. But that's not on you. It's what he thought he needed to do, and it sucks, and it's painful, and it's not fair. But it's not on you. And I'm not going to let Chelsea hurt you."

"Why are you being so nice to me?" I asked, unsure I could speak on anything else he had just mentioned. He was saying all the right things, all the things that I needed to hear, and all the truths that wound between us. But if I focused on them, I would break. So instead, I focused on him.

"You know why," Reece whispered. Then he lowered his head, cursed under his breath, and his lips were on mine.

I stood frozen in his touch, for a bare instant wondering how I hadn't woken up from this nightmare and dream wrapped in one. But then his tongue brushed along mine, and I was lost. I put my hands on his chest, unable to do anything but let him kiss me, and there were no thoughts left, nothing but his taste, his touch. And when reality finally settled in, I pulled away from him, chest heaving.

"Why did you do that?" I asked as I put my fingers over my swollen lips.

"Because I'm a glutton for punishment." And with that, Reece walked back into the building, leaving me alone as my world shifted off its axis.

Chapter 7
BROOKLYN

"He did what?"

I moved to the side as a small child began to skip down the pathway and winced at Aly.

"He kissed me." I tried to whisper the words, but it felt as if I were screaming them across the void.

It didn't matter that we were in a public place, and countless others were milling about as they got their mid to late season plants for their home do-it-yourself gardens, I felt so lost that I could barely even keep up with my own thoughts.

"And? Why? How? How was it? What happened next? Did you talk about it? Is this the first time? Oh my God, I have so many questions and you're not saying anything."

My lips twitched at Aly's enthusiasm, and in that moment, I knew telling Aly first was the right choice.

Unlike nearly everybody else in my life, she didn't know my family. She didn't have a history or a full connection as to who we were. She hadn't dated or been with any of my cousins or numerous other family members. In fact, I was pretty sure the only two people in my family that she had met were myself and Dash. I wasn't even sure if she'd met Dash outside of those few moments where he had given her a look and then shuffled away because we were working.

"I don't think I have any answers to those questions," I said after a moment. I moved closer to her so I could whisper. While I didn't know anybody around us, the pipeline of Montgomery information was oddly quick. You just never knew.

"You have to have at least one answer. So Reece. He's worked with you for how long?"

My teeth worried my lip, and I forced myself to calm down. It was a kiss. An accident. I could talk about it and get over it. Then I'd go home and make way too much bread. "For a while now. He used to be a firefighter. And he's worked with a few other construction crews. Now he does fire restoration and contracting directly with us."

"Ooh. A firefighter. I would say something inappropriate, but I'm sure that has to get old."

"Considering his three younger brothers are still firemen, probably."

"And are they single?" Aly asked, nearly bouncing on her toes as we moved towards the fruit trees.

"I don't know. It's not like Reece and I talk about

personal things. Except that's all we've been talking about lately with the whole Bella situation."

Aly's expression changed. "That has to be terrifying. For both Bella and Reece. But he has a supportive family. Right? And he's not married?"

"I think his parents and brothers are supportive. He gets along with the Montgomerys as we work as a family. Like, he's part of a big family of his own. And no, he's not married, Aly. He kissed me. He's not a cheater."

"That's good. That's good. So, he just kissed you out of the blue?"

When I had shown up to go through a few spreadsheets and talk plants for the upcoming season, I had just blurted out that he had kissed me. She didn't even know Reece, and she was trying to be supportive. And here I was, rambling.

"Not exactly. I mean, there's always been looks."

"Interesting."

I shook my head, my lips twitching even as my stomach revolted. "Not like that. I was with Duke. And we were happy." Or so I thought. "And whenever I saw Reece out he had a different woman each time. Not that it was often, but I've never actually known him to date anybody. He was married for a bit, then wasn't. It's like all of my single cousins who just date around."

"He must have kissed you for a reason. It's not like he just fell on your lips."

We paused by another grouping of trees, and I let out a breath, trying to find something to do with my hands so I wouldn't wring them in front of me.

"Brooklyn?"

"I think he kissed me just to calm me down."

"What happened?"

I let out a shaky breath before going through the long story of Duke, the restoration committee, my baking, and then about Chelsea.

Aly's face paled, before she took me by my arm and tugged me to the side by the employee area. "She did what? Oh, Brooklyn. I'm so sorry. Did you tell anyone in your family what happened?"

"Considering Dash and Lex were there, I'm pretty sure the entire family knows what happened yesterday." I stopped for a moment. "And I've been dodging calls from my parents, so the grapevine has been worked."

"I know Duke's sister's hurting, but what a bitch. And I don't use that word lightly. She has no right to take her pain out on you. You're hurting just as much."

I wiped away tears, angry they were coming again. "I don't know what I did to make her think I deserve that. But she is hurting. And I guess we weren't friends. I thought we were, but we weren't. And that just adds a whole other layer of betrayal and brutality to this grief thing. I want to be angry that he's gone, but that seems selfish."

"It's not selfish to have feelings. And you're allowed to be angry that the life you thought you were going to have is gone."

I looked at Aly then, knowing she was saying the same words my family had said before, but it was still hard to believe them.

"The vitriol in her words. I just don't understand. And she thought that—" I shook my head. "Well, she thought that I was with Reece, and she lashed out."

"Ah. He kissed you, so maybe you think that part of what she said was right? But she's wrong. Even if you and Reece just had sex in the middle of the break room, it isn't any of her business."

I pressed my lips together, trying not to laugh. "I'm pretty sure that's nobody's business other than the fact that I shouldn't be having sex at work. And I'm not. At all. Not with Reece. It was just a kiss."

"Your voice got quite high-pitched just then," Aly said dryly.

I rolled my eyes, feeling slightly lighter and yet still panicked. "I don't know what's going to happen with Chelsea, or what I'm supposed to do about Duke's family."

"Nothing. If that's how they're going to treat you,

and, come on, if his parents haven't reached out either, then that's on them. You do nothing, and you find a way to move on. Maybe not with Reece, but maybe not *not* him."

"It's kind of hard to cut away all parts of a life I thought I was going to have."

"Brooklyn," Aly whispered.

I shook my head and lifted my chin. "I know. I know. I really am okay. Which sounds trite in a way, but I am. I want to be happy. I want to find this new Brooklyn and not cry every time I think about Duke's family. But we're working with a major group that the family happens to run. And not only is it a good project for the community, it's going to bring in a lot of money."

Aly's eyes widened. "Oh. I didn't realize you were talking about Chelsea Rochester."

I froze, ice sliding down my spine. "You know the family?"

Aly pressed her lips together and nodded. "I know of the Rochesters. I'm not in that circle, and I don't want to be, but I know of them. The committee however, they do good work. They're not going to let personal matters get in the way of things. If they did, the circles of old money would never get anything done," she added dryly. "Anyway, let's go look at that list of yours. And you can tell me all about this kiss and if you want it to happen again."

She changed the subject quickly, and I understood, some things were off-limits. But the fact that Aly seemed to know the world of the Rochesters, and all the old money that came with it, was indeed interesting.

"Can I ask one thing?" I whispered.

"Maybe. But there are some things I don't want to talk about. Okay?"

"As somebody who has certain subjects she never wants to discuss anymore, I understand. But, if you know the Rochesters, do you know the Longs?"

Aly's eyes widened. "Yes. Not well, but I do."

"As in Bella Long. Reece's daughter."

"Oh." Aly shook her head. "I don't know Bella, but I know her grandparents. That poor girl."

I reached out and squeezed Aly's arm. "What do you mean by that? Is she okay?"

"I just mean about losing her mother. And Reece is her father? I guess I have been out of that world for a long time now."

I went on to explain everything in detail from the time Bella had shown up at the office until now. "I don't know how it will all work out. What I do know however is that there is a little girl in the middle of all of this, and if Reece is the man that I know, he's going to do all that he can to protect his daughter."

"Now I have even more questions."

"Brooklyn!"

I turned, heart racing at the familiar voice, as the subject of our conversation ran towards us. She'd pulled her hair back in a tall ponytail and smiled brightly. Bella skipped towards us and waved, and I looked up to see Reece walking briskly behind her, an odd expression on his face that I couldn't read.

I hadn't seen him since he'd walked back into the office after kissing me. He hadn't been there when I'd returned. In fact, only Lexington was there as Dash had taken the committee to do what they needed to do, and Reece had gone to the project site.

This wasn't awkward at all.

"Hey there, Bella. How was art camp today?"

"I love it so much. Your cousins are the best. Like legit."

I blinked and looked up at Reece, mouthing the word legit.

He rolled his eyes and held up both hands. "Hello Brooklyn."

"Reece."

And look at that, we were adults, who happened to know each other's names.

"Hi, I'm Aly. I own the nursery. I take it you are Bella and Reece?"

I could feel my face heating as I looked over at Aly, wide-eyed.

"Oh. I'm sorry. Aly, this is Reece and Bella, Reece and Bella, this is Aly."

"Hi. You own this plant shop? It's so pretty. Reece brought me over to help me pick out a couple of things for the yard." She looked down at her feet and squirmed a bit. "I know you helped me and showed me a few things at the house, Brooklyn, but do you think you could help me pick out more? Reece is good at it, but I bet you'd be better."

"And just like that, shoved to the side," Reece said dryly.

"Oh. I'm sorry," Bella said, her face paling.

I could see Reece wanting to curse, but he held out his hand and patted her shoulder awkwardly.

"I was just kidding. Brooklyn here is the best plant person I know."

"Hey, I am the queen of plants." Aly winked.

"Oh, so now we're going to have a competition?" I teased, trying to lighten the mood.

"Well I tend to kill plants, so you both beat me," Reece added.

"You don't kill them, you still have a few things

alive in the front yard," Bella told Reece, as if trying to reassure him.

My heart nearly expanded two sizes.

"Brooklyn planted those," Reece explained.

Bella's gaze turned to me, as Aly snickered at my side. Yes, it seemed I'd have more to explain to my new friend.

"So what are you in the mood for?" Aly said as she clapped her hands. "This girl over here pretty much knows the layout of my shop already. I need to go help a customer over there, though since my team is waving at me, but if you need anything else, let me know. Brooklyn, you've got this?"

I would have thought she was trying to push us all together, but there was indeed a young teenager waving her down.

"I can help, no worries," I said, grinning as Aly skipped off to help her team and actually run her business, leaving the three of us behind.

An awkwardness settled in before Bella leaned to the side and nudged me with her shoulder.

"Will you really help us? I know you're probably busy."

"I'll really help. I was looking for plants for my own yard, because I can't help myself."

"I'm surprised you have any space left," Reece pointed out.

"Excuse me, there's always room for plants."

"Well Reece has a lot of room," Bella mock whispered.

"I'm sure we could find something to fill up those spaces."

"It's the wrong time to plant flowers. Isn't it?" he asked.

"Yes. It's a little late because of the high heat, but there're other things we can do. Don't worry, I promise I won't go too crazy."

"I feel I should just hand over my credit card now."

I held up my hand at the same time as Bella, and I looked down at the girl, realizing I didn't have to look down too far, and we both burst out laughing.

Reece let his head fall back and he groaned. "A menace. Both of you."

"I try," I teased.

"Will you come with me this way? I saw a stone turtle that looked really cool."

"Lead the way," I said, as Bella moved forward, and I glanced over at Reece.

"If you want, I can head out. I didn't realize you two would be here."

He shook his head and pushed a lock of hair back behind my ear. I tried not to lean into the touch, but goosebumps pebbled my skin. "She likes you. I realize that it may be a lifeline, but she's easier when you're around."

"Oh," I said, feeling oddly disappointed.

"And I like you being around too, Brooklyn." He shook his head. "Even though I'm not good for you."

And with that cryptic comment, he moved to follow Bella, leaving me alone for a moment. I had been panicking before over his kiss, wondering how I was going to ever forget it. And now it seemed I had a whole new level of panic to add. Because Reece's daughter liked me. And I liked her just as much. But Bella's father? I could see myself easily falling for him. And that sounded like a recipe for heartbreak.

Chapter 8
REECE

"WHAT DO I have to call them?" Bella asked. She wasn't looking at me, her attention out the passenger side window, but that was fine. After all, with the bright blue skies, and the park filled with a small community event, it was much more interesting than anything I had to say.

"You can call them whatever you need to. Within reason."

She looked at me then, a brow raised.

"I know that look. I see that look in the mirror."

"No you don't," she said, and I let that slide as well. We were not having a good morning.

I'd woken up late thanks to dreams that would not let me out of their grip. There was no need for me to be dreaming of Brooklyn like that. Just like there had been no need for me to grab her like I had and stuff my tongue down her throat. But that was neither here nor there because it wasn't going to happen again.

Of course, my dick last night hadn't agreed with me, and here we were.

Breakfast had been a fight, as Bella hadn't wanted a single thing in my fridge but wanted to go out to a fancy coffee place for a pastry and sugar laden drink. And while part of me wanted to just let her have her way because I was tired, and unsure what to do, I didn't want to set a precedent. Bella was hurting, I knew that. But she was also pushing back with everything she had because she had no idea what the fuck she was doing, just like I didn't. We made a team, a team that I wasn't sure she wanted any part of.

Well too fucking bad, because we were both stuck in this situation, weren't we?

"But do they want to be called grandma, grandpa? Or grandmother and grandfather. That's what I call my mom's parents."

Her voice quieted. As I turned down my parents' street I tapped my fingers along the steering wheel, trying to formulate an answer. My daughter was just as lost as I felt. Just the idea I could say the phrase my daughter scared me. I had lost so many years of her life, she'd had twelve years of thinking I was a deadbeat—or dead.

"You should ask them. My parents are nice, you know?"

"Whatever."

"Bella."

She sighed. "Sorry. I'm sure they're nice."

My lips twitched. "They are. They will be just as cringe as you need them to be."

"We don't say cringe anymore, Reece."

"Well, I do. And I'm not trying to sound like I'm one of the kids."

"Well, good. You're too old for that. What are you, like seventy?"

"I know you're trying to get a rise out of me, but I would look damn good for a seventy-year-old."

"You're not supposed to curse."

I nearly winced but pulled into my parents' driveway. "I'm going to curse a lot. I've had my whole life without a kid there, so I'm not used to holding back. Your uncles are going to be worse." The fact that I'd somehow kept them away from her until this point had been sheer force of will. The art camp was familiar to her as she'd done one similar with her friends before, so that hadn't been a true adjustment. But grandparents and a set of uncles who wanted to shower her with love had been too much for her—she'd said as much.

And now it was time to take that step.

She shifted in her seat and looked down at her hands. "What if they don't like me?"

The softness of her voice nearly broke me, and I swallowed hard.

"Bella."

She didn't respond, so I reached back, and tapped her knee. Her gaze shot to mine in the rearview mirror, and I didn't blink.

"They're going to like you, kid. They're going to love you. And not just because you're mine."

"Are they nice?"

I thought back to the four of us running wild as kids, beating each other up, protecting the others from bullies. The fact that we still gave each other shit and tackled one another because we could. There was no such thing as tackle-free football on Thanksgiving in the backyard. Not for the Fox kids.

"They are."

"It sure took you a long time to think of the answer."

I undid my seatbelt and unclicked hers. "You're an only child, so I don't know how to explain the concept of siblings."

"I'm your only child that you know of."

I winced. "Touche, but we're going to go on the statistical possibility that I don't have any other kids out there."

"That's fine with me. Brothers and sisters seem like a lot of work."

That made me grin. "Believe me, I know. My brothers, your uncles, are a lot. But then again, I think most people in our lives can be. They're going to overwhelm you, but no matter what, they're going to be there for you. So if you need anything, and don't want to come to me, you can go to them. I promise."

"What about Brooklyn?"

I stiffened in my seat, my hand on the door handle. "What do you mean?"

"Can I come to her too? If I need anything." She mumbled the last part, her head down, and I swallowed hard.

"Yes. If you need something, Brooklyn will be there for you. Do you like her?"

"She's nice. And well, I don't know. I like the bread."

That made me grin. "I like the bread too. And Brooklyn is nice."

"Is she your girlfriend?"

I blinked. "No. She's my coworker."

"Okay. Do you have a girlfriend?"

"You know, we've had how many days now alone, and you're just now asking the twenty questions?"

"So the answer is yes?"

"No, Bella. I don't have a girlfriend. You are the only girl in my life."

"That's pretty sad."

I looked at the front of the house and realized that we had an audience.

"Not to worry you, but my parents and my brothers are all in the window staring at us. I have no idea what they did to hold my mother back from running out here and just pulling you out of the car and hugging you."

Bella's face paled. "She's a hugger?"

I pressed my lips together, trying not to smile. "I'm sorry, kid. I think we all are."

"Oh well. The Montgomerys are huggers too."

That made me burst out laughing as I opened the door.

"Don't even get me started on the Montgomerys."

"I didn't realize there were that many kinds of cheese." She laughed with me as we jumped out of the truck. Apparently, the Foxes could not hold my mother back anymore.

"Well, that's a good sound to hear. Hello, Bella, I'm Reece's mother."

Mom moved forward but didn't reach out and hug Bella. Although with the way that she gripped her hands together, I knew she was practically seething inside at not being able to.

"It's nice to meet you."

"Hello, son," my mom said, then went to her tiptoes and kissed my cheek.

"Hello, Mom. You're doing good," I whispered.

"So are you," she said, not bothering to whisper.

"My name's Katherine, and I don't know if you're ready to call me Grandma yet, but you're welcome to call me Ms. Kathy if you like."

"Mom," I put in, but my mom just held up her hand and waved me off.

"Go inside and make sure there's room for Bella to get into the house. Your brothers are annoying me."

Bella's eyes widened, and I just snorted.

"Welcome to the family, Bella," I grumbled.

"Ms. Kathy's nice. I like your name."

Bella sounded as awkward as I felt, and I was sort of grateful that I wasn't the only one in this situation.

"I love your name as well. Now come inside and meet your uncles. I want to apologize now on behalf of whoever raised them."

"Wasn't that you?" Bella asked. My mother gave me a look even as her eyes danced.

"Yes, but as any good mother does, all of their bad traits come from their father."

"I heard that," my dad said as he moved towards Bella.

"Welcome to our home. And I just want to say that it took all within us to keep your grandmother away from yours and Reece's home. You have no idea the energy it took."

I rolled my eyes at them, as Bella found herself standing in the middle of our living room, surrounded by Foxes. I'm sure there was a predator versus prey analogy in there somewhere, but I was too worried about my kid to think any more deeply than that.

By the time Bella was introduced to all my brothers, my mother finally got her hug in, as did my dad. Denver, Rowan, and Aiden all gave her space, and Bella's shoulders relaxed after only a few minutes.

When my mother took Bella outside along with Aiden and Rowan to check out the landscaping, I found myself in the kitchen, with my dad handing me a beer.

"Just the one."

"I know the rules. Plus I'm driving with my kid now."

"Holy cow. Can't believe you made me an uncle." Denver ran his fist over his chest, and my lips twitched.

"Yes, because this is all about you."

"She's beautiful, you know. I assume she got that from her mother?"

"Ha-ha. And you know as well as I do that she looks like Mom."

Denver winced. "I feel like I just went gross there."

"You mother is beautiful, jackass, stop being a weirdo," my dad said as he slapped the back of Denver's head.

I sighed and leaned against the kitchen counter as I

watched the four of them out in the backyard. "I've no idea what the fuck I'm doing, Dad."

"Your mom and I didn't either. By the time we got to Aiden, we just gave up."

"Can I please tell him that?" Denver asked.

I knew they were trying to lighten the mood, but I felt just as lost as ever. I listened as my father and Denver spoke of nonsensical things, each letting the others in the family get the know Bella on their own terms. I knew they'd trade positions soon that way they didn't overwhelm my daughter.

My daughter.

It was still crazy as hell to think those words.

"Bella sure seems interested in landscaping," Denver drawled out, and my gaze shot to his.

"What do you mean by that?" I hadn't meant to snap the words and my brother's eyes widened.

Denver raised a brow. "I don't know. Why do you seem so protective? Could it be that it's because she's spending time with a certain landscaper?"

I set my beer down and turned my back to the others so I could glare at my brother and father. "Where are you getting your information?"

Denver just grinned. "I think you forget that I'm friends with Dash Montgomery."

"I hate you."

"You and Brooklyn, huh? Well, I don't mind that,

but are you sure it's a good time to start up a new relationship?" my dad asked.

"First, I don't know how the Foxes and Montgomerys have suddenly been on the same gossip grapevine shit, but I'm done with it. Second, Brooklyn and I are not together. Bella just formed a connection with her, and while I would've preferred it be with me, my kid seems to relax around Brooklyn. So I'm going to do whatever I can to make sure that Bella is safe and happy."

"Even if you seem to have a connection with Brooklyn as well?" Denver mumbled.

I turned so I could watch the crew in the backyard again, and sighed.

"Brooklyn is a friend. A coworker. And if Bella needs a friend too, then that works for me. But I'm not going to start dating someone because she needs a mom. She had a mom. And I don't think my kid has actually grieved losing her yet."

"Damn," Denver whispered.

"You're not alone, son. We're with you." My dad hugged me tightly, and while I wanted his words to be true, I wasn't sure. Because in the end, it felt like I was standing in an abyss, trying to reach for my kid, for a future that had once seemed so sure and was now clouded with uncertainty. Because I didn't know what would happen if I failed at this, but I'd try my hardest not to disappoint her.

And with that certainty, I moved to the backyard, my brother and father behind me, and went to join the family.

Because my kid was just as lost as I was.

And I knew somehow we had to be found.

By the time we got home, Bella was bouncing in her seat, on a little sugar-high, but seemingly happy.

"And they said I could come by the fire station. I can't believe that they get to go down the pole and everything. It's so cool."

"You do realize I used to be a firefighter too, right?"

"Yeah, but they're still firefighters."

My lips twitched. "Once again, shoved to the side for my brothers."

"I bet you get a complex, don't you? Is that a sibling thing?"

"Look at you with the big words."

"I'm twelve, Reece." She rolled her eyes so hard I was afraid they were going to roll to the back of her head.

"I'm sorry, ancient woman."

"At my next birthday, I'm going to be a teenager and that's when everything changes. At least that's what my friends say. Do you remember being thirteen back when you would chisel words onto stone?"

"I want you to make that old joke around my mother. I dare you."

Her eyes widened. "Ms. Kathy's nice."

"Yes, she is."

We pulled into the garage, and Bella jumped out of the truck without another word. Her mood had darkened with each mile, and I had no idea why. The wild shift in moods made me go over everything we'd said as if I'd triggered something inadvertently. Something was going on in that head of hers, and I needed to figure it out.

"Bella, are you okay?" I asked, but she ignored me, went to her room, and slammed the door.

Pinching the bridge of my nose, I told myself to calm down.

Well, she was one day closer to being a teenager, and I needed to figure this fucking shit out.

"Bella."

"What?" she snapped through the door.

I opened it without knocking, and she glared at me.

"I thought a closed door meant you had to knock. This is my room."

"And you don't get to slam the door. What is going on with you?"

"Nothing. I'm fine."

"That's what you say, but you just slammed the door, and suddenly you're angry with me? I thought we had a good dinner. You liked my brothers and hanging out with my parents. They're your family too."

As her gaze narrowed, I realized that was probably the worst thing I could have said in that moment.

"No, they aren't. They're yours. I don't know them. I want my mom." And with that, she burst into tears.

I moved forward, and even as she tried to shove me away, I ignored her and pulled her into my arms. "You can cry it out, Bella. It's okay."

"It's not okay. I want my mom."

"I'm sorry."

"Don't be sorry. Just get me my mom. You're not my dad." She screamed the words into my chest, and I took each blow, knowing she was in pain. I ignored the actual words, knowing she was just lashing out.

She refused to call me Dad, and that was fine. We weren't there yet. Every time she said Reece instead of Dad, I took it in stride. Because she hadn't known who I was until recently, just like I had no idea who she was. How were we supposed to find our place when we were still so new to all of this? But still, I knew she was hurting, and I had no words. I couldn't make it better. I couldn't make it go away.

"Talk to me. Do you want to talk about your mom?"

"Not with you."

The words lashed out, and I struggled for any sense of control.

"Do you want to call your friend? Your grandparents?"

"Not them. They don't care either."

I froze, my shirt soaked with her tears, and put that information to the side. We needed to dive deep into her situation, I knew it, but in this moment, me pressing for information about her grandparents wasn't going to help anyone.

"What can I do, Bella?" I asked, my voice soft.

"There's nothing you can do. She's gone. And she left me here. And I don't even know you."

I rubbed her back, slid my hands through her hair, and kept her close as she cried into my arms.

The fact that she could even break down close to me had to mean we'd made some progress, right?

A thought occurred to me. One so idiotic that it was going to be a step in the wrong direction, but in this moment, it was all I could grasp.

"Do you want me to call Brooklyn?"

I wanted her to say no. I wanted her to say yes.

She stiffened for a moment, then she nodded against my chest.

I held back a curse, before tugging Bella close and letting her cry it out. Then I picked her up, cradled her to my chest, and carried her to the living room.

"You stay here, let me call her."

Bella didn't say anything as she continued to cry softly into her hands. I wrapped her in a blanket, kept my gaze on her, and pulled out my phone.

My finger hovered over her name, and I told myself this was a mistake.

But I pressed *call* anyway.

"Reece? Tonight was your family dinner, right? How are you?"

"Do you mind coming over here?"

Bella could still hear me, and I tried to sound calm, only I was anything but.

Brooklyn was silent for a moment, and I was afraid she was going to say no. But what if she said yes?

"Let me grab my things. I'll be ten minutes. Max."

"Don't speed." My lips wanted to crawl into a smile, and yet I couldn't.

"It scares me how close I live to you sometimes."

And at that cryptic statement, she hung up, and I slid my phone back into my pocket. I didn't want to crowd Bella, so I stood behind her and watched my daughter, unable to do anything. I'd never felt this helpless in my life, not even when I had nearly died in that fire. The floor had given out but I had somehow survived.

It had changed my career, the trajectory of my life, and yet it had nothing on this.

Nearly ten minutes on the dot later, the doorbell rang, and Bella looked up at me, her eyes rimmed red.

"Want me to let her in?"

"Okay,"

She was no longer crying, and I was grateful I had given her a glass of water. But it felt like there was nothing else I could do.

I opened the door and Brooklyn stood there, a covered plate in hand, and a worried look on her face.

"I was in the middle of making a pavlova, so we get pavlova now."

I blinked as I took the plate from her in one hand.

"Isn't that a meringue thing?"

"It is. I was bored and needed to do something and somehow that ended up with a pavlova."

Without thinking, I pushed a piece of her hair behind her ear and ran my thumb over her cheekbone.

Her mouth parted, her eyes widening.

"Thank you," I whispered.

"I'm always here, Reece. You know that."

And with that, she moved past me. Bella stood up,

blanket wrapped around her, and then Brooklyn was there, arms wide.

"Hey there, girly. What do you say to a movie night?"

Bella smiled, and it was like a kick in the gut. Because my little girl nodded, and let Brooklyn hold her, and it was like the two of them against the world.

And I stood there in an open doorway, a fancy-ass dessert in my hand, feeling lost.

Because it felt as if I couldn't do this parenting thing without Brooklyn, and that was a fucking problem.

Because I had wanted Brooklyn Montgomery for years. Only I told myself she was off limits.

And now there was one more reason that I needed to let her go, and one more reason that I knew I couldn't.

Chapter 9
BROOKLYN

"I'm sorry, Brooklyn. I have to head out of town to go meet with that supplier. They thought they were going to be able to come here, but it turns out they can't. I'm sorry for letting you down."

I wanted to raise my fist to the sky, annoyed with myself for even being stressed out about this, but it wasn't Dash's fault.

"It's okay. I'll figure out something. I can go to this foundation thing on my own."

My cousin merely raised a brow, and I didn't like the look of it.

"Really?"

"What? I can. I'm a big girl. An adult. I don't need to bring a date to this gala."

"The same gala that Duke's family is helping organize?"

I winced, knowing that the reason I had even asked Dash to escort me to begin with was for that very fact.

"Possibly going with a date at all would be bad, right? Like a slap in the face to his family."

"Brooklyn." Dash let out a breath. "You're allowed to move on."

I shook my head. "It's not like that. Plus, I was going to bring my cousin, that's not really moving on." My voice was dry enough that it could start a fire, and Dash merely rolled his eyes.

"It's been a year since we lost Duke. A year in which his family hasn't spoken to me. A year in which they've purposely pushed me away and I was too dumb and broken to notice until it was too late. I am going to attend this charity gala in order to raise money for the historical society as well as the education programs it provides. I've done this since before I even met Duke." In fact, that was how I'd started seeing him to begin with. He'd asked me to dance, and I hadn't been able to say no. Only I hadn't realized our dances would be numbered.

"I know you have, Brooklyn." Dash pulled me into a hug and because I was weak and a little hurt, I let him. Our family was so damn touchy sometimes that it was almost always overwhelming and yet I knew that I could lean on any one of them in a heartbeat—just like I was doing now. He pulled away and looked down to meet my gaze. "This event is important to you and I'm sorry I'm letting you down. However, we have multiple other cousins that would go with you in case you don't want to go alone. Or, and I know this is shocking, you could go with someone not related to you. With the way Duke's sister has already treated you, I don't think you should care one way or another what that woman thinks about you. She *hurt* you. And I'll be damned if she does it again."

And that right there was why my cousin was so misunderstood when it came to other people. He may joke around, and be the life of a party sometimes, but most of the time, he was the one who would break everything in order to make sure that you were safe. And that was why I loved my cousin.

"I'll be okay. I can figure something out."

"Figure what out?"

The hairs on the back of my neck stood on end, and I tried not to turn too quickly. Reece stood in the doorway, head tilted as he studied my face. How could this man know so much about me, and yet almost nothing at all? Or perhaps I was only seeing what I needed to.

I hadn't even realized he was in the building, but I should have.

We were at the main office, going through paperwork and getting meetings out of the way before we headed to our prospective buildings. Reece would be starting on a huge restoration project that was connected to the gala, and I wouldn't be there until the end. After all, you didn't need the landscape architect until there was space for landscape.

"Well well well…" Dash said, the smile on his face so wide that I wanted to slap it right off him.

Because Reece and I still hadn't talked about that kiss. We hadn't done a single thing about it. Instead we had ignored it, pushed it to the side, and pretended it didn't happen.

And if we did mention it, then it would be all too real, and we would have to deal with the ramifications. Instead those simply didn't exist.

The fact that I'd even been in his home afterwards and we hadn't said spoke volumes. After all, Bella had needed me—Reece had needed me—and that was all that mattered.

Bella was all that mattered.

And yet my stomach tightened when I looked at Reece, and I knew this was a problem.

"What's up?"

"I can't go to the gala tonight. You know, that foundation thing for the project you're working on. I have to head out of town right after our meetings. That means Brooklyn has to go solo. Except Duke's family will be there." The bitterness in his tone should worry me, but I only had eyes for Reece. Which was again, a problem.

"It's fine. I can go alone."

"You shouldn't have to," Dash put in.

Damn that man. It wasn't like Dash knew what was going on between Reece and I—not that anything was going on at all—but I swore he could scent it out like a shark with a single drop of blood in the water.

"Is it some fancy ass thing where you have to wear a suit and eat shitty food that comes four sizes too small?" Reece asked, his gaze never leaving me.

"Pretty much. But there's an open bar," Dash put in.

"I'm going there as a representative of the company, and the fact that I'm on one of the smaller subcommittees." I rolled my shoulders back and tried to be calm. "I do good work, but you do have to schmooze. That's why I usually bring Dash. He's good at that."

"I feel like I should take that as not such a compliment, but I'm going to ignore you. Anyway, do you think you can save my cousin, Reece?"

I whirled on Dash. "Really? You're setting up dates for me now? I think I can handle this on my own."

"It's not a date." Dash's eyes widened. "It's just Reece. And free dinner. Bella's with her grandparents tonight, right?" he asked over my shoulder, and I turned to Reece, my heart in my throat. Was my pulse racing?

"She is." His jaw tightened. "It's the one evening for the night where she has to stay with her grandparents. I'm not really too excited about it. We were just getting into a rhythm, and after camp I have to pick her up and drop her off there."

Without thinking I reached out and squeezed his hand. "I'm sorry. You two seem to have been getting along recently. Finding your routine."

Reece looked down between us, but didn't let go of my hand. "We have. It's been working. At least I think so. You've been helping."

At Dash's pointed cough I let go of Reece's hand and took a step back. What was going on with me?

"I'm sorry. But you'll have her back tomorrow, and you'll be able to get to know each other some more. It hasn't been that long."

"No, it hasn't. And our lawyers are still going through the final paperwork and I keep waiting for the other shoe to drop. But I don't want to think about that right now, not when I have to drop Bella off at her grandparents—with people I don't fucking know. When is this gala tonight?"

"At seven."

I glared at Dash. "I can handle this on my own."

"Seems to me you're handling something," he mumbled.

Reece didn't say a damn thing.

"Dash. Go schmooze someone else. I can handle this."

"Again, with the handling. We're going to talk soon." And with that, Dash shoulder bumped me, narrowed his eyes at Reece, and moved down the hall.

What the hell had that been about? He was the one who had wanted Reece to take me tonight, and suddenly he's growly about it. It doesn't matter. It couldn't.

"Don't worry about it. I can go alone. I'm a big girl."

"You can. But I'll go with you. To say thank you for helping Bella." He tacked on that last thing, and it was like a kick to the chest. It shouldn't be. We were just friends. And yet I wanted to feel his lips on mine. I wanted him to hold me close.

And this was the worst possible timing.

"It's really okay."

"Is Duke's sister going to be there?"

I stiffened. "Yes. And their parents."

"Then I'm going with you. You don't need to do this alone. I'll even wear a fucking suit."

The thought of Reece in a suit nearly undid me, but I shook my head.

"I can do this on my own."

"You keep saying that." He reached forward and pinched my chin. I stiffened, my mouth parting. "But you don't have to. So we're doing this. To get it out of our system."

As soon as he said the words I knew he regretted them, but I clung to them, wondering what the hell we were doing.

"Fine."

"I'll pick you up at six thirty."

"You don't even know where we're going."

"I know. I'll do this, I won't have to spend my night freaking out about my kid, and you don't have to face them alone."

"Reece..."

"No. Don't." And right when I felt as if he would lean down and brush his lips along mine, he pulled away and went back to his office, leaving me alone, wondering what the hell I was getting myself into.

"He's going to be at your house when?" Aly asked over the phone as I paced my bedroom, wondering if I was losing my mind.

"He's going to be here in fifteen minutes. My hair is done, my makeup is done, and I have to put on my dress. But now I'm afraid I'm not wearing the right underwear."

"Is there a reason you're worried about your

underwear when it comes to that very sexy, very bearded, very growly man taking you out to a fancy event where there'll be dinner, dancing, drinks, and a hotel room?"

I froze, wondering what the hell she was saying.

"I have no idea what you mean. I was going to wear cute underwear because I like it, and I like it underneath this dress, but it didn't matter before because no one was going to see my underwear but me."

"So you're saying Reece is going to see your underwear."

"I'm not saying that. But. Oh, Aly. There's just this thing between us that we're not talking about, and I have a feeling that if I have one too many glasses of champagne I'm going to actually talk about it, and then he's going to see my underwear."

"Do you want him to see your underwear?"

"Yes!" I practically screamed. "There, I said it. I have always wanted him to see my underwear. And it's a problem. Because he works with me. He's older than me, and now he's a new dad and needs to be focusing on Bella and not the fact that I want him to see my underwear."

"Well. You better wear the good ones. Though I don't know your underwear drawer precisely, I assume you have something lacy that will go with the dress?"

"Aly, what am I doing?"

"You're going to an event where you're going to be stressed out because you have to see people who haven't respected you, and remind you of a painful time, and you're going with a man who you want to climb like a redwood tree, and yet feel that you can't."

"I didn't mean for you to be so precise in your explanation and description."

I ignored Aly's snort. "It's true though, is it not?"

"Maybe. I don't have time for this. I don't have time for this event or dealing with Chelsea and the others. But here we are. I have to go and I'm bringing a date, and they're going to hate me."

"But they hate you already anyway because they're not seeing the truth."

I swallowed hard, rubbing my hand over my chest. And that was the kick of it, wasn't it? They all hated me.

"Wear something pretty, feel pretty. You are young, beautiful, successful, talented, and a good person, Brooklyn Montgomery. You are allowed to desire someone else. You are allowed to be yourself. If Reece wants you too, and you find a way to make it work, even if only for a night, go for it. It doesn't have to be forever. And you're both adult enough to make sure that you can deal with the consequences."

"I don't feel adult enough."

"Trust me, you are. Especially compared to some of the people I know."

"I'm surprised you're not going tonight," I said, broaching the subject that we both were careful about. "I almost asked you to go with me instead."

Aly was silent long enough I was afraid I had said the wrong thing. "I sent in my regrets. But don't worry, I know you can handle this."

I let out a breath and went over my outfit for the evening one more time, before saying my goodbyes and sliding into my dress. I already had on the sexy underwear.

Thankfully I was right on time because the doorbell rang as soon as I walked downstairs. I grabbed my small clutch, and my wrap in case it somehow got chilly in the evening, and opened the door.

Reece stood there in a suit, his shoulders broad, practically straining the fabric, and I nearly fell to my knees.

Dear God.

How was it fair that a man could be this handsome?

It was one of those suits that was narrow in the chest, but not constricting, and he didn't wear those skinny pants that so many others did. These molded over his thighs, but gave him room to breathe. He'd trimmed his beard, but hadn't shaved it completely, and he'd styled his hair so it didn't look as messy as usual.

You could still see his ink, it wasn't as if he would ever hide it, but that just made him even harder to resist.

"Brooklyn," he whispered.

I looked down at my silver dress, the one with the heart-shaped neckline that accentuated my hips, and swallowed hard.

"I've worn it before, but it's comfortable."

"We're going to this gala."

"I know," I said with a frown.

"I have to say that because if I don't, I'm going to take you inside and strip that dress off. You have no idea how hard it is for me not to glide that dress up your thighs and slide my cock right between your legs."

I pressed my thighs together, my mouth parting. "Reece."

He shook his head. "I should probably be sorry for saying that. For being so crass, but I don't fucking care. You know I want you, Brooklyn. And I know you want me."

"I thought we were doing very good not talking about that."

"True. But for tonight? Let's go do this."

I nearly staggered. "Do what?"

"Show the world that you're Brooklyn fucking

Montgomery and you can do anything." And then he took my hand, and I was lost.

"TONIGHT IS GOING TO BE A LONG NIGHT."

Reece, his hand on my waist, stood beside me and let out a deep breath. "Honestly, it sounds like it's going to be an excruciatingly painful night. At least from the speeches so far."

I looked up at him, wondering once again what we were doing. But this was not the time to be too focused on that. Not when there were at least two hundred people milling around us, and we were waiting on the seventh speech of the evening. One where they would congratulate themselves on how gratuitous and giving they were, and would then do their best to one-up one another when it came to donations.

"Honestly, it hasn't been this bad before."

Reece raised a brow at me and looked down at the two flutes of champagne in our hands.

"Are you sure about that? Or were you just infatuated with somebody who was part of this world?"

I wanted to be offended at that, but I looked inward, wondering if he was right. I shook my head. "No. There didn't use to be so many speeches. And it didn't use to be this elegant."

"You have to wonder how much of the donations went to this one hundred dollar a bottle glass of champagne and the tablecloths alone."

I winced. "These were all donated by different families. Including Duke's. It's outside of the foundation itself. They're going to raise hundreds of thousands of dollars tonight to keep children in the arts, to feed them, and to help any after-school programs so kids don't go hungry, and parents can work. They do good things, but it's not always so pretentious."

"And you were going to marry into this family."

My stomach hollowed out at that, and Reece lowered his head and cursed. "I'm sorry. I shouldn't judge. Especially because the man isn't here to speak for himself. I didn't mean to hurt you."

Tears didn't prick my eyes, though I thought perhaps they should.

"I liked coming to these things with him. I felt like a princess. And that we were doing good things. Maybe you're right. Maybe now I'm on the outside looking in."

Reece set down his drink and turned me in his arms, cupping my face. "I was wrong. I'm sorry. You always have a good heart. I'm the idiot."

I looked up at him then, wondering what I was doing once again.

"Reece..." I began.

"Brooklyn. I see you arrived."

Guiltily, I turned to see Duke's family standing there, the Rochesters looking gorgeous in their expensive dresses and tuxes and suits with diamonds covering their necks.

"Mr. Rochester, Mrs. Rochester. I'm glad I was able to come."

"Hmm," the older woman said, her gaze on Reece. "I don't know you."

"This is Reece. He works with Montgomery Construction. And he's lead on the home that is part of the donation to the foundation."

"I see," she said. "You two seem comfortable."

Guilt clawed at me, but I stood straighter. Because this woman, I knew now, had never liked me. I had never been good enough for her son. And now, he was gone, and perhaps I was the one who had moved on too quickly—only I hadn't moved on. I was just standing here with a man who couldn't stop looking at me, but I wasn't with him. Yet, from the look on their faces, I was the terrible woman who had broken their son.

"Reece Fox, I know you," Duke's dad said, and my gaze shot to him.

"You have me at a disadvantage, sir," Reece said, his voice low, assured.

"You should know the Longs are here as well. They

would usually be here early tonight but have personal issues. Personal issues that surround you."

I froze in Reece's hold, just now aware that his hand was still on my waist.

"It's a small world," Reece said, and I wasn't sure what else there was to say to that.

"And it gets smaller every day, Brooklyn." Mrs. Rochester shook her. "When Chelsea came to me and told me that you had found a new life, I was disappointed but not surprised. Now that I see who you're associating with, it can either be a good move for you or not. The Longs have reach in this town."

"As you're talking to a Montgomery, I'm pretty sure that she understands the reach in this town. This town being Denver," Reece said dryly.

I wanted to curl into a ball. I didn't understand what was happening right now.

"You were never good enough for my son," she snapped. "He's gone. And you're here. And I will never forgive you." And with that, she rolled on her heels and stomped off, leaving Duke's father standing there.

"I would apologize for her and my daughter, but they're in pain."

Tears pricked my eyes and I nodded. "I know. You don't have to apologize."

"They need to," Reece snapped.

Mr. Rochester's gaze went to Reece's. "I would be

careful about who you anger. Especially if you want to keep your daughter."

"Are you threatening him?" I asked, taking a step forward.

"I'm just telling the truth. The Longs have connections. Just like the connections you wanted when you were going to marry my son."

"That's not— I didn't—" I sputtered, so fucking confused.

"You're going to want to watch the way you talk to her."

"Don't threaten me, boy."

"I'm not a boy. I'm a father, I'm a friend, and I know people too. If this is how you treat somebody who was going to be your family, I have to wonder how you treat everyone else around you. Now if you'll excuse us, we have a bid to make, as this is a foundation to help raise money for children. Something you don't understand apparently." Reece pulled me away, leaving me staggered, and Duke's father just stared at us, a nonplussed expression on his face.

"Reece."

"Not here. Not now. I can't."

We milled through the event room, and I muttered to a few people, trying to act calm, but I couldn't breathe, couldn't think.

Why did they hate me so much? Were they threatening Reece?

"Don't cry," Reece whispered into my ear, his breath warm against my skin.

Tears threatened to come and I shook my head. "I won't."

"Damn straight. You're stronger than they are."

By the time we made it to the other end of the event center, he pulled my purse from my hand and dug through it for the hotel key.

"I never understood why they gave you a hotel room for helping organize. I guess it's in case you drank too much?"

"Maybe. I don't know." My mind whirled, but then I found myself being practically dragged down the hall, up the elevator, and into the small suite they'd provided.

It was as if I blinked, and I was suddenly standing in the suite, Reece in front of me, his chest heaving.

"We can go. If you want. We can go. But I'm not going to let them have the satisfaction of seeing you break down."

"They hate me so much."

"Fuck them. They don't matter."

"What if they somehow make sure the Longs hurt you? I don't want this to hurt Bella."

He cursed under his breath, took a step back, and

undid his tie. "Fuck them. I'm not letting go of my daughter. Do you get that? No matter what, she's mine. Cassie took her away and hid her for years, and if this is the crowd that they want Bella to grow up in, fuck them. She's my family, she's a Fox. Fuck, she's more of a Montgomery than she is a Long. Fuck them. They're not touching my kid."

My lip wobbled, and I hated myself just then. I had to be stronger than this. "Why do they hate me? I didn't do it. I didn't take Duke away. He's the one who did it. He took his own life, and I don't know why he was hurting so much and why we couldn't see it, but we didn't, and I can't take it back. But I didn't do it. And they can't realize that."

"They don't see you for you, Brooklyn. They never have." He cupped my face, and I looked up at him then, my heart racing.

"We should go home."

"We should," he said. "After." And then his mouth was on mine and I couldn't breathe.

He pressed my back to the door, my chin lifting as he slid his mouth down my neck, over my collarbone. He tugged on the top of my dress, so he could nibble at my shoulder. My hands raced up his back.

"Reece."

"I know. I know." Then he took my mouth again, and there were no words. His hands were on my sides, pulling up my dress slightly, and I spread my legs, letting his knee slide between my thighs. He ground himself against me, my clit pulsating with each movement, and I moaned into his mouth.

"That's my girl. You're here. You're mine."

Oh, how I wanted that to be true. But in that moment I couldn't breathe. I couldn't think about anything else but his hands.

When he slid a hand up my thigh and over me, I let out a gasp.

"So wet. And look at all this lace." He shoved up my dress and went to his knees.

My mouth opened to say something, but then I couldn't do a damn thing. He breathed cool air over my panties, and my knees went weak. When he slid my panties to the side, and began to lick and suck, I lost all sense of thoughts. All sense of decorum.

Instead, he explored me, sucking on my clit and spreading my folds. When he speared me with two fingers, rubbing over a small bundle of nerves on the first try, I came, quick on the trigger.

"You taste fucking sweet, Brooklyn. Look at you when you come, all pink and blushing for me. Look at what you're doing. Do you see my face? You're so fucking wet that you're gushing. And that's for me, Brooklyn. No one else. It's just you and me right here."

I should have been embarrassed, but I couldn't.

Not with Reece there, holding me close. And when he stood up and took my mouth again, I tasted myself on him. He lifted me up by the waist and carried me to the bed. Without words, he stripped me out of my dress, tossing my heels to the side. He shoved off my panties, and I reached around to undo my bra. He threw that to the side as well, and then his face was between my breasts, his beard rough against my flesh, and I swallowed hard. He sucked and he nibbled, biting my nipples. As he met my gaze, his smile was wicked.

There was just something about him, nearly fully dressed with me naked, that left me vulnerable. And yet I knew I was safe in his hands, in his inked, and oh-so-sure touch.

He stood back, stripped out of his jacket, and then his shirt, and I moaned.

"That's a good girl, that's my Brooklyn."

My eyes widened, tears threatening at his words, but then his head was between my legs again, and I couldn't think of anything else. I ran my hand through his hair, loving the way that his dark and reddish hair between my pale thighs looked. He sucked and licked, and before I could tell him to stop, to tell him that I wanted him inside me, I came again.

I never came more than once during sex, and here was Reece Fox making me come twice in a row.

He shoved off his pants, taking his boxer briefs with them, and his cock sprung free, hitting his belly, leaving a trail of pre-cum.

My eyes widened at the length of him, and I licked my lips.

"Reece," I whispered.

"What? You're the one with your hood pierced," he said, leaning down to flick the piercing at the hood over my clit.

"If you keep tugging on that, I'm going to come for a third time," I moaned.

"Good. I'm clean," he said suddenly. "And I don't have a fucking condom."

My eyes widened, and I realized that in this moment we could stop. Him with his hand gripping the base of his cock, the piercing at the end of his dick glistening underneath the light. The hoop matched the hoops in his nipples, and I swallowed hard.

"I can't… I can't get pregnant."

I didn't elaborate, now wasn't the time, and an odd expression covered Reece's face. But he leaned forward and took my mouth with his.

When he pulled back, panting, I tried to catch my breath. "Does that mean I can have you bare? I do realize that even using condoms, it doesn't always work, Bella is evidence of that. But if you want, I can stop."

I shook my head and let him wipe a tear from my cheek. "I want you. In me. And now. There's no risk. I'm clean, but I can't get pregnant."

He nodded. "I'm clean too. I'll take good care of you," he whispered, and in that moment, I knew he meant more than just his touch.

So when I spread my legs for him, and he settled between them, I swallowed hard and kept my eyes on him. He teased me at first, gliding his cock between my folds, both of us groaning, and then he slid into me, inch by inch.

"Reece," I moaned.

"That's it, take me. You're so fucking tight, Brooklyn. And you're going to take me—all of me. Do you see me? Look at my dick. Look at your cunt taking me. Look."

I did as he ordered, my breath coming in pants, as he shifted in and out of me, slowly at first, and then he was seated deep inside of me, stretching me to the point of pain but bliss simultaneously.

"That's it, that's my Brooklyn."

He kissed me again, and then he began to move.

Slowly at first, then harder and faster until we couldn't breathe and couldn't think. And when he shifted, so I was on top, riding him, he played with my nipples, and I did the same to his. A smile curved my lips, and then I was coming again, before Reece pushed me to my back again, one hand around my neck, the other on my hip, and thrust into me harder and faster. And when he came, filling me, his mouth was on mine, and I wrapped my legs and arms around him, needing him more than I could say.

And afterward, both of us panting, he kissed me softly and wiped away my tears before he pulled out of me.

"We need to head back home soon, but first, let me take care of you."

I sat up in bed, feeling oddly bare as I pulled the sheet up to cover me.

"It's okay."

"We can talk tomorrow. But tonight, let me just take care of you."

He kept repeating that, as if he didn't know what else to say. And frankly, I didn't blame him. Instead, I let him carry me to the bathroom where he filled the tub with hot water and bubbles, and moved me inside. I already ached between my legs, but here he was, caring for me. And when he shifted behind me, surprising me, I leaned back against him, his cock already hard against my back. He cupped my breasts, and held me close, and in that moment, I broke down.

"There you go. I was waiting for that." He kissed my temple.

"I'm sorry."

"It's okay. I'm your first since..."

He didn't elaborate, and I was grateful.

Because for some reason Reece Fox understood. He always did.

But I wasn't crying because of Duke.

No, I was crying because I loved the man that held me.

And I already knew what it felt like to lose someone.

And with everything surrounding us, I knew I would have to deal with losing a man I loved again.

Chapter 10
BROOKLYN

We hadn't stayed at the hotel. The idea that the foundation had even spent money for each of the committee members to have hotel rooms in case they had too much to drink was ridiculous. But in the end, we had used that room. And we had snuck out of the building without anyone the wiser. I'd worn my dress, pulled my hair back in a tight chignon, and Reece had my panties in his pocket. Once again, we hadn't spoken.

Because speaking about what was going on between us would actually have to mean something, and that wasn't what we were doing in this moment.

And now I stood in my foyer, with Reece behind me, and I felt more lost than ever.

"I didn't mean to break down like that."

Reece leaned against the wall, hands in his pockets. He had put his suit jacket back on, but hadn't put on his tie. He still had a couple of buttons undone so I could see his chest and the outline of his nipple rings.

I'd always known that Reece had to be a little kinky, but the fact that both of us had piercings, tattoos, and I just had the best sex of my life, made everything a little surreal.

"You needed to." He said it with a shrug in his voice, as if he was used to women breaking down in his arms after giving them the best orgasms of their lives. Not that I wanted to think about him with other women. I knew he had been with other women. Most likely countless women. In fact I had seen him on dates with other people when I had been with Duke. He was a father for God's sakes. Of course he'd had sex. He needed to learn all of those techniques somewhere.

"I'm really not good at this whole awkward morning after thing even though it's the middle of the night. Can I get you some coffee? A whiskey? Something to bang your head against because I'm being ridiculous right now?"

Reece just shook his head, his lips quirked into a small smile as he stood up.

"No. I don't need any of that, Brooklyn. You're doing just fine."

"You don't have to placate me, you know. I do realize I'm being ridiculous."

He shrugged. I wanted to shake him and kiss him. Seriously, something was wrong with me.

"Reece—"

He moved forward then, wrapped his hand around the back of my neck, and crushed his mouth to mine. I moaned against him, unable to breathe or even process what was happening. And then he pulled away, leaving me breathless.

"Stop overthinking."

"You obviously don't know me then."

"Brooklyn."

"No. Don't just say my name and get growly and pretend that what just happened didn't."

"There's no pretending when it comes to you. We both know that."

"And what is that supposed to mean?" I asked, confused.

"It means what it needs to mean."

"If you're going to start sounding like Yoda, you can just leave. We can forget this ever happened and go back to work like we always do."

"And how is that? When we both can't stop looking at each other or saying the wrong fucking thing? This was bound to happen, Brooklyn. I've been trying to keep my hands off of you for years. First because you were too young, then because you were with Duke. Didn't matter that we worked together. I wanted you. And I knew if I wasn't careful, I was going to have you."

Just like that, the man confused me once again.

Why was he so good at confusing the fuck out of me? This man. This crazy man. He never made anything easy.

"I don't know what you're saying, or what you're thinking, but maybe you should just go."

"You're telling me to leave because I said I wanted you?"

"I don't know, Reece. You don't tell me anything. You just growl and then ask me for help when it comes to Bella. That's all you've ever talked to me about. And I don't mind. I love that little girl. She is the sweetest, and she's confused and needs people. So I'll be her friend, but I don't know what to do with you."

His hands still on the back of my neck, he cursed. Then he leaned his forehead against mine, and I wasn't sure what I was supposed to do.

"Somehow that little girl is the best thing I have. The most important thing."

"She is. She's supposed to be. She's your daughter."

"She *has* to be the important thing."

"I know." My heart cracked ever so slightly. This shouldn't be surprising. I knew the answer. I might be falling in love with Reece, but he couldn't afford to fall in love with me.

"I don't want to hurt you, Brooklyn."

"Then don't." A simple statement that was anything but simple.

"I'm not going to forget this though. I don't know what this is, but I can't forget that."

"And you think I can?" I asked, tears filling my throat.

"I know you can't." That cocky smirk on his face made me want to either kick him in the balls or kiss him. There really was no in-between when it came to Reece Fox.

He took a step back, leaving me just as confused as ever. Damn this man. And damn my hormones.

"I don't know what's going to happen. But can you ever?"

"No. You can't. I think that's the whole point of living."

"Astute."

"Are you making fun of me?"

"No, Brooklyn. I'm not. But I don't know what the fuck I'm doing. We both know this is the wrong time for this." Another kick to the heart. "But I don't want to stop."

"Oh."

He raised a brow as he looked at me. "Yeah. *Oh.* I don't want to stop. Meaning I probably should. But I'm not going to."

"Reece—"

"No. Don't speak. My hands on you tonight? That's what we both wanted. The way that those people treated you tonight and how they always have? Fuck them. They don't matter anymore. But I don't know what's going to happen next, Brooklyn. All I know is that I want you, and I know you want me."

"Cocky much?"

"Considering I just had my cock buried balls deep inside you, you know the answer to that."

"Reece."

"What? Did you think I was a sweet, innocent kid who was going to be gentle with you? We both know that's not what you wanted. You might've had boys before, but I'm a fucking man, Brooklyn. And yes, we fucked, and I want to do it again. But I'm not a nice man."

"That's a lie."

"You want it to be a lie. But it's not. I might be a good man sometimes, but I'm not a nice one. Because a nice man would walk away knowing that there could be nothing between us. Not when I don't know what's going to happen with Bella. Her damn grandparents could change their mind before everything is through."

"Are you saying being with me could hurt your chances?" I asked, my heart breaking.

"The problem is I don't know. And I don't know what to do if me wanting you is going to hurt your relationship with Bella. Already, I'm relying on you too fucking much."

"I'll always be there for her. No matter what."

"And the sad thing is I believe you, Brooklyn. Even if I break you, even if I leave you shattered in the tub like you were tonight, I know you'll be there for her. And that's what makes me a selfish asshole."

I leaned forward, reaching out, but he took a step back, leaving ice between us.

"I don't know what to say."

"There isn't anything to say. So how about this, I'm going to go, and I'll see you at work."

"So this was a one-off thing? We're going to go back to normal?"

"There's never been normal between us, Brooklyn, and that's a problem. But I have to think of Bella. And I can't be selfish."

"Being with me would be selfish?"

"Wanting you the way that I do is selfish. I'm an old man, Brooklyn."

"You're forty-one, Reece. You're not ancient."

"Well, I feel like an old man. And I don't see nights of random nameless women in my future. I don't know what that future is, but before Bella, I thought—" He shook his head, not finishing his sentence, and it was as if a cavern opened up between us.

I was terrified that I was the one in his thoughts in

that moment. The one that he wanted when he thought he was ready.

"You should go then."

"If I go now though, it won't be forever. We both know it can't be."

"Make up your mind, Reece. Do you want me?"

"Of course I do. I wouldn't have fucked you and threatened to ruin everything that we already have if I didn't. I just don't know if I can promise you everything you deserve."

I froze, knowing that was the best thing, the most sincere thing he could have said.

"Okay. Okay. Then go, and we don't have to talk about forever in this moment. As long as Bella is number one, I won't hate you in the morning." I tried to smile as I said it. He moved forward and brushed his lips against mine. My knees almost went weak, and I hated myself for it.

"I don't want this to be a mistake," he whispered against my lips.

"Then we don't make it one. We can be adults about this."

"I'm a jealous man, Brooklyn."

"And?"

"I can't picture you with anyone else."

"Do you really think I would sleep with anyone

else? It took every ounce of my soul in order to give myself to you, Reece Fox."

"You have no idea what that does to me."

"Then I better be the only one in your bed. If we ever get there."

"Damn straight." He kissed me again, then took a step back.

"I'm going to go, before making another mistake."

"Another?" I asked, my voice hollow.

"Waiting so fucking long was my first." And with that, he left me standing in my entryway, alone, faded, and yet empty at the same time.

That seemed like the perfect description of everything that it meant to be me and Reece.

"Did you hear that the Franklins have decided to sell?" my mom asked as I sat on their couch, knees under my chin, and a glass of wine in my hand.

My eyes widened at that.

"Really? Why?"

The Franklins were my parents' neighbors, an older couple who truly hated everybody near them. Honestly, I didn't know why they had stayed in this neighborhood for so long. They disliked anybody who wasn't like them, constantly tried to get the HOA to kick out my family because we were loud, inked, pierced, and had motorcycles coming to the house every once in a while depending on who visited. Not to mention nearly all of my family was bi, pan, or gay. I had multiple family members who were in poly relationships, and had kids within those triads. My parents' house was large enough with enough acreage that we even had Montgomery events on the property. The Franklins hated it and had tried to block off the entrance to our back road, our *private* back road.

"What finally convinced them to sell?" Nate asked as he walked into the living room and sat on the couch. He practically shoved me out of the way when he did, and I narrowed my eyes at him.

"Hey. Don't spill the wine."

"We couldn't have that." Nate rolled his eyes and I leaned forward to scrub some paint off of his forehead.

"Did you even shower before you got here?"

"Of course I did. Paint just gets everywhere. I'm in the middle of a scene that's bothering me. Though I think this paint has to do with the kids at camp."

I opened my mouth to ask about Bella, then realized I probably shouldn't. Asking about her would have my entire family on my heel. We really were a nosy bunch.

"Be nice to your brother, and your sister," my mom said as she sank into her chair. My dad came into the room, handed her a glass of wine that he had just refilled, and took another seat.

Tonight was all about Montgomery family dinner, although I knew my other brother, his wife, and a couple of cousins would be visiting soon. Just because it was our particular family dinner didn't mean it was just the ones I had grown up with underneath this roof.

"Your uncle bought them out," my dad said as he grinned.

"Which uncle?" I asked, surprised. I set my glass down so I wouldn't spill it, and put my feet on the ground.

"Wes, of course. My twin likes to one-up us."

"How did Uncle Wes finally get the Franklins to sell?" I asked.

"I don't understand exactly how your uncle can do these things," my mom said dryly. "But if anyone could do it, it's Wes and Jillian," she said, speaking of my aunt.

My father, Storm Montgomery, was twins with Wes. My mom, Everly, had Nate and James before she had married my dad. I had come along later.

My brothers' half-siblings lived in the area, and usually made it to family dinners, but they were all with their individual families for the evening. In fact, the eldest was on vacation with his husband—another reason that the Franklins have hated us.

"Seriously though, how did they sell?"

"You're going to have to ask them," my dad said as the doorbell rang.

My eyes widened. "How many people are coming to this dinner?" I asked with a laugh.

"Your uncle wanted to tell the story, meaning he's bringing some of the kids."

"You say kids as if we're not all in our thirties." Nate said dryly.

"Addy and Cody are still in their twenties, stop taking my youth away from me, child," Mom said with a laugh. She stood up, roughed up my brother's hair just a bit, and then moved to the entryway to greet the others. I gave my brother a look, he crossed his eyes, and we moved to follow.

Nate's twin James moved in, signing quickly as his wife Sarah said her hellos as well.

James moved close to me and hugged me tightly. "Hello baby sister," he signed as he moved back.

James had cochlear implants and could hear most sounds but not all tones. He preferred to sign, and I signed back to him. We all signed when we were near James, and the entire family—cousins and all—had learned over time. It reminded me that Reece had learned to sign when he had become friends with Nate, and then therefore James. That man was always so surprising.

And I needed to get him off my mind, because I swore my mother could read my thoughts, and she kept giving me curious looks. My family had liked Duke well enough and were ready to welcome him to the family. They had been just as lost as I was when Duke had died. I wasn't sure what I was supposed to say when it came to my relationship—or lack thereof—with Reece.

After the others came into the house, Uncle Wes and Aunt Jillian followed with both Addy and Riley. I squealed, and held them close, loving my cousins. While I was friendly and friends and practically sisters with the majority of the female cousins in my family, Riley and Addy and I were the closest.

As our fathers were twins, we always joked that we were closer in genetics than anyone else.

With the group of us, we were loud, most likely annoying, and yet another reason that the Franklins were selling.

"Where is Cody?" my mom asked.

Aunt Jillian hugged my mom tightly and just smiled.

"Cody's out on a date but he sends his love. We sort of surprised you with this family dinner and we're crashing yours. Sorry about that."

"We're here to annoy all of you, so that's all that matters," Riley said with a wink.

Riley had to be the most bubbly of all of my cousins. She ran the art gallery—and therefore saw Reece every time that he dropped off Bella. And it had been Riley that I had spoken to in order to get Bella back into the camp. She had numerous questions, and had been very careful about them so far, but from the way she was looking at me, I knew I wouldn't be able to hold her off for long.

Addy was slightly quieter, and traveled often, and I was so grateful that she was here.

I loved the girls, and having grown up with two older brothers, it was nice to have them in my life. It's like I had sisters, rather than just the annoying stinky brothers I knew.

"Okay, everyone into the living room and open dining room, I have cheese," my mom said.

"There's a reason why he married you." Uncle Wes kissed my mom smartly on the mouth and then ducked my dad's fist.

They all joked and moved into the living room, and I rolled my eyes.

"And to think, Uncle Storm dated our mom first," Riley teased.

I shuddered. "Why do you always bring that up? I don't need to know what my dad and Aunt Jillian did."

"I'm just saying, it's all in the family," Riley teased.

I shoved at her shoulder playfully, and they rolled their eyes before we moved into the living room.

"By the way, I invited Reece and his daughter to dinner," my mom began, and I froze. "I know that things are a little tumultuous, and he has an amazing family, but I met Bella when I went to help at art camp, and she was the sweetest. But they couldn't come today. He did say he would come next time though." My mother gave me a pointed look, and I tried to stare anywhere but at her.

Reece had been invited? He hadn't told me.

My stomach ached, and I tried to look like I wasn't going to throw up.

"Okay, we're going to talk about this soon," Riley whispered against my ear.

I ignored her and listened in as Uncle Wes told the story of how he finally got the Franklins to sell.

Apparently all it took was back taxes and forgetting to pay mortgage payments.

"Seriously? They kept calling us low lives, and they weren't paying their bills?" my dad asked.

"Are they okay?" The worry in my mom's tone just reminded me how amazing that woman was.

"Oh, they're fine. They had plenty of money in the bank, they just didn't want to pay the man." Uncle Wes rolled his eyes.

"Typical," Nate muttered as he looked down at his phone.

"Well, what are you going to do with the property then?" Mom asked.

"Well, I figured I can get one of the construction crews to clean it up, and we can make sure a Montgomery family in need takes it."

"I want it," I said, raising my hand.

As Uncle Wes worked and owned Montgomery Inc, he just stared at me.

"What? I think it takes youth and new knowledge in order to make the place special." I pressed my lips together so I wouldn't laugh, but Riley and Addy burst into giggles anyway.

"Ouch. Are you calling me old?" Wes asked.

"That means you're calling me old too," my dad said.

"Totally." I shook my head as everybody either groaned or laughed.

"Actually, I've always loved that house, and the property itself. Even though we weren't supposed to actually be on it, it was fun when we would dare each other." I gave my brothers grins, and they each flipped me off.

"Hey, be kind. And we all knew that you were trying to get on their property," Mom said dryly.

"Well, the good news is I was thinking of you, Lex, and Dash. I know you've always loved the house," Uncle Wes said, and I smiled.

"Really?"

"Of course. And frankly, a few of the outbuildings have a lot of fire damage, and I don't know if they can be saved. Your man Reece would be the perfect person to help out with that."

"Oh, he's not my man." I blurted the words and everybody stared at me before Riley put her hands over her mouth, and Addy giggled.

"Hey, let's get more cheese," my mom said, trying to save the conversation, but there was no saving it.

"Oh? Is there something we should know?" my dad asked.

"We're pregnant," Sarah blurted, and James just grinned like a kid in a candy store, and suddenly all attention was off my snafu, and on the fact that I was about to be an aunt.

Tears pricked my eyes and I ran past Nate, practically shoving him out of the way and held Sarah close

"Congratulations."

"Thank you. And you're welcome."

I rolled my eyes and hugged my sister-in-law tightly.

All conversation turned towards the new baby, and

the fact that my parents were about to be grandparents. However, right as we moved into the dining room for dinner, both of my cousins pulled me into the hallway.

"Okay, spill," Riley ordered.

I shook my head. "No, we should be focused on the fact that we're having a new baby in the family."

"There's always going to be another Montgomery in this family, but, are we about to have a Fox-Montgomery?" Addy asked.

"Ooh, that's a good one," Riley said as she held up her hand. The two high-fived, and I glared at them.

"Stop it. This isn't the place."

"What happened? Just tell us. Was it good?" Riley asked, her voice soft.

I pressed my lips together, before I closed my eyes, and nodded dramatically.

The girls squealed and did a little dance in the hallway, and I sighed.

"I have no idea what I'm doing. The foundation gala was terrible, and then we were kissing, and there was a bathtub and well." Since everybody was still focused on Sarah and James, I quickly explained what happened with Duke's family, Reece, and what had happened when he had taken me home.

My cousins stared at me, slack jawed, and I winced.

"What, say something."

"I want to punch Duke's family, but I feel like that would be wrong," Riley said.

"They were always rude to us, and now I can hate them. I can hate what happened to them, but I can also hate them." Addy nodded tightly. "And as for Reece? Oh my God. He's so hot."

"Shush," I snapped quietly. "I don't know what's going to happen. I don't know what we're doing. And this is the worst place to talk about this."

"Yes, it is. And so we'll have girls' night tomorrow. And we'll spill about everything."

"Like how about the fact that I'm surprised you're even here because you're usually attached by your mouth to Patrick?" Addy said dryly.

Riley blushed. "I can't help it. My boyfriend's adorable. And I love him."

I sighed happily.

"I love you for loving Patrick too. However, we should probably get back before they start questioning things."

"Oh, little sister, we're questioning things," Nate said as he leaned against the doorway.

"Stop. Don't say anything," I said to him, pointing at my brother.

"Oh, I won't. Although, I like Reece. And I like his

little girl. She has spunk, and is fantastic at drawing. She's been working with Oliver."

My heart squeezed and I moved forward.

"Really? I didn't want to ask and be weird about it."

"Bella has so much talent. Once camp's over, you should talk to Reece and make sure she takes lessons with us. It's not something we normally offer, but since she's Reece's, and yours in a way, we're there."

"Nate—" I shook my head, my throat tightening. "I don't know what's going to happen. He might have to fight for custody, and I'd just be in the way."

My brother moved forward and pinched my chin, forcing me to look up.

"You're never in the way. You were never in the way with Duke and his dumb-ass family. And you're not in the way with Reece. I know he has a lot going on, and I'm going to give him some grace for that. But if he fucking hurts you, I'll break him."

"Nate."

"No. I get to be the big brother here. Just like I'm the big brother for you two," he said to Addy and Riley.

My cousins snorted in unison.

"We have a younger brother that tries to act like the big brother."

"Hey, our fathers are twins, the genetics are twisted

enough that I'm going to be the growly big brother for all of you. Don't disappoint me."

"And how is it our fault?" Addy asked, brow raised.

"It's not. It's always going to be the man in your life's fault. Or the significant other in your life, depending on who you're dating. However, just be careful. I love you, little sister. And I like Reece. And I like the fact that he's stepping up and proving to be a really fucking good dad. This is messy, little sister."

I sucked in a deep breath, as Riley moved forward, and wiped a tear from my cheek.

"It's okay to be messy. Okay to make mistakes."

"Okay, frazzled Ms. Frizzle," I said with a laugh.

"It's true you know. Now, let's go eat some cheese and celebrate a new Montgomery. And don't worry. I really like Reece."

"So do I. I think that's the problem."

My brother's eyes darkened, and then he wrapped his arm around my shoulder, and led me into the dining room with the others.

My relationships had always been slightly complicated, and it seemed like it wasn't going to get any better.

But even this dinner, the one that I had needed to get away from thinking about Reece and what would happen, had already been wrapped around him so tightly, there had been no escaping.

And if we broke something, if we hurt each other, it would twist so many other avenues.

Yet I knew I loved him. I had been falling for him in increments for far longer than I care to admit.

And now I needed to deal with it.

Even if that meant walking away.

Chapter 11
REECE

THE SCREAM WOKE me and I leapt out of bed, practically tripping over my feet. Gone were the days where I'd sleep naked or even in boxer shorts. Now I wore an old T-shirt and long pajama bottoms. We were going on eight weeks of Bella being under my roof, and we're still finding a rhythm.

But this was the first time I had heard my daughter scream.

I practically slammed through the door as I went into her room, the nightlight radiating a small space, and went to the side of Bella's bed. She was tangled in her sheets, her hands in tight fists in front of her, and she continued to twist within the blankets, alternating between screaming and crying.

I sat at the edge of the bed and reached for her shoulders.

"Bella. Wake up. Bella baby. You're okay. You're safe. You're home."

I kept saying random words out loud, hoping they

would pull her out of her nightmare, and that they were even the right words to say.

Home. My daughter was home.

And this is where she would be until she decided she was old enough to move out and start her own life. But that could be years from now, and I couldn't even dare think about those moments in time.

Bella shot up, her forehead connecting with my chin. Stars danced behind my eyelids, and I held back a curse. Bella didn't seem to notice though. She stared at me with wide eyes, tear-stained cheeks, and shook in my arms.

"Bella. You're awake. What's wrong."

"I miss my mom." Then she burst into tears. My arms went around her automatically, but I had no words to say.

Of course she missed her mom. She hadn't spoken a damn thing about her since she'd moved in, though I had tried. My own mother had thought maybe therapy would help, but finding a routine between the two of us had been hard enough. And while I knew it had to happen eventually, I hadn't wanted to start things off on the wrong foot. Maybe I had made a mistake. Then again, I was damn good at making mistakes these days.

"Do you want to talk about it?" I asked, my voice gruff. Was that the right thing to say? Should I let her cry it out? I wasn't good at this. How was anybody supposed to be good at this? What did you do when the daughter that you hadn't known existed until two months ago starts crying in your arms because she misses her mom. The woman that I hadn't seen in years, who had lied to me and everyone else about Bella's existence.

I couldn't hate Cassie. I couldn't even judge her. Not anymore. Not when our daughter cried in my arms.

"No. I don't." She buried herself into my chest, and stilled, not sure what to do. Bella and I were still figuring things out. It didn't even feel like we were friends at this point, let alone father and daughter. She told me about her day when I forced it out of her. I knew her friends' names—Wyatt and Natalie—because I pried. I knew she liked to draw and paint, but she didn't bring anything home from camp. Although the Montgomerys said that there would be an art show at the end of the summer where I would be able to see her work. I didn't feel like enough though.

I didn't know anything about my kid, but I was trying to learn.

I knew she liked lactose-free milk over regular milk even though she wasn't lactose intolerant. I knew she loved all forms of sourdough, and Brooklyn was well on her way to teaching her how to make a starter. I knew my daughter wanted to learn how to plant flowers, and it was Brooklyn who was teaching her.

I knew my daughter liked English and science but not history or math. I had found that funny because it was usually one or the other not a mix of creative and analytical. Then again, I was a decent mix.

I was learning bits about my daughter, but sometimes it didn't feel real.

I didn't know when she would call me Dad or if she would ever. And I didn't know what the hell to do about the fact that I was falling in love with Brooklyn Montgomery, and when I fucked that up, it would hurt Bella. Because somehow the relationship I had formed with my daughter had been irrevocably tied to Brooklyn.

But all of that didn't matter in this moment, not when my daughter was crying in my arms.

"I'm here if you need me," I said softly, confused, and feeling helpless.

My mother told me being a parent meant feeling helpless ninety percent of the time, but I didn't believe her. Maybe I should have.

"Why is she gone?" she asked softly. I swallowed hard. I was afraid to move and startle her. If I did, then maybe she would stop talking to me.

"I'm not good at figuring out why life is the way it is or why sometimes fate is an actual thing. I will tell you it's not fair. And I'm sorry. Your mom should still be here. You should still have her in your life. But if you think about it, part of her is still here. She is inside you. You don't have to not talk about it. I'd love to hear more about your mom. What she means to you."

"If she was alive then I wouldn't know you. Wouldn't that make you mad?"

My arms tightened around her for a moment, and I swallowed hard.

"I would like to think that one day you and I would have found a way to each other. I love having you in my life, Bella. But I wish your mom didn't have to die for that to happen."

"She was really nice. She baked cookies, but sometimes they were burned. Not like Brooklyn's. And she liked to sing. I loved her singing."

I rubbed my cheek over the top of her head. "I remember. She used to sing karaoke. And forced me to go out."

Bella pulled back, her eyes wide. They were still glistening with tears, but not as puffy. "Really? You sang?"

I nodded, though I cringed. "Your mother could sing. I'm decent at it, but not as good as her. She was the bright light, I usually just growled the bass level."

"That sounds fun though. I wish I could see."

I frowned, thought back to any posts we might've

made. "My brother might have a video on his phone somewhere. He never deletes anything. I'll check, okay?"

She nodded, her eyes sad. "Okay. Thank you, Reece."

It was like another kick to the stomach, the fact that she called me Reece. But she wasn't so angry now. Not so sullen. Maybe she still resented being forced to live here, with things that weren't her own, but we were trying.

I got her a glass of water and tucked her back in. Thankfully she went right back to sleep.

It wasn't until I got into bed myself that I realized she hadn't told me what her dream had been about. Only her mother.

And the fact that she was gone.

"That's rough, buddy," Gage said as we looked over yet another set of IKEA instructions.

"Why do you sound like Zuko?" I asked.

"Because he's the best villain to hero arc out there? And the best animated character ever." Gage grinned, and I rolled my eyes.

I had known Gage for a while now. Of all our friends that had a connection to the Montgomerys,

Gage was actually closer in age to me than the others. We had seen enough shit out there that things got a little hairy.

And of course because it was Denver, the small town that it was—insert sarcasm here—Gage had a connection to the Montgomerys as well. His younger brother Patrick was madly in love and dating Riley.

I didn't know Riley well, but she worked one-on-one with my daughter at the art gallery that she ran, and I knew she was one of Brooklyn's closest cousins.

"Seriously though, she okay?" Gage asked.

That was the thing with Gage. He gave me shit just like I did the same for him, but he was a good man, and really cared about his friends. He took care of everybody around him, to his own detriment sometimes, and I was grateful I had someone else to talk about this with. Sure, I had Brooklyn and my family, but my family always thought I was a good guy—even when they were rousing me—and I couldn't talk about everything with Brooklyn, not when my feelings towards her were complicated enough.

"I think she's okay. I don't know. She doesn't really fucking talk to me." I kept my voice down since Bella was in her room sketching. She told me she would come back out soon to help with the bookshelves, but I wasn't going to pressure her. She'd had a rough night after all.

"My brother has the name of a decent family and child therapist. So I figured I'd see if I can get on their books. Or if they have a recommendation."

Gage nodded solemnly. "It's a good idea. I mean, I have no idea how to handle kids at all, and I know this is completely new for you. But her having someone to talk to outside of this would be good."

"She has Brooklyn at least," I blurted.

Gage raised a brow. "Oh, really. How often is she here?"

I flipped him off. "Stop."

"No, really. I overheard Riley telling Patrick that Brooklyn was hanging out with you more, but I didn't hear the details. You and the Montgomery then?"

"Stop eavesdropping on your little brother and his girlfriend."

"It's not eavesdropping when they don't fucking care that I'm in the room." Gage rolled his eyes. "We were over at the parents' house, and I can't seem to get away from the lovebirds."

"Something wrong there?" I asked, not really that curious about the younger couple. I liked Gage, and he was a good man, but Patrick annoyed the fuck out of me. He was like one of those frat guys who smiled a little too brightly and always got what he wanted.

Sure, the kid worked hard, sometimes, but he went through life pretty easily. Though from what I could tell he treated Riley right, so that was fine with me.

"Don't get on a new subject. You and Brooklyn?"

I looked down the hallway, grateful that Bella's door was still closed. "I think we're seeing each other."

"You think?"

"I don't fucking know. We don't go out, because my nights are now spent with Bella, but Brooklyn comes over here, and we went to that gala together."

"Are you sleeping together?"

"Say that a bit louder with my kid in the house."

"You do realize you're going to have to have the talk with her, don't you?"

"With Brooklyn? Yes. I realize that. We're sleeping together, and we don't talk about what it really means. But that sounds a little too much like talking about your feelings, and I'm not in the mood for that. Not with everything going on."

"I was actually talking about the fact that you will soon have a teenage girl in this house, but good to know about you and Brooklyn."

I closed my eyes as my stomach twisted. "Yes. I realized what talks are going to have to happen. They have a book called *What to Expect When You're Expecting*, but not *What to Expect When You Find Out You Have a Twelve-year-old Daughter*."

"Maybe in a book about adoption?" Gage held up

both hands at my glare. "I'm being serious. People adopt children who aren't babies. Maybe there's something for you in there."

I sighed and pulled out my phone. "I'm making a note to look it up. Thanks."

"I am trying to help. I may be an asshole, but I'm your asshole."

"If you continue to flutter your eyelashes at me, I'm going to think dirty thoughts."

"Just as long as those dirty thoughts also include Brooklyn."

Gage ducked my fist, and the Allen wrench fell from his hand as we continued to laugh.

"What's so funny?" Bella asked as she skipped into the living room and smiled.

I gave Gage a glare and looked over at my daughter. "My friend is just being an idiot. How's the drawing going?" I asked, hoping to change the subject.

She shrugged. "Good, I think. Can I help?"

"Have at it. You must be better than your dad at building things," Gage said, pointing to one of the boxes.

Both Bella and I stilled at the phrase "your dad", but I waited to see what she would say before I made a move. When she didn't say anything, I knew it wasn't time to dwell on the casual mention from Gage. We were so good about calling me Reece, but Bella would always be my daughter. And now we were finding our path.

"Excuse me, it's my literal job to build things."

"Then why aren't these shelves already done?"

"Because you're distracting."

"You just think I'm pretty."

Bella burst out into laughter, the sound like literal bells, and I just sat there, watching my kid be big.

How the hell is this my life?

"Okay, hand me the directions, Bella, let's get these shelves up."

"And they're really for me?" she asked, the hesitancy in her tone killing me.

"Of course. You keep getting books, and I want to make sure they have a place that isn't the floor. You have to take care of them."

"Grandma and Grandpa only let me use the shelves in the library. I couldn't have anything in my room."

I held back a scowl and told myself I didn't need to complain about those two. They would still be in her life, and there was no changing that. And though I hated their attitude, there's nothing I could do about it in that moment. "Well, we can't fit every bookshelf that we might want in your room, but we do have my office, and the loft upstairs. They can hold a few bookshelves."

"So we can buy more books?" she asked, her smile bright.

"That's it, kid. Use that smile and you can get anything that you want," Gage said.

I glared at my friend. "Really?"

"Hey, I'm the fun uncle. I'm supposed to be the one who annoys you. And to make sure that my girl gets everything that she wants."

"You know, Uncle Aiden said that he was my fun uncle."

"Yes, by blood. I'm the fun uncle you choose."

"But then there's Uncle Dash, and Uncle Lexington, and Uncle Crew, and Uncle Connor, and Uncle Colin." She continued to name more Montgomerys as Gage laughed, and I just shook my head.

Somehow this kid of mine had gained a whole extra family when we hadn't been looking, and I would forever be grateful for the Foxes and the Montgomerys in my life.

"What about Uncle Patrick?" I asked, ribbing Gage.

"He's nice too. But all he does is suck face with Riley." She rolled her eyes, and I stiffened.

"Really?"

"Not really. I mean sometimes." Bella shrugged, playing with a screw. "Riley's really nice. I love her. She is so organized, and makes the art classes fun. But her boyfriend always shows up and tries to distract her. She doesn't get distracted easily though."

"It seems that my brother is still the peach that he always was." Gage rolled his eyes, and Bella widened hers.

"He's your brother. Oh."

"What, didn't think an old man like me could have a little brother like that?" Gage asked.

"No, you're just so pretty."

I was grateful that I had already swallowed the sip of water I had just taken, because I burst out laughing, tears threatening as Gage scowled at me.

"Thanks for that," Gage said with a sigh. "I am pretty."

"Pretty old," I muttered.

"Hey, just because I have more silver on my temples than you doesn't make me any older. In fact, you're older than me."

"Really? That's old," Bella said, and I didn't know who was more offended in that moment, but when the doorbell rang, we didn't have much time to care.

"I'll get it," Gage said, but I shook him off.

"My house, remember?"

"Okay, here, Bella, help me actually finish these bookshelves or we're going to be here all night."

I shook my head, loving the way that Bella leaned

into Gage, both of their heads down as they looked over the instructions.

For a man without kids, he was sure good with them. Then again, my brothers were the same. We were all learning this on the fly, and I was grateful for the family we were making.

I opened the door without looking, and my heart left my chest.

"Brooklyn."

She smiled at me, the sun right on her freckled face.

"I should have called, I'm sorry. But I figured since I was driving by I would come annoy you. And really just check on Bella."

With Bella's attention on Gage, I leaned forward, took Brooklyn by the back of her head, and pushed my mouth to hers.

She moaned into my mouth, that moment of surprise simmering between both of us, as I deepened the kiss.

When I pulled back, we were both breathless.

"Oh."

"I'm glad you're here." I said the words, and I meant them. I had no idea what the fuck I was doing, but I could not keep my hands off of her. It was going to be a problem, but I didn't care in that moment.

"I'm glad I'm here too."

"Brooklyn!" Bella said as she moved between us and threw her arms around Brooklyn. Brooklyn, the woman that I was falling for, immediately softened and hugged Bella tightly. They were nearly the same height, with Bella being tall for her age, and Brooklyn being so short, and it was another kick to the gut.

This time, not just because of who Brooklyn was, but because I had lost so many years. So many fucking years that I wouldn't have of Bella's childhood. But I wasn't going to lose any more.

"Well, what do we have here?" Gage drawled out. I elbowed him in the gut, but of course the man's eight pack didn't move an inch.

"I was just here to check in, and annoy you." She winked at me as she said it and I ignored the heat my chest.

"You're never annoying. Come on, Gage and Reece are trying to build a bookshelf for me, and I don't think they're doing it right."

"Well, as the landscape architect versus the actual person who builds things for a living, I'm here to help."

"Stay for dinner?" I asked, my gaze only for Brooklyn.

"Of course I will," Gage answered, and I laughed, but Brooklyn nodded.

"Of course."

And as I closed the door behind her, and nearly

swallowed my tongue, I told myself that I needed to tone it down.

"Does Bella know that you're in love with the woman that seems to be her best friend?" Gage whispered under his breath.

"I'm not in love with her."

"You can lie to yourself but don't lie to me. You know I hate liars."

I gave Gage a look, but pulled my attention quickly back to the two in the living room.

"I don't think it's smart to fall in love with Brooklyn. She's too fucking young."

"I don't think she has a problem with that."

"It wouldn't be fair to Bella."

"As long as you don't keep secrets or lie, I don't think Bella's going to care."

"Damn it. I don't know."

"Better figure it out. You're a dad now. Things get complicated."

And that seemed to be an understatement.

"You know, if you put the sticky wallpaper or drawer inserts on the back panel before you nail it in, it's like a backdrop."

"Really?" Bella asked, eyes wide.

I resisted the urge to groan. "We're not going to add pink and sparkles are we?" I asked as Gage laughed at my side.

"I'm not a pink girly," Bella said sarcastically.

"I have a couple of samples in my car. Mostly because I couldn't help myself. I knew you were doing bookshelves today, and you know me, I love a project. Yay, crafts."

"Really? Thank you. Can I use them, Reece?" Bella asked.

"Anything. *Seriously.* As long as you say thank you."

"Thank you, Brooklyn. *Seriously.* Thank you." She threw her arms around Brooklyn again, and my heart slowed.

"I would have those talks soon," Gage whispered.

This time I didn't elbow him, because he was right.

We were going to have to have so many fucking talks.

"I can go get them from your car if you want. And that'll give you and Reece more time to make out." She winked she said it, and took Brooklyn's keys, leaving me slack jawed, and both Brooklyn and Gage laughing their asses off.

Well, it seemed at least one conversation might have been tabled.

By the time the bookshelves were in place—complete with a sage green and gray pattern background, it had been dinner time, so we ordered in, and enjoyed dinner out on the back porch. It was a little too hot for it, but Gage had set up some fans and had told countless stories to make Bella laugh. Then all four of us had ended up in a water gun fight, because why not, plus Uncle Gage had brought some over. Apparently he'd thought I had an eight-year-old son instead of a preteen daughter, at least as a joke, but in the end, it had been the perfect gift.

Gage had left soon after the fight, and after Bella had showered, she'd fallen asleep hard, the day full of activity.

That left Brooklyn and me in my bedroom, the door closed, and a question on my lips.

"I should probably go," Brooklyn whispered.

I moved forward and cupped her face. "You don't have to. Bella knows that you and I are..."

Brooklyn's lips quirked into a smile. "That you and I are what?"

"That we are what we are. And she doesn't seem to mind."

"I guess she doesn't. Do you mind?"

"I want you, Brooklyn."

"I want you too. And it sort of scares me."

I ran my thumb over her lips. "It scares me too. But I guess we'll figure it out just like we are everything else."

She let out a long breath and leaned into my touch. "We never did talk about before."

I frowned for a moment before the memory kicked in.

"We don't have to if you don't want to. I don't want you to hurt."

"I'm okay. Really. But if we are what we are, as you say, maybe we should get a few things out in the open."

"I'm not with anyone else."

"Same here. And we've established that. But Reece, I want you to know that I don't want to hurt Bella. I promise."

"Neither one of us would be here if you did." And that was the complete truth.

"I want to be a mom. One day. Only it's not going to come like it does with most people."

"Brooklyn, the way I became a father wasn't exactly routine either."

She smiled then, and reached down to play with my belt loop.

"I have an oddly shaped uterus and a few other complications that means I can't get pregnant. And even if somehow I can miraculously get pregnant, I can't stay pregnant. I've known since I was twenty-two that there were issues, and that means every time I get somewhat serious with somebody, I have to explain to them that the way that they become a father isn't going to be the route of easiness."

"I'm sorry," I whispered. I cupped her face, and kissed her softly, before pressing a kiss to the tip of her nose, each eyelid, and then her lips again. "I'm sorry. That must've been painful to hear about."

"I'm sorry too. And it was."

"Brooklyn. Look at me." She did, her eyes so full of emotion that it took everything in me not to hold her until the end of times. "I care because you care. But it's not a deal breaker for me. Do you understand?"

She swallowed hard. "Okay."

"Good. Now, we're going to have to be quiet. Something that neither one of us is very good at. But I don't want to traumatize any other people in his house."

She smiled then and I leaned down and captured her lips.

The first time we had been together was hard and fast, and then slower, as we had explored one another in the tub. And over the past couple of weeks when we had stolen time when we could. Moments in her bed and mine when Bella was at camp, or when she was with my parents. But we had never been together in the darkness underneath my roof, with my kid down the hall.

Parents did this all the time, but I was new at this, and Brooklyn wasn't her mother.

That's something I would have to deal with later, just the mere concept of it. But for now, I pushed those thoughts from my mind and focused on the woman in my arms.

She tugged on my belt loops, and I pulled back, stripping my shirt over my head. She leaned down to lick at the hoops at my nipples, I groaned at the tug and slid my hands up her shirt to cup her breasts over her bra.

"Reece."

"Quiet," I whispered against her ear before nibbling at her earlobe. She was so damn sexy. It was sometimes hard to breathe, and as we stripped each other naked, I didn't care. All that mattered was she was in my arms, and now in my bed.

After I threw my jeans to the side, she knelt at my feet, and my brows lifted.

"Baby, you don't need to do this."

"But I want to."

"Be careful of the hoop though. Don't want to hurt those pretty teeth of yours."

"Well, if you make me gag and my eyes water, we're going to have a problem."

I licked my lips and pressed the tip of my dick against hers.

"I'll be gentle. I promise."

"Liar," she teased, and then swallowed the head of my cock into her mouth. I groaned at the sensation, her tongue licking at the tip, flicking the hoop, and I nearly came just then. My hands went down to her breasts, pinching slightly knowing she liked just that slight edge of pain. Never too hard, never too rough. I knew exactly what my Brooklyn wanted.

She continued to bob her head, and I wrapped her hair around my fist, forcing her to stay still.

"Open wide, but I don't want to hurt you."

She nodded, even with my dick in her mouth, and swallowed. That sent my cock farther down her throat, and both of us groaned.

I couldn't thrust into her like I wanted to, not with the piercing in. I could take it out next time, and we would go rough and hard and just on the edge of pleasure, but for now, I went slow, loving the way that she swallowed me whole, her nose pressed against the base of my groin in the patch of hair there.

"That's it. Take all of me." I tapped her cheek with two fingers, and she hollowed them, tightening her hold, and then I slid out of her before repeating the action. Her nails dug into my thighs, and I smiled, knowing that she was all mine. And when I was ready to come, I pulled out, gripped the base of my cock, and tugged her up.

"Reece," she whispered against my mouth.

"Be quiet, Brooklyn. You have to be quiet."

I explored her mouth with my own, both of us breathing heavily. I had the fans on, the sound somewhat muffled, but we needed to be quieter. I shoved her onto the bed, went down to my knees, and buried my face in her pussy. She put a pillow over her face, moaning my name into the fabric, and I continued to lick and suck my feast. She was sweet, swollen, and all mine. I spread her before me, both of us shaking, as my tongue lapped at the tiny ring on her hood.

"I fucking love this," I whispered, as I sucked her clit into my mouth, loving the way she arched. Her thighs clamped around my head, and I smiled as I continued to eat her out, until she was coming, her orgasm gushing over my face and soaking my beard. I loved the taste of her and I needed more, so when I stood up and placed the tip of my dick at her entrance, both of us froze.

"Bare again?" I asked.

She nodded, and without another word, I slammed into her. She was tight, oh so fucking tight, and it took a moment for her to stretch, to accommodate me. She liked it when I went fast, when I went just hard enough for a moan to escape us both, and so that was what I did.

Anything for her.

I asked each time before we made love to see if she wanted me to use a condom. And each time she said no.

We were both clean, had been rechecked just in case, and just the fact that her bare cunt was around my cock was nearly enough to send me over the edge.

So when I leaned down over her and captured her mouth with mine, as I continued to piston in and out of her, neither of us could say a damn thing.

When I pulled out of her again and flipped her over, she gripped the bedsheets and arched her back for me. I slid my hands over her hips and entered her from behind, each having to muffle our own groans.

"We're going to wake her up," I whispered.

"Then be quiet, and fuck me already," she said with a laugh.

I pressed her head down into the mattress, forcing me to go deeper. She covered her mouth so she wouldn't scream out, as I continued to pound into her. I flicked my fingers over her clit and the piercing there, and she came again, burying her face into the comforter. I pulled out and somehow was able to find the energy to cradle her in my arms before we fell onto the bed. Our hands roamed all over each other, kissing, touching, kneading. We ended up on our sides with her leg wrapped around my hip, as I slid into her slowly, our gazes meeting.

I moved inch by inch, filling her until we could barely breathe, and all that mattered was she was mine, and there was nothing more I could take.

And when she came again, clamping around my cock, I followed, filling her with my cum, branding her as mine. She whispered my name against my mouth, and I held her close, a bruising force that sent us both into the abyss.

And as we came down, our breaths panting, our heartbeats in sync, I knew I was in trouble.

Because I had done the one thing I had told myself not to do for nearly a decade.

I had gone and fallen in love with a Montgomery.

My Montgomery.

Chapter 12
REECE

After another week of routine that didn't feel like routine, I now found myself at a rented out park in the middle of summer for the Montgomery family picnic. Bella stood by my side, practically latched onto me, and I couldn't help but notice her wide eyes.

"Are they all really Montgomerys?" The incredulity in her voice made my lips turn up into a smile.

"Not all of them." A group of brunettes with blue eyes and wide smiles walked past, each with plates of food in their hands, and waved even as they continued their conversation.

"Perhaps a majority of them are Montgomerys, but like us, there are more than a few friends of the family invited."

The morning after Brooklyn had spent the night, we had woken up and made breakfast. Bella hadn't blinked an eye at the fact that Brooklyn had still been there. In fact, the kid had just been ecstatic that she didn't have to eat my breakfast. I hadn't thought I'd been doing badly, but of course, Brooklyn was the best. She made cinnamon rolls from scratch, and I swore if it wasn't for the fact that my job took a lot out of me, and I spent so much of my time fucking Brooklyn, I would probably gain weight by being with her. She made such damn good baked goods, that it was a little stressful. But I knew interesting ways to burn calories.

She'd ended up inviting us to this picnic, and I knew she had been nervous. Because she would have invited us no matter what. I had been to countless Montgomery events like this, where they would invite the entire family and as many friends as they could possibly fit and feed. There wasn't an entrance fee, but everybody did their best to pitch in, because it wasn't as if the Montgomerys were millionaires or anything. Of course, I knew a couple were thanks to their jobs and families. But what made the Montgomerys work was that they were a blue-collar family that worked their asses off for each other. So everybody pitched in, and Bella and I had brought drinks.

Heading down to the Costco in order to buy in bulk was really the only way to make certain things work. We dropped them off when we had first come in, and a few younger Montgomerys had shown up and taken everything off with their dolly, as if they had done this a thousand times before. And frankly, they had this down to an art at this point. So that was probably more true than not.

There was a bouncy castle for the kids, a full beach volleyball section, another place for flag football, soccer, and field hockey. I had a feeling if there had been a way to do something like this at an ice rink, Montgomery hockey would be a thing.

There were different food stations surrounding the park so there wasn't a hold-up in one area. As well as drink stations, and seating areas for those who needed a moment to breathe. The elder Montgomerys were usually found there, with a grandchild or great-grandchild on their lap. And if my eyes weren't deceiving me, I knew there were more than a few pregnant Montgomerys at this event.

"You made it," Brooklyn said as she moved forward, and I held up my arm. She slid right next to me, as if we had been doing it a thousand times, and we froze at that moment.

We hadn't actually spoken about the fact that we would be coming to this, not quite together.

But as soon as one of the Montgomery cousins caught the action, the cat was out of the bag.

"Oops," Brooklyn whispered, and now the Montgomery wildfire grapevine would be quickly approaching its magnitude for the fact that Brooklyn had just held on to and kissed the cheek of Reece Fox.

"Well, this is going to be interesting," I said dryly.

"My parents love you. Don't worry. I mean, I would worry a little bit."

"Oh, is this one of those meet the parents things?" Bella asked.

I coughed and Bella grinned. Brooklyn moved away from me so she could hug Bella tightly. The way that those two leaned into one another as if they'd known each other their entire lives did something to me I couldn't quite name.

They were friends. My relationship with Brooklyn made things tricky, but I knew Bella could rely on Brooklyn no matter what. I would just have to do everything in my power to make sure that stayed the same even after I ended up fucking things up with her. Because I didn't do serious relationships well. And I was more than likely going to fuck this up.

That was why dating somebody I worked with, who was practically my boss, and connected to my life in multiple ways was a bad idea.

And yet all I wanted to do was bring Brooklyn back to my side so three of us could walk through the picnic and spend the day together.

I was in quicksand up to my neck, and there was no getting out.

"This isn't going to be awkward at all," Bella said with a laugh, and I glared at my daughter before kissing the top of her head.

We both froze in the action since we were still getting used to this whole connection thing, but she smiled up at me.

"I see Wyatt and Natalie over there. Can I go?"

I looked over at the soccer area where Bella's friends who I had met a couple of days ago stood and waved.

I nodded and pulled away. "Sure. Just stay on the grounds and where a Montgomery adult can see you, okay?"

"Even if they're strangers?"

"A Montgomery is never a stranger," Brooklyn sing songed.

"I bet you have that embroidered on a pillow," the dryness in my voice could not be matched.

"My mother does." She fluttered her eyelashes, before hugging Bella tight.

"Seriously though, if you need anything, all the Montgomerys look alike, so you'll be able to figure out who's who."

"You need name tags."

Brooklyn snapped her fingers and pulled name tags and a marker from her pocket. "I have those. Sorry, I forgot to give them to you."

"I'm not wearing a name tag." I raised my brows when Brooklyn merely wrote my name out and slapped it on my chest a little harder than she should have.

"Deal with it."

Bella put hers on and grinned.

"Aw, you look great, Reece."

"Thanks. Glad to know who's in charge."

"Brooklyn. Duh." She rolled her eyes like the twelve-year-old she was and skipped to her friends.

I looked down at Brooklyn and put my hand over her name tag.

"Just making sure it's on correctly." I patted her breasts a couple of times, and she rolled her eyes.

"Nice."

"Hey, stop pawing at my cousin," Dash whined.

I froze, and remembered exactly where we were.

"Oh. Hey."

"Hey there. So, bringing the boyfriend. Should be interesting." He ducked Brooklyn's fist, but didn't get out of the way of Riley's kick to the shin.

"What the hell. Why am I going to be bruised at the end of this?"

"Because you suck at sports," Addy said with a roll of her eyes. "Seriously. Why are you so mean?"

"You guys are the ones hitting me." Dash rubbed his shin and gave me a wink.

"Good luck with the Montgomery gauntlet." He dove through the crowd then, both cousins chasing after him, and I gave Brooklyn a look.

"Is there a gauntlet?"

"I would like to say no, but maybe." Her eyes widened, and the blood drained from her face. "Well, maybe there will be a gauntlet."

I turned, afraid to see one of her parents or brothers there with a hatchet or something, but instead I just blinked as my parents and three brothers walked towards us.

"Did you know they were coming?" I asked.

"No. Did you?"

"Of course not. I would've warned you. And it's not a Fox gauntlet. I promise you."

"I don't know if I actually believe you with that," Brooklyn said softly, and then my mother was there, her arms wide.

"Your mother called me and invited us, and so I'm here to annoy my son."

My mom leaned down to hug Brooklyn. The woman I was falling for smiled brightly. "I like the sound of that, Mrs. Fox."

"Call me Kathy."

"Maybe we'll stick with Mrs. Fox because I'm afraid." Brooklyn laughed, and my chest squeezed.

"Whatever you'd like. Do you know my sons?" she

asked.

"We've met. Hi, Fox brothers."

"So, which of your cousins is single?" Aiden asked, and thankfully Denver slapped the back of his head so I didn't have to.

"Maybe we should have color coded our name tags for that," Brooklyn said before sliding her tongue over her teeth.

"There are name tags?" my dad asked. "Thank God. I thought keeping you four straight was hard, but the Montgomerys are ridiculous."

"We really do like to procreate, don't we," a deep voice said and I turned, not realizing I was still holding Brooklyn to my side as I did.

Storm Montgomery moved towards us, broad shoulders, sure stride, and looked as if he could bench press a Mack truck. Or maybe I was just seeing things.

"Good luck," Rowan whispered, and I stepped on his foot.

"Hello there, Mr. Montgomery."

The other man just rolled his eyes. "I have been Storm to you since we met. Don't go all Mr. Montgomery now that you're seeing my daughter."

"Dad…" Brooklyn began.

"No no no, let him tease. This is what I like," Brooklyn's brother Nate said as he came forward. Then Nate's twin James as well as James's wife came over, and finally, completing the mass introduction, Everly Montgomery moved forward.

"It's good to see you, Reece." She kissed my cheek, and I hugged her tightly.

"Good to see you too. Thank you for the books, by the way."

"I mean, there's a new reader in your life. Of course I'm going to make sure Bella has books. Where is she?" Everly asked as she searched over the crowd.

"She's hanging with her friends on the soccer field," Brooklyn said, as she pointed. "And I do believe Lexington and Mercy are keeping watch."

"Oh, good. While we don't have security, all the adults are on watch to make sure the kids are safe."

"Considering you have a security company in the family, I'm pretty sure you have security," I said dryly.

"That is true," Nate put in. "And remember that. There's family members that can look up anything. Find anyone."

"Did you really try this whole acting intimidating thing on my wife?" James asked, and then he ducked Nate's flying fist. The two started to wrestle, and my brothers moved forward, trying to join in.

I pinched the bridge of my nose and let out a breath. "They do realize that we're not teenagers anymore?" I asked my mother.

"Didn't you tackle Denver like two days ago?" Brooklyn asked, and I scowled down at her.

"I thought you were on my side?"

"How close to his side are you?" her dad asked, and my gaze shot up to him.

"Um."

"Oh, look at that. In your forties and you still get all flustered when it comes to meeting a girl's parents." My mom clapped her hands, and I rolled my eyes.

"And with that, I'm going to go get a drink. Have fun making my life hell."

"I can't help it, I live for these moments." My mom patted my cheek and then pushed me towards Brooklyn. "Go, save yourselves. I'm going to go see what's wrong with the other children in my life." She sounded so put upon, that I couldn't help but laugh.

Brooklyn dragged me towards the beverage area, laughing. "Okay, that was ridiculous, and I love them. But wow. I didn't expect them all to be there in one little spot. It's better when it's in small spurts."

"And with the way that some of your cousins and uncles are glaring at me, suddenly I'm not just the guy that works with the Montgomerys that used to be a fireman in their neighborhood, now I'm the one who dares to touch their precious Brooklyn."

She winced, and I moved closer to the table, getting her a can of hard seltzer, and me a beer.

"I didn't mean to make this a big thing. You've just always come to the picnic, and I guess hiding what we are would've been awkward."

I cursed under my breath. "I don't regret it. I just didn't think it through."

"Same here. But Bella seems okay with it, right?" The caution in her voice nearly broke me.

"I think so. I've never dated someone while I was a dad."

"And I've never dated a single dad before."

"I guess we'll make things up as we go along?"

"Yes. And by the way, I should also warn you that one of my cousins who didn't know the backstory, invited Duke's parents."

My hand clenched around the beer can, and I let out a breath before I accidentally burst.

"Oh?"

"They were immediately apologetic, and sorry they didn't hear the news. But it's not like they can uninvite them."

"They would have some nerve showing up."

She rolled her eyes though I still saw the pain in them. "Like they would come to something so lowbrow as a picnic."

"There's nothing low about you or the Montgomerys, baby."

"I'd like to think so. Either way, if they show up,

we'll deal with it. But that's another added layer you know. You and me, even though it's been over a year."

I ran my thumb over her chin and nodded, studying her face.

"As long as you're okay, same with Bella, that's all that matters."

"I am. I'm not that same person, I'm not broken."

"I don't think you ever were, Brooklyn."

"Thank you for saying so."

I leaned down and brushed my lips against hers, ignoring the whistles and the cat calls.

Then Bella was at my side, grinning.

"I love it here. You guys sure know how to have a party. Can I have something to drink?" Her gaze went straight to the seltzer in Brooklyn's hand, and I scowled.

"Let's get you something non-alcoholic," I said dryly.

"Of course. I don't want to drink. It makes you stupid and I would rather be on a sugar high."

"Honestly, I'd take a sugar high too." Brooklyn winked, and we moved towards the drink area, and then the food. People came and went, either looking completely shocked that Brooklyn and I were together, or as if they had known and suspected all along.

I didn't know what the hell we were doing other than this felt good. Almost like we were a family.

Though it was way too fucking early to be thinking that.

But as we moved about, and I joined in a football game, regretting it instantly because I was at least twenty years older than some of these Montgomerys, I couldn't help but know that my kid was safe here. Not only would Brooklyn do anything to protect her, but so would every Montgomery, and those connected to the Montgomerys. I hadn't gone into this summer knowing what my life would look like. I assumed it would be more work, countless destroyed buildings, and bureaucracy.

Now I had multiple lives to think of, and two women in my life who altered the trajectory of my eternity. At the end of the summer, Bella would start school, and we would finalize the paperwork of what this new family meant. Only I wasn't sure what that meant for Brooklyn.

Because as the two smiled at each other, I was so afraid of what would happen if Brooklyn and I called it quits. Because we weren't serious, and there were too many complications in front of us. She was still healing, and we worked together. I was a ready-made family, and I wasn't sure she was ready for something like that. Nor did I know if I wanted anything like that either.

But the two of them were already a unit.

And if I wasn't careful, I'd break that.

So maybe, just maybe it would be better if I broke it off sooner rather than later. That way the two of them could remain friends. Because if I waited any longer, I'd shatter the three of us. And I couldn't do that to Bella, not again.

Chapter 13
BROOKLYN

WITH MY SOURDOUGH cooling on the racks, I quickly checked my phone, and knew I had a little bit of time before I needed to head to Reece and Bella's.

A smile covered my face slowly as I realized that yes, it was indeed Reece and Bella's. She was making a mark on it for sure. Not only were there bookshelves, but Reece had taken part of the game room/man den that he'd had for so many years and added a mini art studio.

From what Reece had told me, Bella enjoyed doing her art in private. Although Riley had mentioned what exactly Bella got up to, I knew Reece wanted to be part of it.

He was trying so hard to be a good dad, even though he had been thrown into it so quickly. Soon the school year would start and he'd have to figure out how to deal with homework, after school activities, friends, weekend plans, and moments where their tentative trust would break.

Bella hadn't been grounded yet, but one day she would be. All kids did something that led to being grounded or getting in trouble. I knew that my parents, as well as his own, had sent over a few books. Even Gage had shocked me by handing him a book about adopting older kids. Reece hadn't looked surprised though, so maybe the two had spoken of it before.

He was doing his best, and though I didn't think Reece thought it was enough, I knew it was.

I knew they were taking steps to finding their path, and there would be more obstacles to come, and tonight was one of them.

Although the grandparents didn't seem to want custody, and had blatantly said so at one point, they were still demanding a dinner.

I wasn't sure how Reece was going to stomach it because I knew that he had issues with them that stemmed from long before Bella had even been born.

I didn't like the way Bella's shoulders caved in when she spoke of them. Or when her gaze would go distant, as if she wasn't even sure that they cared about her. I could have been projecting, but I wasn't so sure.

It wasn't going to be easy, I knew that. But as someone who came from a loving family, I understood how sometimes those connections were needed more than anything. My brothers' birth father hadn't been the greatest man, and they had never even met him.

But their half-siblings—people I called siblings myself because that's who the Montgomerys were—had been dealt a much harsher blow.

Sometimes cutting off people who did their best to belittle and break you was the only way to make life work. I hoped that wouldn't be the case for Bella, and tonight's dinner would be part of that. I would be going over there before the dinner to help Bella with her hair because she had asked, and although Reece was trying his best, he could not braid to save his life. I knew he was trying though, because the night before last, we had sat in bed and watched a movie after Bella had gone to sleep, and he had played with my hair until I had nearly dozed. He laughed, kissed my neck, and then kept me awake far longer than either one of us had planned.

I hadn't meant to be in a relationship with Reece, and yet here we were. Not quite a family, not quite a label. But something. And because Bella was involved, it was inherently serious. It should scare me, and frankly, part of it did, but not everything. Some things felt as if I had been waiting my entire life for these moments.

I moved into my bedroom, opened up my closet door, and stared at the box that I had put there for good reasons.

I shouldn't open it now. It would do no good for

anyone, but if I didn't, it would lurk in my thoughts for the rest of the evening. And that wasn't something I was sure we could do in that moment.

I went to my tiptoes and reached for the pale blue box with light white flowers, and pulled it down from the top shelf.

I sank onto my fluffy armchair next to the bed and near the big window in my room. With trepidation and shaking fingers, I opened the lid and set it on the thick armrest. The top photo took my breath away as it always did, and I let out a deep breath.

Duke's face stared up at me, his eyes dark, the smile there not quite reaching them. Was it my own knowledge that brought those thoughts to mind, or had he really been unhappy? I pulled out the framed photo from soon after we had gotten engaged, and traced his face with my finger.

I had missed the signs. There was no denying that anymore. I had missed things.

Duke had been hurting and I hadn't seen it.

My therapist as well as the grief support groups that I went to all explained to me that it wasn't my fault. That he had hidden himself for a reason. But part of me knew that I should have seen more. That same part told me that I was most likely projecting what I thought I should have seen for the years we were together.

Holding back tears because they wouldn't help anyone in this moment, I went through the rest of the box, letting the memories fly through. They hurt, and always would, but grief, while everlasting, wasn't always equal in its righteousness. I would always miss Duke. And the person that I had been when he had been alive and mine would always love him. But I wasn't that person anymore. I was a different Brooklyn Montgomery, haphazardly put together in some aspects, but not the woman that Duke had left behind. He was no longer here, and the person with hope in her eyes holding that man wasn't either. And that was okay. Well, it was never okay that he wasn't here. And I would hate those moments and that feeling for the rest of my existence. But the woman I was now, that woman was in love with a far different man. Older, wiser, and just as broken as me.

I didn't know what I was supposed to do with those thoughts. Because I didn't know if he loved me. Not the bravest concept, but what else was I supposed to do. I couldn't wallow in what I didn't know.

After taking a long breath, I packed away the ticket stubs and ribbons from gifts that he'd given me over time. I had chosen to keep them, including the fancy wrapping paper, much to my father and my brothers' eye rolls. But my mother was the same way, and I had kept little mementos of our time together.

But Duke wasn't here anymore. And while a part of me would always love him, I wasn't in love with him anymore. To do so would remind me that I had been broken, and I wasn't that person anymore. This new person had a whole new life to live. And that was scary as hell because I didn't know what that life would be like with a certain single dad.

I shook my head, and put everything away, before setting the box back in its place.

If Reece ever asked about it, I would tell him. Keeping secrets like that would help no one, but it wasn't that I kept it for reasons that would break me. No, it's because I kept a part of who I had been. Not who I was now.

My phone buzzed, my timer going off to tell me that I needed to head out soon.

"Goodbye, Duke. I loved you."

I didn't cry when I said the words out loud. And I felt like that was a bigger step than before.

With a calming sigh, I quickly finished getting ready and headed to Reece and Bella's.

Bella opened the door before I could even ring the bell and she bounced on her heels.

"You're here. I'm glad. I really want to learn how to do that mermaid braid."

I smiled big and reached out, tugging on the braid she had done over her shoulder.

"You did great with this."

"This is just three pieces. Anyone can do that."

"Not anyone," Reece said, his voice slightly growly. He leaned over Bella and kissed my temple. "Thanks for coming. I'm a failure when it comes to these things."

"You're not."

"He kind of is," Bella teased, and then skipped out of the way as Reece threatened to tickle her.

The two just looked so freaking adorable together. They were making so such big strides in their relationship, and I was honored to be a witness—and perhaps a small part—of it.

"Are you ready for dinner tonight?" I asked, and Reece just gave me a look, as we headed into the living room where Bella had all of her hair things out.

"It's going to suck," Bella said.

"I don't think you're supposed to say suck," Reece added.

"Aren't you the parental unit? You should be the one who knows these things."

"I'm new at this parent stuff," he said with a laugh.

They were laughing at this. I loved the fact that they were so cute together.

"I'm just saying, you should know these things."

"Fine. I know you shouldn't be saying suck, especially because these are your grandparents."

"You don't even know them."

"That's what this dinner's about," he said with a shrug. "I'm going to get to know them."

"I don't know if they want to get to know you. This is probably just to see how you are with me. They don't even want me, but they like to control things."

I paused in the act of braiding her hair, my throat tight as I looked at Reece.

He looked ready to curse or perhaps punch something, but instead he let out a deep breath, and squeezed Bella's shoulder.

"I don't know if that's all true. But either way, you've got me kid."

"You've got me too," I blurted, not knowing if it was the right thing to say, but I didn't want Bella to feel alone. Especially not tonight.

"Will you come?" Bella asked as she looked at me, her teeth gently biting down on her lip. "You don't have to, but maybe it would be better if you did? That way, Dad's not alone. And well, I'm not alone?"

I froze, my hands nearly shaking. As I looked up at Reece, his eyes were just as wide as mine felt, and I swallowed hard.

"This seems like a thing for family," I said slowly. Reece wasn't saying a damn thing, and I ignored the odd whine of my heart in that moment. It would be silly to want anything more than that.

"But you're one of my best friends. And you know me and Reece. I don't know. I just want you to come. But you don't have to."

"Come," Reece ordered, his voice a deep growl. He reached out and pushed my hair back from my face. I loved the gesture usually, but in that moment it just confused me.

"I don't want to make things confusing."

"You won't. Come. We'll do dinner, and from what Bella says, it'll probably be something boiled and disgusting, so we'll get ice cream after."

"I can do ice cream." I let out a deep breath, unsure if I was making a mistake. I looked down at the billowing linen slacks and soft top I wore and cringed. "Is this okay for dinner?"

"You look beautiful. I always love your style."

"You're about my height you know. You can borrow a few things."

"But I don't have your boobs."

"Please don't say boobs in my presence," Reece said with a dramatic sigh. "At least until you're thirteen. It's on my list to have those discussions when you're older."

Bella met my gaze, and the both of us burst out laughing. That poor man and his lists. They were going to blow up in his face, but he wouldn't be alone in that.

"Okay, if you think I look good enough for dinner, I can come."

"That's great. Let me go get my sketchbook, then we can go." Bella hugged me, whispered, "thank you," and ran to her room.

"You do look good enough for dinner."

I ignored the innuendo in his tone and pressed my fingers against his lips as he leaned forward to kiss me.

"How are you going to introduce me to Bella's grandparents?" I asked slowly. "I'm not asking for a relationship, I just don't… God, no. More like what we're going to do for Bella."

He had stiffened as soon as I asked the first question, and my backtracking probably hadn't helped.

"How about our friend. And somebody that we care about?" I let my hands drop and swallowed hard.

"Good answer."

Bella cleared her throat. "If you two are done making moon eyes over each other, let's go. They hate when we're late."

Reece sighed. "We won't be late. But let's go."

"And now when we give them the bread that you made as a thank you gift, they'll know that you made it, and we didn't just pick it up at a store," Bella said as she got into the back of the SUV.

I slid into the passenger seat, when Reece closed both doors for us, and sighed.

"I really hope we're not making a mistake," I told Bella before he got into the car.

"We aren't. But I think Reece is going to need you."

I turned, frowning. "What are you not telling me?"

"Nothing you don't already know." She shrugged, and went to her sketchbook, as Reece got into the driver's seat. He raised a brow in question, and I shook my head, not even sure what I could say in that moment.

I was going to a ridiculous family event and hadn't planned on it. That seemed to be the case day by day for the two of us these days. And I didn't like it.

What were they going to think of me? They'd already met me of course, but I was Reece's coworker then.

Thankfully, I had cleaned the dirt out from under my nails, but I still looked like I played in the garden all day. Because that's what I did.

And here we were, heading towards the same neighborhood that Duke's family lived in. The homes were huge, on large swaths of land, and could easily be a few million dollars each. I was so far out of my depth it wasn't even funny. But then Reece squeezed my hand, and I realized that I wasn't the only one nervous.

We pulled up to the mid-century Gothic home, with an actual honest-to-God turret, and I blinked.

"Is that a turret?" I asked, my voice dry.

"Yep. Grandma won't let me use it. It was for her office, and the front sitting room. Although I don't think anyone actually sits in it." With a dramatic sigh Bella got out of the SUV, and I gave Reece a look before I scrambled to follow her.

Reece was out of the SUV and by Bella's side before I could blink, and I went to Bella's other side, showing that we were a team.

We might look like a family, but I didn't want to confuse Bella, her grandparents, or even me for that matter.

We were Bella's team and that was all that mattered.

The door opened and a man who could only be labeled as a butler stood there, with his thin nose in the air. "Bella. It's good to see you are well."

"Hi Henry. Are Grandmother and Grandfather here?" she asked.

I knew she was trying to sound as if she was strong and unworried, but I heard the unease in her tone. I squeezed her hand, and she leaned her shoulder against mine for just a bare moment. The butler however saw the action, and his eyes narrowed.

"They are in the dining room, waiting for you. As it is summer you do not have coats, but is there anything I could take from you?"

I didn't know if I was supposed to give him my purse or not, but I kind of didn't want to give it up. Instead I just smiled awkwardly, and Reece shook his head.

"No, thank you."

"Bella knows the way."

I wasn't sure if he was rude or not that he wasn't showing us, but then again, I had only been in a few homes that had a butler. Duke's family had one, but I had always been with Duke, or Chelsea. Then again, I hadn't been back since the funeral.

I pushed those odd memories from my mind because they didn't matter anymore, and followed Bella into the dining room. There was a full spread of silver platters laid out on the mahogany table, as both grandparents stood by the window, a drink in hand. He had an Old Fashioned, she a Dirty Martini, and I tried not to smile.

Duke's parents had always said those who went dirty with their martinis must be dirty in morals, and I had thought it was a joke at the time. Perhaps the upper echelons had their own pretentious ways to judge each other. I myself loved a Dirty Martini, and an Old Fashioned. Right then and there, I could use either one of those. I had no idea what I was doing here other than being here for Bella, and yet, I felt like I needed to go home. It was a little too much for me.

"Grandmother, Grandfather. We're here."

"You do not need to announce yourself like a ragamuffin, Bella." Bella's grandmother shook her head and set her glass on the side table. Her grandfather did the same, before leaning on his cane. He didn't move towards us, and I had a feeling he probably shouldn't be standing as he was. Then again, I didn't know the recovery time for a hip replacement. It had been over two months now, but I hadn't seen these people since before the surgery. I knew Bella had only once, so maybe this was normal now.

"Thank you for your text by the way that you would be bringing another person. Thankfully you did it ahead of time so we had a place setting. But texting, Bella. Really?"

"I'm sorry," I blurted. "That's my fault. It's good to see you both again, Mr. and Mrs. Long."

"Ms. Montgomery. I didn't realize that coworkers came to family events," Mrs. Long practically snarled.

"Barbara, dear. Don't you see the connection? It seems that Reece is spending no time trying to replace our dear Cassandra."

The blood drained from my face as Bella let out a soft squeaking sound, but then Reece was there in front of us.

"Reginald, Barbara. Thank you for the place

setting, but if this is going to be how you both act, we're not staying."

"Do you think you can dictate how we are around our granddaughter?" Barbara asked.

"Please stop fighting. I'm sorry. I just wanted Brooklyn here. She's my friend."

"Is that what she calls herself?" Mrs. Long sneered. I had no idea how many martinis this woman was on, but it had to be more than a few.

"You know what, let's just call this a wash, and I'll be out in the car." I squeezed Bella's hand, but she refused to let go.

"No. This is my friend. You wanted us here for dinner, and we're here. Why are you acting like this?"

"Why do you think we're acting like this? You are the one who wanted to have this dinner, Bella. We told you at the start of the summer that this was how it was going to be. Your mother is no longer here, and we do not have to deal with this kind of insubordination anymore. We didn't want to raise a child again, not when we have our future in front of us. And now your father has finally stepped up to the plate."

"Watch how you talk to my daughter," Reece snapped. "In fact, don't talk to her at all."

"What are you going to do? Use those workman hands to beat me up?" Mrs. Long slurred.

"Barbara, settle down." Reginald shook his head,

as bile rose in my throat. I pulled Bella into my arms, wrapping one arm around her waist and keeping her close by. I wanted to tuck her behind me, but I didn't think she would budge.

"I'm sorry," Bella burst out, tears sliding from her eyes.

"This was a mistake. Not even a little mistake."

"Why did you even want us to come if you were going to react like this?" Reece spit out.

"I wanted to see if my granddaughter was whole and happy. It seems that you're right on track for raising her into a Fox." He spoke the word Fox like it was derogatory, but in my estimation, the Fox half of her was the only thing keeping her steady. I finally pulled Bella behind me, and looked at Reece, wondering what the hell we were going to do.

"No. You do not get to speak to your granddaughter in that tone."

"My daughter is dead," Barbara shouted. "She's dead, and I'm not dealing with *that*." She pointed at Bella as if she were a monster, and I snapped.

"Don't you dare talk to her. Or even look at her. What is wrong with you?" I asked.

"You don't even belong here. Thinking you can step into my daughter's shoes."

"I'm not doing anything of the sort. But I care for

Bella. She's my friend, and I don't let anybody talk to my friends with that kind of menace."

"Oh, the Rochesters were right about you. Always clinging to social status. But you're not getting any of our money through Bella. She gets nothing. Our daughter is dead, and I'm not dealing with her mistakes."

It was Bella's grandfather who said that last part, shocking me. Bella let out a wail, and I turned, putting my back to them as I pulled Bella close.

"We're leaving," I whispered.

But then I turned at the sound of glass shattering, and realized that Reece was right in the old man's face. He hadn't touched him, but Mr. Long had dropped his glass, shaking.

"The next time you speak to me it'll be through our lawyers. Bella is mine. I'm going to take care of my kid always. If you even dare to contact her, my lawyers will be on you so fast you'll have to get your other hip replaced. You get me, old man?"

"Don't you dare speak to my husband like that."

"Lady, I'm not some kid that you can try to whip about. I don't know what this dog and pony show was for, but I'm done. Fuck you both." And with that, Reece whirled, and I tugged Bella towards the front door. Without saying a thing, Reece moved towards me, pulled a crying Bella into his arms, and tucked her underneath his chin.

Tears threatened, and I quickly opened the door, ignoring Henry the butler, and ran towards the SUV so we could get Bella situated.

"I'm going to sit in the back with her," I said, and Reece just nodded tightly.

We buckled Bella in, and I held her close as she cried silently, and then Reece was in the front seat, tires squealing as he pulled out of the long driveway.

He didn't say a damn thing, but the white on his knuckles told me that he was ready to hurt someone.

I wasn't sure if there was anything I could say, so I just held Bella as she finally quieted, and pulled away, wiping her tears. She stared out the window, but I took her hand, tangling her fingers with mine. When Reece parked near an overlook where we could see the sunset, I let out a shaky breath, and he turned off the engine.

Without a word he got out of the SUV, and I undid Bella's seatbelt. "Let's go get some fresh air."

"Okay."

The smallness of her voice nearly broke me, and I kissed her temple, before Reece was there to open up her door, and pull her out of the car. I followed, sliding my hand into Reece's as he helped me out of the large SUV. He closed the door behind us, and the three of us stood on the lookout, with Bella between us.

"I'm sorry," Reece said, his voice shaky.

"I am too. I wanted to show them that you weren't a monster. That you weren't what they said you were. And I just wanted my grandparents. I knew they didn't love me. They never did. They call me Mom's mistake."

"I'm going to go back and kill them," I blurted. Reece gave me a look that I couldn't decipher, but Bella let out a shaky laugh.

"I don't want you to go to jail. I'm sorry though. For what they said."

"I don't have any words," Reece finally let out, before turning her so she faced him. Bella's back was to me, so I could see Reece's eyes.

And it was right then and there that I knew without a doubt I loved him. No matter what happened now or in the future, I loved this man.

"We're going to have a talk about what those people said. I know we talked about therapy, but maybe it's time we both go," he said dryly.

Bella let out a watery laugh. "Yeah, maybe. I know Mom used to go."

That surprised me but I didn't say a word. From the look on Reece's face, his thoughts aligned with mine.

"Good. Then maybe we can figure out what to say. As for your grandparents, I'm going to talk to my lawyers, and we're going to make sure that we never see them again. Not until they apologize or get their heads out of their asses. And I do realize that I keep cursing around you and threatening them, but it's been a day."

That made me laugh, and thankfully Bella did too. "You're allowed to curse. You're the parental unit."

"I am. I'm your parental unit. I'm going to take care of you, kid. Always." Reece met my gaze, and I wasn't sure what he wanted to say, but there wasn't anything to put into words. Not between the two of us. I felt like an outsider being there, as this was such a private moment. But I didn't want to be anywhere else.

"You're mine, you get that right? I lost so many years, Bella. I'm not going to lose anymore."

"Is it okay if I call you Dad then?" Bella asked, her voice watery.

"And there you go," I said with a laugh, before I burst into tears.

Reece gave me a look, his eyes full of unshed tears, before he pulled Bella into a hard hug, kissing the top of her head.

"Yeah. Call me Dad." He cleared his throat, before he opened up one arm and pulled me into the hug with them.

"Sorry. I get emotional. And it's been a weird night." I tried to laugh it off, but he kissed the top of my head as well, and then the three of us were standing there and holding one another, this moment forever etched into my memories.

"Does this mean we can get ice cream now?" Bella asked against Reece's chest, and this time it was Reece who laughed, and a little bit of the darkness began to lift. Not enough, it would never be enough, but we were a unit.

"Ice cream. Maybe dinner first."

"Let's do ice cream first. We deserve it," I teased.

"Anything for my girls," Reece said, and I ignored that familiar twinge. Because these two were a family. Finally. And every ounce of me ached to join them. I just didn't know if it was for the best. But I ignored those thoughts, and smiled at the man that I loved, and the little girl who had far too quickly taken my heart, and smiled.

They were a unit, and I would do anything to protect them.

Even if it meant walking away. But for now I wouldn't tell them that. No, those private thoughts were just for me.

Chapter 14
BROOKLYN

REECE

I will pick up chicken.

ME

As in fried chicken?

REECE

Do you have a problem with fried chicken? I could get grilled chicken, but I thought you said you wanted the spicy kind.

ME

Fried chicken's amazing. I just didn't know if you were buying raw chicken and planning on cooking it.

REECE

Why would I say we were going to get takeout and then buy raw chicken?

ME

You said you were going to get food.

REECE

Are we really fighting about chicken, Freckles?

ME

We're not fighting about chicken. But I'm about to fight about Freckles.

REECE

You know you like it when I call you Freckles. Especially when I whisper the nickname right before I eat you out and lick those freckles that nobody else sees.

My cheeks burned so badly that they hurt. I looked around frantically, hoping nobody could see exactly what he was texting me.

ME

Since when do we dirty text?

REECE

An old dog learns new tricks. Of course, now I'm hard while I'm walking around this fucking project site.

I looked up from the bed of my truck and searched the opposite end of the project site. I gave him a little wave, and though he didn't wave back, I swore I could see his brow rise from far away.

REECE

Get back to work, boss. Or I'll have to spank you.

ME

I thought you liked it when I spanked you.

REECE

We both know you like being over my lap. With your pretty little ass going a pretty little pink.

ME

Yes, because you working with a hard-on is totally going to make the day go quickly. As it is I'm going to have to change my panties.

REECE

Brooklyn Montgomery. Don't make me come over there and show the rest of our team exactly who you belong to.

I shivered, then put my phone in my back pocket.

We were getting used to this whole being together while working thing. We no longer had to even pretend to hide it considering the entire team knew we were together. As soon as we had shown up to the family picnic as a couple, there was no hiding. Neither one of us had truly thought too far into the future of what that meant. We'd accidentally fallen into this, and I wasn't even sure when our relationship had begun. Because it was a relationship. He didn't call me his girlfriend, he called me *his*. And that was all the label that I needed. We were exclusive, we put Bella first, and I had a feeling we were as serious as we could get. I didn't need a ring, or future promises. I'd had that before and everything had failed. All I needed was a commitment, and fidelity. Both things that he was giving me. And I could return the favor.

Of course that meant I had to deal with the countless teasing from my siblings, cousins, and friends. Our friend groups were so connected and woven together, that there was no hiding from it. Everybody wanted to know details, and neither one of us were ready to give in.

The only people that mattered in this relationship were the three of us.

Bella and I were friends, and Reece and I were, well, we just were. I was so damn happy. Happy enough that I was a little worried because things seemed to be going well, and that's when things in my life usually tended to explode. But I didn't want to focus too hard on that.

"Hey there," Aly said as she came forward, and I pushed thoughts of Reece and whatever our relationship was out of my mind.

"Hey, I didn't know you were doing the delivery today."

Aly pulled her hat off of her head, folded the brim, and shook out her long hair.

"It's been a long day, and I was tired of looking at

the books so I told my usual delivery driver that I would handle it. That means he's in the green house, working on what he can, and I get to be out here in nature." I looked at the older building that sat on a decent acreage, and then at the three other buildings we had been working on over the past year, and smiled.

"Suburbs is nature now?"

"We live in Denver, so yes. We're right next to the city, right next to actual nature and full on national parks, but any form of plants that I can get at this point is my favorite thing."

"That sounds like a plan. Which projects then are you here for?" I pulled out my tablet, going through what I had.

"Project F? I don't know how you label these, since we're in nearly a cul-de-sac."

"Okay, that's right over there, two houses down. We had that huge fire that came through the brush area a couple of years ago, and we're working to make everything come back again."

Although we lived in a lush area, there were still fires that latched onto the dryness of some parts. As soon as fires broke over the tree line over the mountains, it was scary. I still remembered living near Colorado Springs with two of my cousins when the fire had nearly taken out the Air Force Academy. I was just glad that nobody had gotten seriously hurt, but there had still been countless properties damaged, and acreage that was just now starting to come back. One of my other cousins worked with an animal refuge that had done its best to keep as many unharmed and alive, and I had donated my time to help them.

We lived in a fragile ecosystem, and although my family did build on land, we did our best to use the land that had already been taken by humans, and give back to nature as much as possible. I used native plants whenever I could convince the clients, and also added as much as I could to help the erosion issues and any potential fires.

"I remember it out here," Aly said, pulling me from my wayward thoughts.

"It was scary for sure, but we're nearly done with a few of them. We still have two more buildings that Reece is working on. One he doesn't think he's going to be able to do any restoration on, and it kills me. It was one of the most beautiful structures in the area, but the fire just took the soul out of it." I pointed to the project house on the opposite end of the street from us, and Aly sighed.

"I would say good bones, but even those look a little charred."

"Reece is over there now, doing what he can. I just don't know."

"Well, speaking of Reece..."

"No you don't. You already know as much as I do about that man." I paused. "Okay, not that much. But there isn't going to be any details now. Let's work with your beautiful plants."

"I've got it," Dash said as he came up to Aly and bumped his hip against hers. She rolled her eyes and shoved him playfully.

"Hi Dash. Look at you, looking pristine where everybody else has been working."

I looked at my cousin and grinned. "You do look kind of spiffy. Getting glam for someone special?"

"Oh, there's no one special in Dash Montgomery's life. From what I can tell he likes them all special."

"I don't know if I like the fact that you two are ganging up on me," Dash said with mock severity. "I'll have you know I was in a meeting, and then had to deal with that court thing."

I nodded, having forgotten it was on the schedule.

"Everything okay?"

"Everything's perfect. We are good to go. However, I hate these pants, so I'm going to get them all filthy so I can tell myself it's okay to buy another pair."

"You are as bad as I am when it comes to that," I said with a laugh.

"What can I say? I'm pretending to be frugal. Okay, Ms. Aly, you tell me where you want these, and I will get to work. Reece said that he needed you at project site B," Dash called out.

"Really? Oh, did they get the inspection through?" I asked. Project site B was the second burned building that might be a loss, and we were still waiting on a few things before we could even begin.

"Yes, you can go in. I already did and the place is going to need a lot of work. But be quick, because I have no idea where your plants go."

"I'm so glad that you offered to help then," Aly teased.

"I'll be right back. Promise." I waved to them and made my way to the project house, knowing that our family was working ourselves a little too thin. We considered this branch of projects one major endeavor. We had finished up the smaller projects, as well as the one that my cousin Lexington had been working on so hard last year. Honestly, we had been moving through everything as quickly and competently as possible. But I would be glad when we were done with this set. It was a lot of back-breaking work, and we weren't even close to being finished.

"Hey, Brooklyn, over here to check out the corpse?"

I frowned at Jesse, one of Lexington's team members.

"Really? You're calling it a corpse now?" I shivered

at that, not surprised the team had found another way to add a nickname that weirded me out.

Jesse shrugged in answer. "I don't know if Reece is going to be able to fix the place. That fire took it out hard core. And this one isn't even as bad as the one he's at."

"So he's not at *this* project house. I thought Reece wanted me to be here."

"Reece is on his way, don't worry. You love birds can have some privacy. I'm going to go help Dash with the plants."

I rolled my eyes as he went to help Dash and walked into the small house. There wasn't a front door anymore, and everything that the firefighters had put it through had pretty much ruined most of the uniqueness that made this house a home. It hurt my heart that there didn't seem like there was anything we could do, but between Lex and Reece, they could usually think of something.

I moved into the living room and froze as the sound of a huge crack echoed through the area. Somebody shouted, and I whirled, wondering which house it was from. Then a shadow split over me, and I tried to move out of the way. Three huge beams that had been part of the roof tumbled forward, and my foot slipped, tripping over an upturned board. I hit the floor, splinters digging into my palms as the first beam slammed right over me. Part of it hit my shoulder, and I screamed.

The other two hit each other, slowing down somewhat, but were still coming at me from the second story. It all happened so quickly, that it felt as if with each breath, there was no escaping it. I tried to get up, but the first beam pinned me down, but then Reece was there, strong hands on my arms, as he pulled me out, and the other two beams slammed into the floor with a breathtaking speed, shards of wood flying everywhere. Reece covered my head and shoved us both to the ground, keeping me safe.

My heart thudded in my chest as I looked up and him, wide-eyed.

"What the hell were you thinking being in here?"

"Are you serious right now?" I pushed him away and winced at the blood on my hands. "I'm in here because we already had the major inspection done. I'm allowed to walk in here. I'm the one who fucking owns it."

"You could have been killed!" Reece practically shouted in my face. We were both kneeling on the ground, and I moved away from him, standing up without putting my hands on the floor. People were shouting now, running towards us, and I couldn't even look at Reece.

He'd saved me, but screaming at me in front of everyone else? What the fuck.

"Are you okay?" Dash was there, looking down at my hands and cursing. "We should take you to the doctor."

"I'm fine," I said, ignoring the ache in my shoulder. "I just need to wash my hands or something."

"You should go to the fucking doctor," Reece snapped.

I looked at him then, my eyes narrowed. "I think you've done enough yelling. If you'd like to yell some more, go find the inspector who fucking lied."

"Freckles, don't be stupid. You're hurt. You're going to the doctor."

Silence settled over the entire place, every single member of *my* team staring at us in shock. This. This was why I had tried not to want Reece. Why I'd tried to keep my eyes off of him. Because when things weren't going well, we fought. And he acted like *this*.

And I'd always be the person too fragile to stand up for myself.

Or I had been.

I saw the fear in his eyes. I only wished I could latch onto it. To lean into it. But I didn't think that was an option. Not now.

"I'll take her," Aly said as she came to my side. "No need to act all growly. She freaked me out so I get to take my new best friend to check out that noggin of hers."

"No one says noggin, Aly," Dash drawled, trying to lighten the tension.

Reece didn't say a damn word. Instead he turned on his heel and walked away, leaving me alone with my team. And there were no other words for that.

IN THE FORTY-EIGHT HOURS SINCE THE UNFORTUNATE work incident, my entire family had shown up, at least my immediate family and a few cousins. They all came to the house, making sure I was fine, and I held up the small bandages on my hands, and sighed.

"No stitches, no broken bones. Just a couple of bruises, and an annoying splinter."

I repeated that statement to the point that I could say it in my sleep.

And Reece hadn't shown up.

No, apparently he was giving me the space I didn't know we both needed.

He had texted, at least he had done that.

A simple text saying he was glad I was okay, and that I should get some rest.

Away from him.

He didn't say that last part, but it sure as hell felt

like it. However in this moment, I wasn't exactly alone. Aly paced by my side in the kitchen, worry on her face.

"He's scared," Aly said after a moment, eyes narrowed.

"I don't care. He doesn't get to yell at me." That was when I realized that tears were sliding down my cheeks, and I didn't know if it was fear or anger, and I hated it. Hated it all.

Aly handed me a tissue and I wiped my face, annoyed I'd cried at all. At least it was in front of her and not any of my family. "Reece yells. He's a growly asshole, but he was worried about you."

"I may not be his direct boss, but I am part owner of this company. He doesn't get to do that."

"No. He doesn't. He needs to hold his temper. But he was scared. We all were. We had no idea what happened, but then you screamed, and we were all running over there."

I looked down at my hands and let out a shaky breath. I'd thought of nothing else these past two days and come to the realization I should have in the heat of the moment. "Reece pulled me out of the way. From the second beam. I could have died, and I can't even focus on that because I'm too worried about the fact that my boyfriend is yelling at me."

I wiped away my tears, this time knowing they were full of anger.

"You can yell right back. It's okay."

"No, it's really not. But I don't know what to do with him, Aly."

"Do you love him?"

I swallowed hard, unable to say the words aloud, but she saw the answer, nonetheless. Without a word, she hugged me, telling me I wasn't alone. I was a Montgomery, after all, one was never alone—something Aly had seen firsthand when the family phone tree and chat group had been enacted when I'd been hurt. That at least brought a smile to my face and once Aly left to head to the nursery, I knew I needed to get my act together and either get to work or reach out to Reece. There didn't seem to be another option.

Anger and confusion warred within me. What was I supposed to do? Lean on my boyfriend. The one who didn't want to be called boyfriend. Because neither one of us wanted labels. No, this was just a reminder that life was complicated, and I was going back to work today, and everything would be fine. The inspector had apologized, but I didn't think that was enough. Neither did Lex and Dash.

In fact, we were going through every step that we had taken after that particular inspector, and repeating everything that we could. It was just a freak accident, that's what I kept telling everyone, and that's what the evidence seemed to prove, yet it seemed that the house there wasn't the only thing that had broken.

My doorbell rang, and I frowned, wondering which Montgomery it was this time. I opened the door, careful of the bandages on my hands, and sucked in a breath when I realized who stood there.

"Brooklyn!" Bella launched herself at me, but Reece caught her at the last moment.

"She's hurting, Bella. I don't want you to jostle her."

Bella frowned, her eyes wide and sad, and I opened up my arms. "I could do with a hug though." Then Bella was there, holding me tight, and I let out a shaky breath.

"Dad said that you needed some time," she whispered, and my heart did that little clutching thing at the sound of her calling Reece Dad. From the way that Reece's eyes warmed for an instant, before they went to their normal glower, I knew he felt the same.

"I'm really okay. It's a long day at work, but I have sourdough bread to keep me company."

"Will you help me make a starter?" Bella asked.

"Bella—" Reece began, exasperated.

"I said I would. Don't worry. We will make you a baking star."

"Why do I feel like there's going to be flour all over my kitchen?"

I looked at Reece then, my arm wrapped around Bella's waist, hers around mine, and smiled. I hoped it reached my eyes. "Hi."

"Hey Freckles. Sorry it took us so long to get here. I wanted to make sure you had time to rest."

I knew it wasn't quite the truth, but with Bella here, there wasn't much else to say. "I'm really okay. I could have gone back to work today, but my dad yelled at me. Lex yelled at me, and Dash scowled. There's a lot of yelling going on."

Reece's jaw tightened, and he gave me a slight nod. "I was scared," he whispered. "I shouldn't have yelled at you in front of your team." He looked at Bella and sighed. "I shouldn't have yelled at all."

"In the heat of the moment, I understand the yelling. I shouted as well, but we're going to need to figure this out." I looked between the two of them. "I think all three of us are going to need to figure this whole thing out."

"That means talking about relationships," Bella said slowly and dramatically. "Using real words and everything. Don't worry, I have a book on this." She sounded so serious, that I had to press my lips together so I didn't laugh.

"God save me from you two working as a team." Reece shook his head. "I'm sorry, Freckles."

"Apology accepted. And I'm sorry for storming off.

I think I was embarrassed that of all the people that a house could fall on, it was me. The one who tries to be the big boss."

"We all know that Lex is the big boss that likes to move you all around like chest pieces," Reece said dryly.

"Okay, fair." And then I was in Reece's arms, and he kissed the top of my head, and Bella held me close.

"Does this mean we can get ice cream?" Bella said softly, and I couldn't help but laugh.

"Tomorrow, kid. You two can go get the ice cream that you've promised each other."

I looked up at him then and smiled. "Really?"

"Don't look so surprised. You and Bella said you wanted a girls' trip, and I need to help my brothers out at the station with one of their enrollment gigs. So I do assume you're going to bring me ice cream as well."

I laughed and finally pulled them into the house fully.

"Of course we'll bring you ice cream. Bubblegum, right?"

Bella made gagging sounds as Reece didn't even bother to answer. Instead, he went to my kitchen, began to make coffee, and poured milk for Bella. He was there in my kitchen, acting as if he knew what he was doing, and comfortable with it.

I would never understand this man, not fully, but I truly wanted to figure him out.

"Ice cream tomorrow for you two, but tonight, movies, popcorn, and we'll order a pizza."

"Yay for junk food," Bella said as she danced around the living room.

"Do I get a say in this?" I asked, laughing.

"Not in the slightest." Reece leaned forward and kissed me softly on the mouth and just like that, the tension that had been riding my shoulders began to ease. "I'm sorry, Brooklyn."

I cupped his face, his beard soft under my hands. I should tell him I loved him, but I didn't. The words would come, but in this moment, it just needed to be us.

"It's okay. You should have yelled. Maybe not those exact words, but screaming was a must."

"I don't know what I would've done if you'd been hurt even more than that." He let out a shuddering breath and kissed my temple. "Just be careful with trees or anything else that could hurt you while you're at the job, okay?"

"You're the one who works with fire, I should be more worried about you."

He kissed me softly again, and I ignored Bella's fake gagging behind us.

"Go sit down, let me take care of you." I met his

gaze then and tried to understand exactly what he was saying.

"Can Bella and I pick the movie?"

"Nothing animated," he said with a sigh, then he went back to the kitchen and continued to get things ready.

I sank into the couch next to Bella, wondering how this had happened. It wasn't one quick moment, not even a purposeful path. I was surrounded by two people I adored, two people I loved. And we needed to figure this out. As Bella went through the movie selection, I knew we could.

We were doing good, the three of us, and nothing could take that from us.

Chapter 15
REECE

"She's really okay?" Rowan asked, his frown looking far more permanent than usual.

"Yes. Thank God. If she wasn't, I wouldn't be here."

"It took an enormous amount of pull to even get you here in the first place. But don't worry, we're excited for training."

Even though I could hear the roll of his eyes as he said that, I ignored it.

Brooklyn was safe, and she hadn't been hurt that badly. Yes, a few bruises, and her palms had been scraped up, but it could have been so much worse. I still wasn't sure how I had been able to get her out in time. I'd ended up with a bruise on my thigh by throwing myself on the ground as I had, and I wasn't as young as I used to be. Being in your forties when you throw yourself on the ground meant that you could break a hip. At least that's what my youngest brother kept saying.

"Well let's get this over with," I said dryly. "Because I want to head over to my actual job and see the girls."

"Look at you. Your girls. How is my favorite niece?"

"Your favorite and only niece is doing pretty good. We're about to do the whole back to school shopping thing, and I'm terrified."

I shivered even as I thought it. I hadn't thought of back to school anything in over twenty years. I felt far older than I should in that moment. And yet, waking up that morning with Brooklyn in my arms hadn't felt too bad. I hadn't felt old at all.

"You should ask Mom." Rowan lifted his chin, and I turned to see both of our brothers walking towards us. The three of them didn't work in the same firehouse. While some family members could probably make it work, my brothers each did better in different stations. That way, they didn't have to worry about somebody getting promoted over them. Sure, they were all at different ranks now, but they weren't in the same chain of command.

"What are you asking Mom to do?" Aiden asked as he took the apple from my hand that I had just picked up. I scowled at him, but didn't care. As long as Aiden was eating fruit instead of junk food, I counted it as a win. Much like it did when it came to Bella.

"Back to school shopping," I said with a laugh.

"Mom would like that. So would Brooklyn." Denver raised a brow, and I knew he was fishing.

"Just ask," I bit out.

"Are you going to ask her to move in?" Aiden asked.

"Are you going to ask her to marry you?" Rowan asked at the same time.

Denver just stared at me. "Have you told her you loved her yet?"

All three of my brothers, as well as a few other people in the station house stared at me.

"Don't you all have somewhere to be?" I barked out at those who weren't related to me, and they immediately went back to cleaning.

Denver beamed. "Just like you were when you worked here. Look at you, fitting into those boots."

"Fuck off. And she was engaged just over a year ago, and I don't think putting a ring on her finger right now would be the best thing."

Denver said. "I think you're wrong."

"I think you should just have her move in first," Aiden said.

"With Bella there?" Rowan put in, and then the three of them were having a lightly heated argument, and I didn't have any input.

I was fucking in love with that woman. I was going to tell her. My brothers didn't need to know that.

Mostly because they'd accidentally spill it. At least Aiden would. He wouldn't do it on purpose, but things happened. And I needed to finally tell her that I loved her.

Moving in and marriage, that would take a moment. Bella came first, and I liked where we were at.

We were figuring out who we were as a family, albeit a different one.

I never expected to be a father, not after so many years of being single, but here I was, a father, in love with a slightly younger woman, and happy.

I ran my hand over my chest, and ignored my brothers' pointed looks.

"We're fine. We're figuring things out. Stop being nosy."

"You're the one who told us to ask," Aiden whined, even though I knew he was just exaggerating.

"Where is Bella?" Denver asked. "I thought my favorite niece would be here so she could hang out with her favorite uncle."

"You mean me?" Aiden put in.

I ignored their bickering once more, and sighed. "My girls are out getting ice cream. They promised themselves a girls' day, but with the accident at the job site, they'd had to put it off. Now Brooklyn and Bella are out and they promised to bring me ice cream after we finished this up."

"Wow. It must be serious if the two of them are out by themselves."

"I trust Brooklyn no matter what. Hell, I trust her more than you," I said, pointing at Aiden. He flipped me off, and yet, the smile on his face told me that he knew I was kidding.

"I hope she brings us ice cream," Rowan said, and I ignored them once more, before heading to the conference room so we could go over the class for the day. I was only one of the speakers, not the major educator, and for that I was grateful. It had been a while since I had been an active duty firefighter, but I still trained enough that if we needed volunteers, or there was a natural disaster, I could suit up if needed. Though now with Bella in the picture, I wasn't sure. Yes, my family and Brooklyn could take care of her when I was gone, but I didn't know if I wanted to risk myself like that. Not with people in my life that I wanted to come home to.

I leaned back against the wall, as the rest of the class ended, and checked my watch. They should have been here by now. I hadn't been craving ice cream, but suddenly I wanted it. And I wanted to see my girls.

I pulled out my phone to call and see where they were, when it lit up with Lexington's name.

I answered, an uneasiness settling over me. It could be anything. He was my boss after all. But I didn't think so. Not with that odd sense of foreboding.

"Lex? What's wrong?"

"They're both fine."

"What the fuck?" I asked and I was already moving towards the exit and my SUV before Lex even continued. My brothers were on my tail, the tone of my voice seeming to pull them out of whatever the hell they had been fighting about.

"Bella and Brooklyn were in her car when somebody T-boned them at a stop sign. The guy was going fast, and it..." He stopped speaking before finally continuing. "It hit the driver's side, but both of them are okay. They were taken by ambulance to the hospital." He named the emergency room, and bile slid up my throat.

The driver's side. Brooklyn was... Meaning Brooklyn's side. My daughter was tall enough now to sit in the front seat, so I'd never had to deal with car seats or the like other than when I had been at the station teaching young couples how to work with car seats to begin with. But with the way that Lex kept saying that they were okay, I couldn't help but not believe him. Especially because he said the word ambulance.

"Why were they taken by ambulance if they're okay?"

"What hospital," Rowan asked as he took my keys before I could even say anything. I scowled at him, but got into my passenger seat, my brothers getting into Denver's truck. They would leave the other two here, and we'd deal with it later. But without words, we were on the move. I named the hospital, and Rowan nodded, before peeling out of the parking lot, the other truck behind me. I knew they would tell the station what had happened, and hell, the accident had probably gone through the radio, but it hadn't been in their area.

I tried to catch my breath, but all I could think of was both of the people that I loved more than anything, were broken and bloody, and all because someone had to run a fucking stop sign.

"Bella has a broken arm and Brooklyn is cut up and a little bruised. Even more so than before. I'm her emergency contact, so they called me. My parents are already on their way here, same with her siblings. But Reece, I know you're Bella's emergency contact, however, whatever was in their system wasn't updated. They called her grandparents."

I slammed my fist into the dashboard, cursing. "Fuck."

"Just get here. They're fine. I promise you."

"If my little girl has a broken arm, then she's in pain. And she's not fine. And how many cuts and bruises does Brooklyn have?" I asked, my words clipped.

"Just get here."

With that, Lex hung up, leaving me seething.

"The call went to Bluetooth, so I heard all of that," Rowan began.

"Just drive safely, we don't need another accident."

Even though the words felt as if I were dead inside, I was trying. Damn it, I was trying.

It didn't take long to get to the emergency room, as every worst case scenario rolled into one another, and there was nothing left in me but to have my knees buckle. I jumped out of the truck, nodding at my brother, knowing he would deal with parking and everything else. As I ran into the emergency room, I didn't even have to wait long. Storm Montgomery was there, a glare on his face, and he lifted his chin.

"He's with us," he said to the front desk, and then the nurse nodded, and I followed him down the hall.

"Brooklyn's down here, but I know you need to get to Bella first. Her grandparents are in the waiting room on the other side." Storm shook his head. "They took one look at her and left."

I nearly tripped over my own feet, and stared at the father of the woman that I loved.

"What?"

"I don't know what they were thinking, if they were

scared, or just don't fucking care. But they're pacing in the private waiting room, and my wife is in with your daughter right now. We said that you two were engaged, and that's why Everly's in there and not a social worker." Storm said the last part so low that I could barely hear, and I swallowed hard, nodding tightly.

"Thank you," I whispered.

"Just go get your girl, and I'll check on mine. And then, you can come and check on her too."

Feet heavy, I moved past the open doorway, and into the next, knowing that if I went into Brooklyn's room in that moment, I would fall to my knees and not be strong enough for my little girl.

Because if I looked at Brooklyn in that moment, I would fail at being the father I needed to be. Bella needed me to be strong, so I would be, and then I would hold the woman that I loved. The gasp that escaped the room nearly made me pause, but I ignored it, knowing that Bella had to be scared.

Brooklyn wasn't alone, and I would be there soon. But I needed to see my daughter.

She looked so small in the hospital bed, with a temporary cast on her arm. She spoke in quiet tones to Everly, before she looked up and smiled at me.

Fucking smiled.

"Dad. You're here. Is Brooklyn okay?"

I looked at Everly and gave her a tight nod. "Thank you. If you want to go check on your daughter…"

"I will. We were just making friends. But I'll be back." Everly stepped toward me and went to her tiptoes to kiss me on my cheek, and my shoulders relaxed ever so slightly. She was just like her daughter in being able to calm me, calm people. But I only had eyes for Bella in that moment. I moved forward, wanting to pull her close to make sure she was alive, and safe, but I didn't want to hurt her any more than she already was.

"Brooklyn's parents are with her, and I will go check on her, but I needed to see you first."

"You should see her. I don't want her to be scared."

Her eyes were wide, a little watery, and I cursed, before going to her other side without the broken arm, and holding her close. I did my best not to make her shift, and she sank into my chest and let out a deep sigh.

"I was so damn scared that I lost you, Bells."

"I'm okay. Brooklyn did really good. She took care of me even when my arm hit the dashboard."

"I'm going to find your doctor and nurses, and I'm going to get everything that I need to know about this, and then you're about to be pampered like nobody's business. Just wait until your grandma and grandpa hear about this and get here. You're going to be so spoiled. It's going to be insane."

I was trying to make light of it, even though I felt like I wanted to throw up.

"If you marry Brooklyn, I get another set of grandparents. I really like Everly. And Storm is really nice and pretty."

I rolled my eyes. "We need to talk about your ideas of pretty," I said dry.

"And I like calling Ms. Kathy Grandma. You think she'll be okay with that?"

"She'll be damn fine with it." I wasn't sure how I was able to speak with my throat so tight, but I nodded at the top of her head.

Before I could say anything else, the doctors and nurses were there, and they explained about the clean break, the lack of surgery, and the fact that Bella was young and strong and would heal quickly. By the time my parents and brothers were allowed back, I was able to break free, with instructions in hand, and went to check on Brooklyn.

Bella was safe, in good hands, and I needed to see her. I hated that I hadn't even been near her yet, but it wasn't as if they were in the same fucking room. As it was, if it wasn't for Storm and Everly's lie, things could have been even more complicated.

Before I could get there though, the two people I

did not want to see most in the world, stood there, chins lifted.

"I see you finally showed up." I ignored Mrs. Long and stared at the older man. "Is there a reason you left her alone in that room?" I asked, my voice shaky.

"She was just fine with that other woman. And I didn't like seeing her hurt like that."

"Of course we didn't," Mrs. Long added, surprising the hell out of me.

I stared between the two of them, not understanding them at all. Who the hell were these people, and why could I never get a read on them?

"I don't know what the hell is going on, but my daughter was hurt, and she's safe now. I know you want to walk away, and maybe that would be better for everyone, but we're going to need to figure this out. You too. I don't know what that means, but for now, I need you to get out of my way."

"She got hurt under your care," Mr. Long snapped.

"She did. Because kids get hurt. And the woman that I love got hurt. It was an accident. One that someone else caused. But I will die before I let anything happen to them. Even from you. I know we need to talk, but that's my kid in there, and that other door holds the woman that I love. And I need to see her. If you are going to make things more difficult, you need to leave."

They didn't say a damn thing, instead they stared at me, before finally walking away, leaving me in the hallway, wondering what the fuck I was supposed to do.

That's when I realized that I had practically shouted those words, and countless nurses, doctors, and Montgomerys were standing there, wide-eyed. And finally when I took two steps forward so I could see into Brooklyn's room, I saw her sitting at the edge of the bed, stitches on her forehead, and the side of her arm, with wide eyes.

I ignored the others, knowing that this wasn't going to be easy, but I took a few steps in, needing to breathe.

"I take it you heard all of that?" I asked, before moving closer. I was standing right above her, hovering. She had been hurt, waiting, bruised, and it took all within me not to pick her up just like I wanted to do Bella.

"You were kind of shouting it."

"I didn't actually mean to scream like that, but I was fucking scared. And pissed off."

"When you walked by like that, I thought you hated me. Because of the accident." I caught her hurt. Shame coated me, and I realized I had made the wrong decision. I had thought by leaving her with her family when I could focus on Bella and not want to throw up, I had been doing the right thing. Only in the end, I had hurt her more.

I cupped her face, careful of her stitches, and leaned down to brush my lips against hers.

"I'm sorry, Freckles. I didn't mean to do that. I needed to check on Bella, and I knew if I walked in here, I'd break down like I want to right now, and then neither one of us would be strong enough for that little girl in the next room."

She let out a shaky breath, before smiling softly up at me.

"I guess that's a good answer. Because I thought you would be so fucking angry with me. I didn't see the car. I didn't know it was there until it was too late."

"Lex told me what happened. It wasn't your fault. But if I find that guy, it's going to be a problem."

"I'm pretty sure that he has a host of other problems that have nothing to do with us. But is she okay? I keep wanting to go in there, but nurses and doctors keep coming in and then Montgomerys." She gave an exaggerated eye roll. "I just want to make sure she's safe."

I kept my palms on her cheeks and let out a deep breath.

"She's safe because of you."

"I didn't do anything. I'm the one who got her in an accident to begin with."

"It could have been worse. We both know that. But she's safe. And you are too. Although every single bruise and cut on your body makes me want to strangle someone. You're going to have to be patient with me. I'm not good at this kind of thing."

"And what thing is that?" she asked, eyes wide.

"You heard what I said out there. This whole love thing. I didn't mean to fall in love with you, Freckles. But I don't want anything else. I just want you. So you better be damn okay. And you better forgive me for having to walk past your door."

"I forgave you the moment you did it. I know why. And I love you too. I didn't mean to. You're growly and old and mean, but I love you."

She was crying and laughing as she said the last part, and I rolled my eyes, knowing that my nosy brothers, her family, and countless others were listening in. I was going to hear about this for years. But I didn't care. Instead, I lowered my mouth to hers and kissed her softly.

"I love you."

"Yay!" I whirled to see my daughter on Denver's phone, waving. "It's about time."

I scowled at my brother.

He just shrugged. "You wouldn't let me bring her over, and I figured she should be part of this. It's a momentous occasion."

"I would ask for time alone but I don't think you're ever going to give it," I said dryly.

"Never," Bella and the others said simultaneously, and I laughed before leaning down to take Brooklyn's lips again.

I moved out of the way when the nurses came back, and knowing that Brooklyn would be discharged soon, I went back to check on my daughter, and did my best to figure out this whole single dad thing. But as my family and Brooklyn's surrounded me, I realized I wasn't doing this solo. And I never had been. And when Brooklyn was finally discharged, and we waited for Bella to be ready, I held onto the woman that I loved, and we made plans for our future. Something I never would've expected even this past spring.

But the two girls in my life were anything but expected. And I knew the path in front of us was never going to be boring.

Chapter 16
BROOKLYN

My knees dug into the pillow, and I lifted my chin, tears falling down my cheeks. He wrapped my hair around his fist, and I swallowed hard.

"That's it, Freckles. Take it. Take all of it. Do you want this dick? You take it."

I eagerly took more, letting him take control. After months of dancing around each other, and settling into this new life of ours, I wanted Reece to do what he did best.

Take care of me.

"Look at you down on your knees. Are you wet? Touch your pussy for me. Show me how wet you are."

I blinked up at him, his cock halfway down my throat, but did as he asked. Well, ordered. I let my fingers slide down my belly, over the thatch of curls, and dipped my finger into my cunt. Everything ached, I was sore from the night before and swollen. I loved this man and everything he did, and not just when it came to getting me off. But damn did the man know how to fuck.

And the fact that he was teaching me to think all of these naughty thoughts in words I never used to use, just told me exactly how much I loved being with this man.

I slid my finger out of myself, and showed him, even as I bobbed my head, taking more of him in.

He smiled, and then pulled the back of my hair hard enough to make me pause, before he leaned down and took my fingers into his mouth.

"Sweet and tart. My favorite combination. Now, are you ready for more?"

Eyes wide, I had to wonder exactly what kind of game we were playing. We both liked blowjobs and that's something I never thought I would say in my life, but I knew how close he was. His balls were tight, his cheeks slightly ruddy. He was ready, but I knew this wasn't where he wanted this to end. No, he wanted to come inside me, and not down my throat again.

I pulled back, needing to breathe, my eyes watering, and kissed the tip of his dick.

He smirked at me. "I take it you like the fact that I took the piercing out?"

"Just for this."

"It will go back in soon. Don't worry, I'll take care of you."

"That I have no doubts about." Then he was back down my throat, and both of us were moaning, though it was hard to breathe around his girth. And when he slid out of me, having made me gag more than once, I found myself in his arms, my legs wrapped around his waist. He kissed me hard, tongues clashing, and I couldn't help but scratch my nails down his back. My clit ached, pulsating with each heartbeat, and I wanted him inside me.

Then I was somehow bent over the armchair, ass in the air, and he was gripping me hard.

"Look at you, dripping for me."

"Reece."

"I've got you. I've always got you." And then he was inside me, hard, thick, and there was no more thinking. My toes barely reached the ground, so I arched my back, taking him deeper. He slid his finger over my clit, swiping at the hoop there, and I shivered, my pussy fluttering around his cock as I came.

"So fucking tight. That's my Brooklyn. That's it. Take me."

He moved, both of us moaning, the sounds of our lovemaking filling the empty house.

But then he pulled out, leaving me aching.

"We're not done," he growled, before tugging me onto the couch behind him. He laid back, his dick standing at attention, and I went to sit right on top of it.

"No, my face."

I've raised a brow. "Excuse me? I thought you wanted to come."

"I need to taste you first. Sit on my face, Brooklyn."

Both of us laughing, loving these rare moments of time where we could just be ourselves, alone in a home that was constantly full of people, I felt at peace. I scrambled on top of the couch, grateful that it was wide enough for this, and bent so I was facing his cock, and I hovered over his face.

"Just tap my thigh if I suffocate you."

Reece's warm breath against my thigh as he laughed made me smile and shiver. "And what a way to go," he growled, before giving my cunt a long swipe of his tongue.

I shivered, then he was feasting, sucking and licking, using his fingers to spread me. And since it was there, I gripped the base of his cock and began to have my taste. I bobbed my head, doing my best to focus on him, but it wasn't easy when he was doing the goddess's work to make me come. I could barely breathe, either with him in my mouth, or just with the panting involved, and when his lips circled clit, my tugging at the ring, I came on his face, loving the way he'd groaned. The pre-cum on the tip of his dick settled on my tongue, salty and slick, but before I could have more of him, he shifted us again. Laughing because we were ridiculous and knowing that if we weren't careful, he wasn't going to last much longer.

"Okay, now you can sit on me," he said, as he sat on the couch with me hovering above him. Even though he was already wet from my mouth and my pussy, he spit into his hand and ran his palm over his length.

"Why is that so hot?"

"Because you're dirty. Just like I like you."

I leaned down and took his mouth, before I slid myself over him. I was already swollen, aching, but it didn't matter. I just wanted him.

He gripped my ass, massaging me as I rolled my hips, not bothering to lift up and down. But that was just fine, because I was ready to come. And finally, he licked at my nipples, and I came again, this time crying because I wasn't sure how it was even possible, and then he followed. I buried my face in his neck, tears leaking, as he held me to his chest, his cock twitching inside me as he filled me with his cum.

"We're making a fucking mess," he growled against my ear, and I smiled against him, unable to speak.

"You just sit there for a minute or two, and I'll take care of you."

"You may have to burn this couch."

"No we won't. This is my game room couch, in the man cave. It's why I scotch guarded it."

I laughed against him, wondering what I had done in a past life to earn him.

"I love you," I whispered as I pulled back, his semi-hard dick still inside me.

He pushed my hair back from my face, studying me with such an intense gaze I wanted to duck my head. But he lifted my chin with one hand, his other hand lazily playing with my breasts.

"I love you too, Freckles. Having a rare moment with you where we're not trying to be quiet in the shower or the bedroom is nice."

"Fucking like bunnies in a house that neither one of us live in. Sounds pretty fun," I teased.

We were indeed in my old home, and while we were on his couch, it was one we had moved over here so I could bring my better couch to his home. Our home.

We were going to sell this one soon, and figure out what to do with some of the old furniture, but having a moment where we could just fuck like bunnies without having to deal with anyone walking in was nice.

Although, more than a few Montgomerys had keys, so that might be an issue, but I wasn't going to think about that.

I kissed his chin, and laughed because it was still wet from my pussy, his beard drenched. I blushed all over, and he clucked his tongue.

"I'm a little too old to start over again right now," he growled. "So when we get to the shower, I'm not going to be able to fuck you like I want."

"If you weren't already somewhat inside me right now, I would close my legs. I don't think I could take another orgasm. Not that I don't love them."

"We should embroider that on a pillow."

I shoved at his chest, and then we were both laughing, taking extra care as we stood up. We might be on a scotch guarded couch with a towel, but it was still messy.

We cleaned up, and thankfully, we were able to just kiss softly in the shower. We had a timetable, and both of us spending time to get each other off wasn't going to happen even though we had just spent the morning enjoying every inch of each other.

Dressed, I put in my final earring, and headed out to the living room.

"It's weird to be in here, and know that I've baked so much sourdough, and yet my starter isn't here."

"Jane Dough is safe at the house, so you don't have to worry about it."

"Her. The sourdough starter is a her," I corrected, knowing it annoyed him to no end.

"You're trying my patience, Freckles. But we will be good. I'm going to miss this house when we sell it."

"We'll just have to rent hotel rooms." I paused, a mischievous smile on my face even as his eyes darkened with lust. "Or, you know, Bella will be out more. On dates."

He scowled at me, and tapped my nose, a little harder than I was expecting. "We don't talk about that. My precious daughter will never be dating."

"You go on and think that. I totally believe you."

"You're lucky I love you, Montgomery."

"I love how I'm always Montgomery when I annoy you."

"How the hell I work with all of you, I'll never know." Then he took my hand, and we headed towards his truck.

"Do you think my old neighbors know that when they see your truck here, you're fucking me?" I asked with a laugh.

"Well if you say it any louder, they will now," he said dryly. He helped me into the truck, then walked around the front to get in himself. As always, I had a truck of my own and could get in by myself, but I liked that Reece took care of me. It was nice just to relax.

We still worked together, still fought when we butted heads, but the team liked when we irritated each other. It meant that we were finding the best possible answers for things. We were making things work, and it was as if we had been together all along. I hadn't known what I was expecting when it came to Reece, but this moment in time was never it.

He had never been in my dreams because I would never have thought big enough for him. And yet I couldn't wish for anything less now.

"We are headed to Natalie's house, right?" he asked, speaking of Bella's friend.

"You know it. A fun slumber party before we have to deal with homework again."

The school year was frustrating for all of us because we were learning a new routine. Bella had good days and bad. She loved school because she loved being with her friends, and the Montgomerys and Foxes had enveloped her easily. She honestly was never alone. We went to therapy, individually and as a group, and we were a family. I would always be Brooklyn for her, and that was fine with me. She had a mother, one that we spoke of often, because I knew she missed her. Maybe one day she would call me something different, but I was perfectly fine being her Brooklyn. Just like I was Reece's Freckles.

We'd had one more dinner with Bella's grandparents, and it hadn't ended in screaming or tears. The Longs were learning to mourn in their own way, and I had a feeling they realized that they were getting older, and the last connection to their family would walk away if she needed to. I wasn't sure we would ever leave Bella alone with them, but it wasn't as fragile of a connection as it had once been.

I hadn't seen the Rochesters since the gala, and I knew I would see them again at another event, but they didn't matter to me. They couldn't. They weren't my family. I had my family. One I had put together myself. One where I was wanted. My sourdough had a home, my family loved me. This man, this man who thought he was Atlas, the world on his shoulders, loved me, and I was safe.

The box in my closet would forever be closed. Those memories no longer hurting, but of the past woman I used to be.

I was happy, I was in love, and one day I would be Reece's wife.

I had everything I needed.

"After we pick up Bella we're heading to your parents' for dinner. It's okay that we're not bringing something with cheese, right?" Reece asked with a groan.

"I promise you, you do not have to eat cheese in order to be part of my family."

"I don't think that was written precisely in the bylaws," he said dryly.

"It's okay, I'll protect you from the Montgomerys."

"And I'll do my best to protect you from the Foxes. But they still scare me." I grinned as he stopped at a red light, and leaned towards him.

"Kiss me?"

"Always." A soft kiss. "Forever."

Chapter 17
DASH

"That's it. You know you want it."

She rolled her eyes, her lips quirking into a smile. "Really? That's the line you're going with? Oh, you know you want it. You want it so bad. Here, come and take it. It's so big and meaty."

With my dick in hand, I paused and couldn't help but burst out laughing.

"Are you serious right now?"

"Of course I am. Your jeans are past your hips, your is cock is pressing against my stomach, and I can't believe we are once again doing this."

I leaned down and bit her jaw. "Because it's what we do. And you like it."

"Maybe," she said, drawing out the word. Then she lifted her chin, and I nibbled up her neck, needing her taste. Damn, I always needed her taste.

"Why is it that every time I'm ready to go out or get ready for the day, you show up, and suddenly your pants are down and all I want is your dick."

"Irrefutable proof. You want my dick."

She looked down between us, at the way we were so close, her legs wrapped around my waist, with her back against the wall. Her panties were already shoved to the side, her skirt rocked up to below her tits.

"You're ridiculous. And I don't usually wear skirts."

"I really like this dress." I fingered the lace over her breasts and swallowed hard. "Easy access."

"Slut."

"So? You like me slutty." Her eyes danced and I leaned down, taking her mouth. She arched against me, my cock sliding against her pussy. We both froze, as the sensation was the best fucking thing I had ever felt in my life. And that meant we were missing a clear thing.

"If you stick that in me without a condom, I will haunt you until the end of your days."

"On it. Swear to God. There is no way I'm fucking you bare. Not that it wouldn't be the best damn thing. Because oh my God, just the thought of fucking you without a condom sort of makes me hornier."

"I did not realize that could actually happen."

"One second." I held my dick to my stomach, got the condom from my back pocket, and proceeded to sheath myself. She'd been busy while I'd been taking care of us, and had pulled down the top of her dress so her tits were out, playing with those perfect nipples of hers.

"Okay, now I'm going to come in this condom instead of you, and we're going to have a problem."

"Then come on, Montgomery, fuck me."

With a grin, I took her mouth again, both of us moaning. I slid the tip of my cock against her entrance. We both froze, the groan escaping my throat guttural. Her pussy slid over my cock, greedily taking me in. I was a monster, we both knew it, but then again, she was the same as me. We were each other's monsters and could only have each other in the dark, a secret and a masterpiece all in one. And I wouldn't have it any other way.

"You have to move faster."

"I'm taking my time. Let me take my time."

"You're ridiculous. And if you don't get that cock in me and start moving, I'm going to have to take matters into my own hands." She leaned down and gripped the base of my cock. I closed my eyes, loving the touch of her small hand over my length. Her fingers could barely wrap around me, and I wanted to be prideful and puff up my chest, but that would force me to move, and I didn't want to be anywhere else but deep inside her.

"Please. Move."

"As my lady wishes," I whispered before shoving home.

She let out a scream, and I latched onto her throat, sucking and nibbling, as I stayed where I was, her pussy fluttering around my cock. I slid my hand between us, my thumb brushing over her clit. And when she came, that sweet cunt of hers squeezing my dick, I nearly joined her.

"You play dirty."

"Damn straight I do," I groaned.

"I love what that piercing does."

"I know you do. You come so prettily around my cock."

"I don't know how I could possibly do that being all sweaty, but again, you're not moving." She pushed up my shirt and flicked my nipple, tugging at the ring slightly.

I groaned at the flash of pain, leaned down, and bit her lip.

"Ouch," she said.

"Poor baby. Let me kiss it and make it better." I licked at the sting before taking her mouth with mine. I ground against her, my cock still deeply embedded as I rotated my hips, using the friction against her clit to nearly send her over the edge again.

"Watch me. Eyes on me."

"Damn you, Montgomery," she mumbled, and I smirked, leaning down to take her lips once more. We moved as one, my lips on her breasts, tugging on her nipples. Licking over her collarbone, my hand between us. Hers rested on my shoulders, fingernails digging in. There were no more words, no more thinking, just breathing. Just us. And when I pulled out of her, she whimpered, but I couldn't help it. I needed more.

"Face the wall. I've got you."

"I know you do."

I ignored the hitch at that, because I knew what she meant. She pressed her hands against the wall, and I took her hips, sliding deep inside from behind. We both stood there for a moment, a groan escaping, as her body softened to accommodate me.

"That's it. That's my girl."

"Not yours," she whispered, and I nodded against her, kissing her shoulder.

"That's a good girl."

"There you go," she said, laughter in her tone. Then I moved, one hand tangled with hers against the wall, the other on her hip as I glided in and out of her, a hard and fast rhythm that left no time or moments for words. She came again, clamping on my cock, so I pushed harder, a bruising force that I knew would make us both ache in the morning. But I didn't care. I needed to mark her, to claim her, to fuck her into oblivion. When I finally came, I gripped both hips and slammed home so hard that she shook against me. My dick twitched as I filled the condom, and I leaned down, breath coming in pants and chest heaving as I tried to formulate words. But there were no words.

Not when it came to Aly.

"Well then, Dash Montgomery. You seem to have reached a new level."

I snorted, kissing her shoulder again, before sliding out of her. Her pussy practically dragged against me, and I moved my hand to cover her, gently patting her over her cunt.

"You're swollen. You're going to hurt tomorrow."

She turned in my arms and shifted so she pulled her dress to cover those beautiful tits of hers.

"Maybe. If I have to sit on ice because you fucked me too hard, we're going to have a problem. I have inventory tomorrow."

I rolled my eyes, before I took care of the condom. I twisted it at its top and tossed it in the trash can near us. We were still in her bathroom, not the sexiest place in the world, but it made for easy cleanup. I tucked myself back into my boxer briefs, did up my jeans, and tried to straighten my shirt. We both look wrinkled, rumpled, and like we just fucked.

But it wasn't the first time. And knowing us, it wouldn't be the last.

"It's not my fault that your pussy can take a pounding."

"You say the sweetest things. I mean, what would you like me to say in response? Oh, Dash, your cock is so big that I can barely even walk."

I lifted an eyebrow and licked my lips. "Well, you're going to walk out of here bow-legged."

"You wish."

She still hadn't adjusted her panties, so I slid my hand up her dress and speared her with two fingers. She gasped, her pussy clamping over my fingers as I ground the base of my palm against her clit. She came again, her eyes rolling back as she nearly fell. Her knees gave out, and I caught her with my free arm, keeping her steady.

"Well look at that. Bow-legged after all." I slid my fingers out of her cunt and rubbed her wetness over her lower lip. Her tongue darted out to taste herself, so I moved my hand to lick my own fingers clean.

Her pupils dilated, and we both stood there, her leaning in my arms, me letting that tartness settle over my tongue. I already was at half-mast again and this woman was a problem.

"Well, I guess you did help me with my headache from earlier."

I threw my head back and laughed, and finally helped her stand up completely. She adjusted her panties and pulled down her dress. She still looked well fucked, there was no denying it.

"Well, I have another solution to your headache if you need it."

She rolled her eyes. "I don't swallow, big boy."

"Oh, that's sad, but thank you for the compliment."

"You're adorable. Now, we need to leave my bathroom without letting the others know we've been in here."

"They've been in the backyard, and nobody's walked past, I would've noticed."

"Would you?" Aly asked. "No, I'm going to trust you on that."

"This is why we work."

"Secret and yet not secret," she agreed.

"If they find out, they'll have questions, and you know my family."

"I'm getting to know them. My family has a different set of questions." She crossed her arms. "But don't worry. You're secret's safe with me."

I swallowed hard and nodded. "Good. As long as we don't catch feelings." I tapped the tip of her nose, and she glared.

"You're the one who's going to catch feelings, Montgomery. I'm just using your dick."

"You're welcome to use it any time, Aly. But remember, feelings ruin everything. This is just going to work between us until we find whatever's next."

"Stop stressing out. I know what friends with benefits means. We fuck until we don't. No feelings, just friendship. If we need each other's help with something, other than sex, we're there. But as soon as one of us finds the one, we're done. No feelings, no promises, just friends."

"That's how I like it." I held my hand up, and she looked at it, then rolled her eyes.

"Really?"

"What? Celebratory post orgasm high five sounds like a decent deal."

A laugh spilling out of her, she returned my high five, before walking out of the bathroom. I followed her, grateful no one else was in the hallway. By the time she was in the kitchen working on something, and I was in the backyard, beer in hand, our friends hadn't even paid attention to us. They didn't know that I had just fucked Aly in her bathroom.

Or that I was probably going to do it again today.

Our situation was perfect.

No ties. No complications. No issue at all.

Others might say being a single Montgomery was

difficult, because everybody kept dropping like flies, but not me. I was Dash Montgomery. I knew exactly what I was doing.

Next in the Montgomery Ink Legacy series: Dash gets his HEA in His Guilty Pleasure

If you'd like to read a bonus scene: Check out this special Epilogue!

Bonus Epilogue
REECE

"Is it supposed to look like that?" Bella looked over my shoulder, going on her tiptoes, and nudged me out of the way. I sighed and took a step to the left.

"I don't think so. Maybe. We've watched her do this how many times?"

"You would think we would know better, but sadly we don't. I think it's fine. And we just have to do the shaping now?"

"Oh, yes, this is the candy cane. But after you do the butt fold."

I blinked and slowly turned towards my daughter.

"The butt fold?"

Her cheeks blushed, and I held back a laugh. My little teenager embarrassed easily, at least when it came to me. Apparently. She could shrug off anyone else, but I tended to embarrass her like any dad could.

"You know, you fold over the sides before you roll it."

"Like a blanket. Or a hot dog." Has she ever used the word butt fold?

"I don't know. Maybe it looked like a butt once. Why are you being so mean?"

"I'm not being mean. But that was hilarious. Mostly because now every time that I see Brooklyn do this, I'm going to think of a butt."

"I'm glad I can help you in your relationship."

"You like Brooklyn. Right?" I asked, oddly worried. Brooklyn had been part of Bella coming into my life since the start. In fact, I knew that I wouldn't have the relationship I did with my daughter without Brooklyn being there.

Brooklyn and Bella had their own relationship. Not quite mother and daughter because Bella had her mother but close enough. It wasn't a relationship that they could put a label on, but they were learning. And if today worked out, there would be a whole new label to that relationship. One that made me kind of nauseous because everything could go topsy-turvy and end up exploding after this moment if we weren't careful.

"You're looking a little green there, Dad."

Dad.

I tried not to preen at her using the word. It was still relatively new between us, but she called me Dad. Not just Reece. Not old man. Not something mumbled under her breath that would probably get her in trouble.

"Help me make this butt fold, then the candy cane, and then we'll stick it in the fridge."

"We've got this. Maybe. Probably not. But she'll like it anyway. She loves you. It's what sappy love does."

My heart beat rapidly in my chest, a smile playing on my face.

"Yes. She does love me. I'm a pretty lucky guy. I have this annoying teenager here, and a woman that loves me. One that makes a damn good bread."

Bread we were trying to do ourselves.

"Okay, we can do this." I clapped my hands together, flour billowing in the air, and Bella coughed dramatically.

"Stop it," I growled, without any malice in it. We followed the directions as purposeful as possible, and I tried to remember everything that Brooklyn had done in front of me, since she made bread practically daily, and yet, I knew we would probably fail. We would try though. For her.

"I'm just glad that Brooklyn gave me some of her starter to make my own, so we didn't have to filch hers."

I raised a brow. "Do you really think I would touch

her starter? She takes care of that thing better than she does the plants that she's put in this house."

Brooklyn didn't live here permanently yet. She still had her old place but rarely stayed there. Eventually, all of her indoor plants had migrated to my house. And she'd already started on the landscaping. Using my labor, of course, but I had to remind her that I was old, and could break at any moment. Then she'd tackle me to the ground and prove exactly how young I could be.

I swallowed hard, remembering that last time when Bella had been with my parents, and Brooklyn and I had enjoyed our time alone. But thinking of that wouldn't be good for this moment.

Instead, we wrapped up the dough, and put it in the fridge, and hoped that it turned out, but if it didn't, it was just bread. There were far more important things going on, namely, what was going to happen later tonight.

"Let's clean up. Then you were heading out with Uncle Dash and Uncle Aiden."

"I like them both."

"Honestly it scares me that those two have become friends. I don't know why I'm even letting you go along with them."

"They won't let anything happen to me."

"No, but they'll corrupt you. My precious, innocent baby girl."

Bella blinked at me slowly, before she burst out laughing. I couldn't help but join in.

Bella was a sweet kid, innocent, but just as mischievous as Aiden and Dash. They got along great, and they were all heading to a game later. I would never be able to show my family or Brooklyn's how much it meant to me that they had opened their arms to Bella. Without a second thought, she was theirs just as she was mine.

Our lives had changed dramatically over time, and we're still figuring things out, but I would forever be grateful that I wasn't alone in this.

And once we got through this evening, I would never be alone again.

At least I hoped not. Hell, now I was stressing myself out.

"Go shower and get ready. You can't stink when you go on your date tonight."

"Excuse me? You're saying I smell bad?"

"If the lack of deodorant fits."

I reached for her, and Bella squealed and scurried out of my reach. The front door opened, and Brooklyn walked in, her eyes wide at the situation.

"What did I miss?"

"Your boyfriend stinks," Bella said as she ran upstairs after giving a wave to Brooklyn.

The woman that I loved turned to me, a smirk on her face. "Well, I see you guys have had a good day so far."

Oddly nervous, I wiped my hands on the dish towel and moved forward. I cupped her face, lowered my head, and brushed my lips to hers.

"Welcome home."

Her eyes widened. "Thank you. The meeting sucked. And I don't think we're getting the contract."

I kissed the side of her mouth, her temple, the tip of her nose, then her lips again. She moaned into me, her fingers hooking in my belt loops.

"That's fine. We didn't like them anyway."

"Still, that's so kind of you. But true. I just hate losing."

"They're not going to go to any of your family, meaning they're going to get subpar service, and get what they get. It's what they deserve."

"You do say the nicest things after a long day." She kissed my chin, then looked over at the kitchen. "Why is there flour everywhere?"

I winced, annoyed that I hadn't finished cleaning it up. "Bella and I are trying something out, and if it fails, just know that I love you."

Her eyes widened and she patted my chest.

"Baking? That is the best thing ever. And I'm never going to get tired of you telling me you love me."

"I love you," I whispered, before nibbling on her earlobe.

"Hey, there is an impressionable child in the house!" Bella called out before she continued to stomp down the staircase.

"Stop pounding the stairs, Bella."

"I'm just walking."

"Sure you are," I said dryly.

"Whatever. Stop making out."

"Never." I dipped Brooklyn in my arms and captured her lips with mine. She wrapped her arms around my neck and kissed me back before laughing.

"Gross," Bella said, though she was still smiling.

"Did you finish your homework?" I asked.

"Yes. You already asked me before we started baking."

"I'm just trying to trip you up."

"I lied one time about not finishing my homework and now it's a thing."

"You're not going to lie again, are you?" I asked.

"No. Because you didn't let me make up the assignment, and I had to deal with doing that extra paper."

"And you kicked ass *and* got a passing grade. It's a win-win. Don't lie to me."

"Fine. Fine. Uncle Dash said he's nearly here, so I

will see you guys later." She came up to Brooklyn, wrapped her arms around her tight, and stood there, letting out a deep sigh.

If the kid spoiled tonight, I was going to be angry, but not really.

Brooklyn gave me a weird look, before hugging Bella tightly. They were practically the same height now, since Bella was growing like a weed, and Brooklyn would always be my pixie queen.

"Have fun tonight." Brooklyn cupped Bella's face and grinned. "You watch your uncles. They're insane."

"Of course. I'm in charge."

"Dash is in charge," I said.

"No, Aiden is," Brooklyn corrected.

Laughing, Bella hugged me, and I kissed the top of her head.

"Be safe."

"Always."

She opened the door, and I walked behind her, waving at Dash who rolled down his window.

"There's my favorite niece!"

I shook my head, knowing that our family connections would never be simple. Because Dash wasn't her uncle, wasn't even Brooklyn's brother. And he already had nieces and nephews, though technically only because of his cousins and second cousins. She was biologically

Aidan's niece, so that worked, but the Montgomerys loved to make things confusing. I waved them off, knowing that if they came in to say anything, we would never get out of here, and I had plans with Brooklyn. So when she gave me a weird look, I tired to look like I wasn't nervous.

"They were running late. That's why they didn't come inside."

"If you say so. It was just weird."

I shrugged. "They're weird." They drove off, and I could hear Bella's laughter through the open window, before I closed the door.

"Now. Let's get you out of those clothes."

Brooklyn's eyes widened. "Well then. An empty house? Where are you going to fuck me next?"

"I was thinking I was going to take you out to dinner. I have reservations at Pierre's."

"Really? I've always wanted to go there. But it's hard to get reservations."

"I know a guy."

And I did. But I'd used up one of my favors to get there. It was fine though, Brooklyn was worth it.

"Come on, we only have a couple hours, but I apparently need to shower."

"Well, why don't I shower with you."

I groaned as she pulled at my belt loop, tugging me upstairs.

"If we're late, you're going to have to deal with Pierre."

"You know the chef personally?" she asked me.

"I know a lot of people."

"So I hear. However, I can make this quick."

I looked down at her dilated eyes and snorted. "We both know that's not the case."

"Try me."

She giggled as she ran upstairs and I followed her, my gaze on that sweet ass of hers and the way it moved in her jeans.

We weren't quick, in fact, with Bella on her knees and my cock in her mouth, we were never quick. But we'd ended up showered, well-fucked, and a little exhausted. I couldn't help it, she had been bent over, my hands on her hips, my dick sliding slowly into that sweet cunt of hers, and we lost all meaning of time.

Thank God I had a tankless water heater.

By the time we got dressed, and did so separately because me watching her slide herself into that slinky black dress would've made me bend her over the chair and fuck her once more, we were right on time when we headed to the restaurant.

"I love that you found this dress in my closet and brought it over. Sneak."

"You should just bring all of your clothes over at this point," I said with a shrug.

"I know. I know. Bella's fine with it, I'm over there every night anyway, but I don't know what to do with my house."

"You can rent it out," I said, my fingers tangling with hers as we followed the maître d' to our table.

"True. And you know the Montgomerys know how to deal with that."

"You guys can plan anything, I believe in you."

"It's just a big step."

I faltered, and I had to clear my throat before helping her into her seat and pushing it closer to the table.

"Is it too quick?"

"No. We've already talked about it, and I'll make it happen. We've just been busy."

I reached across the table and squeezed her hand. "Good. Because it's time. You having your clothes at two places has to be annoying."

"I'm going to miss my landscaping though."

I winced. "We would move into your place, but—"

"You have twice the amount of room, a bigger yard, and Bella's already safe there. It makes no sense to move into my place. I get it. I'm just going to have to figure out what I can transplant, what cuttings I want, and how I'm going to work landscaping into a tenant contract if that's what happens."

"Good thing you're a landscape architect."

"I know, right?"

The waiter came over, and we ordered our drinks, heard the specials, and I tried not to tap my foot in impatience. I wanted tonight to be perfect, but I knew perfection didn't exist. Meaning as long as Brooklyn enjoyed herself, that was all that mattered.

I wasn't good at this. I never had been. I felt like an old man, trying to catch up with the past I had nearly lost out on, and here I was, trying to take leaps when I wasn't sure if my hips and knees could take it.

By the time we finished dinner, I was full, and Brooklyn was giddy, but thankfully had only had a single glass of wine. I didn't want the rest of the night to end too early because we had drank too much. But we had been careful, and now it was the second phase.

"Walk with me," I whispered.

"Were you planning this walk? Is that why you picked out wedges for me?" she asked, showing me her foot.

"I'm diabolical like that."

"I like planner Reece."

"Good to hear it." I brought her hand up to my face, and kissed the back of it, then her fingers. Her mouth parted, her eyes widening as I did and we walked along the path in the park behind the restaurant. It was a full moon tonight, and a cloudless sky, so one barely needed the streetlights in order to see. To the west was a vast darkness, the Rocky Mountains doing their thing. A mysterious and moving moment of time that spoke to the beauty and the uncertainty of nature and the earth.

Everywhere else felt like the city, and where people had congregated. There were others walking along the path, but I only had eyes for Brooklyn.

And suddenly I was fucking nervous.

"Are you okay?" Brooklyn asked. "I mean, I've loved this date, and the surprises, but you seem stressed out. Do you want to talk about it?"

I squeezed her hand, and we made it to a park bench.

"I'm fine. Just thinking."

We were underneath an old willow tree, one that didn't quite belong here, but had been planted and cared for over time. We were alone, just the two of us, and I knew this was the moment.

She frowned at me, worried that I hadn't said anything, so I swallowed hard and went to one knee.

Brooklyn's eyes widened, and she put her hands over of her mouth.

"We both know I'm not good at this shit," I growled.

A laugh escaped her, and she lowered her hands and ran one through my hair. "Reece..."

"I never meant to fall for you. I'm the grumpy

asshole of the group, and you were the vivacious, brilliant, and full of life woman who can push her away through anything. I've already done this before, and failed. I thought it was over. I thought I would walk into the rest of my life, content in my friendships and whatever the hell I had left. But you and Bella have changed everything. We're a family, Brooklyn. And we are because of you."

"Reece. You're the reason that I can *be*."

"No, it's all you. Don't you understand that? Bella and I would've found our way, but you were the one that made me realize that I could be a father. You were the one that brought Bella out of her shell. And I love you for that, but that's not why I'm in love with you. I love you because of the way you smile. Of the way that you have faced adversity and loss and thrived. Of the way that you stand up for your family more than you even stand up for yourself. I love your freckles. I love your laughter. I love the way that you can keep anything green alive when I try to kill it. I love your bread, I love your aversion to beeswax. And I love the way that you make me hard just by breathing near me."

"That is quite a list," she teased.

"I should have written this shit down. And I probably shouldn't be fucking cussing."

"You wouldn't be my Reece without it."

"Brooklyn Montgomery. I love you. Bella loves you. And she wants you to be part of this family. And the only reason she's not here right now is because I wanted you to know that I'm not asking you to be Brooklyn's mom. Not alone. I'm asking you to be my wife because I love you. Because I'm not whole without you. Yes, we will be a family, and I know we already are. But I'm asking you to be my wife because I want you to be mine just like I'm yours. And that's separate from who we are as a family. I hope you realize that. So marry me, Brooklyn Montgomery. Marry me and let's connect the Foxes and the Montgomerys in a weird-ass way that's going to be complicated and loud and ridiculous. Because I love you. And I already call you mine. And now I want to call you my wife."

Tears slid down her cheeks and I swallowed hard waiting for her answer.

"I really think that Brooklyn Montgomery Fox has a nice ring to it. So yes. Yes, I'll marry you. I fucking love you too, Reece, you growly asshole."

I threw my head back and laughed, before I slid the ring onto her finger, stood up, and took her in my arms. I twirled her around, our lips connecting, and I knew that this was the moment.

This was the moment that my life had changed once again.

"I could kiss you forever," she whispered.

"And now you can. You're stuck with me. And a sullen teenager. I'm sorry."

"Don't be sorry, because I'm taking it. I'm taking all of it."

"Good. And tomorrow, Bella and I are going to show you that we can bake bread. Maybe. It's our engagement present."

"Sure of yourself, are you?"

"Fuck no. We probably messed up the bread, but we're trying."

"I can't wait to be your wife. And to be Bella's mom. So that way she knows that she is loved by more than one."

"Damn straight. Thank God you said yes."

"Thank God you were such an asshole to me for so long so that way we waited for each other."

"I tried my best," I teased.

And she kissed me once more, and I was lost.

I'd caught myself a Montgomery. And thankfully she seemed to be the sanest of the bunch. But in the end it didn't matter. Because I had a feeling that Bella and I had just become Montgomerys right along with them.

And that was just fine with me.

Next in the Montgomery Ink Legacy series:
Dash gets his HEA in His Guilty Pleasure

A Note from Carrie Ann Ryan

Thank you so much for reading **KISS ME FOREVER.**

I'd had idea for this story a few years ago and it took me awhile to find the perfect hero. Reece flew off the page and I KNEW I loved him and wanted his story to be perfect.

Hence why it took me far too many drafts.

As for Brooklyn…she has my heart. She always will. I adore her and what strength she held so close.

Next time? Dash..oh Dash. His story is going to be…interesting. Are you ready for His Guilty Pleasure?

And while we're here…Jamie is heading up to Wyoming to get her own story in Accidental Runaway Groom. ALL THE THINGS ARE HAPPENING!

The Montgomery Ink Legacy Series:

Book 1: Bittersweet Promises (Leif & Brooke)

Book 2: At First Meet (Nick & Lake)

Book 2.5: Happily Ever Never (May & Leo)

Book 3: Longtime Crush (Sebastian & Raven)

Book 4: Best Friend Temptation (Noah, Ford, and Greer)

Book 4.5: Happily Ever Maybe (Jennifer & Gus)

Book 5: Last First Kiss (Daisy & Hugh)

Book 6: His Second Chance (Kane & Phoebe)

Book 7: One Night with You (Kingston & Claire)

Book 8: Accidentally Forever (Crew & Aria)

Book 9: Last Chance Seduction (Lexington & Mercy)

Book 10: Kiss Me Forever (Brooklyn & Reece)

Book 11: His Guilty Pleasure (Dash & Aly)

Book 12: Maybe it's You (Riley & Gage)

Loved this dynamic? Read the first chapter of this second chance, small town, contemporary suspense romance: **The Forever Rule.**

Next in the Montgomery Ink Legacy series:
Dash gets his HEA in His Guilty Pleasure

If you'd like to read a bonus scene:
Check out this special Epilogue!

If you want to make sure you know what's coming next from me, you can sign up for my newsletter at www.

CarrieAnnRyan.com; follow me on twitter at @CarrieAnnRyan, or like my Facebook page. I also have a Facebook Fan Club where we have trivia, chats, and other goodies. You guys are the reason I get to do what I do and I thank you.

Make sure you're signed up for my MAILING LIST so you can know when the next releases are available as well as find giveaways and FREE READS.

Happy Reading!

From The Forever Rule

ASTON

The Cages are the most prestigious family in Denver—at least according to the patriarch of the Cage Family.

And the Cages have rules.

Rules only they know.

I ALWAYS KNEW that one day my father would die. I hadn't realized that day would come so soon. Or that the last words I would say to him would've been in anger.

I had been having one of the best nights of my life, a beautiful woman in my arms, and a smile on my face when I received the phone call that had changed my family's life.

The fact that I had been smiling had been a shock, because according to my brothers, I didn't smile much. I was far too busy being *The Cage* of Cage Enterprises.

We were a dominant force in the city of Denver when

it came to certain real estate ventures, as well as being one of the only ethical and environmentally friendly ones who tried to keep up with that. We had our hands in countless different pots around the world, but mostly we gravitated in the state of Colorado—our home.

I had not created the company, no, that honor had gone to my grandfather, and then my father. The Cage Enterprises were and would always be a family endeavor. And when my father had stepped away a few years ago, stating he had wanted to see the world, and also see if his sons could actually take up the mantle, I had stepped in—not that the man believed we could.

My brothers were in various roles within the company, at least those who had wanted to be part of it. But I was the face of Cage Enterprises.

So no, I hadn't smiled often. There wasn't time. We weren't billionaires with mega yachts. We worked seventy-hour weeks to make sure *all* our employees had a livable wage while wining and dining with those who looked down at us for not being on their level. And others thought we were the high and mighty anyway since they didn't understand us. So, I didn't smile.

But I had smiled that night.

It had been a gala for some charity, one I couldn't even remember off the top of my head. We had donated between the company and my own finances—

we always did. But I couldn't even remember anything about why we were there.

Yet I could remember her smile. The heat in her eyes when she had looked up at me, the feel of her body pressed against mine as we had danced along the dance floor, and then when we ended up in the hallway, bodies pressed against one another, needing each other, wanting each other.

And I had put aside all my usual concepts of business and life to have this woman in my arms.

And then my mother had called and had shattered that illusion.

"Your father is dead."

She hadn't even braced me for the blow. A heart attack on a vacation on a beach in Majorca, and he was dead. She hadn't cried, hadn't said anything, just told me that I had to be the one to tell my brothers.

And so, I had, all six of them. Because of course Loren Cage would have seven sons. He couldn't do things just once, he had to make sure he left his legacy, his destiny.

And that was why we were here today, in a high-rise in Centennial, waiting on my father's lawyer to show up with the reading of the will.

"Hey, when is Winstone going to get here?" Dorian asked, his typical high energy playing on his face, and how he tapped his fingers along the hand-carved wooden table.

I stared at my brother, at those piercing blue eyes that matched my own, and frowned. He should be here soon. He did call us all here after all."

"I still don't know why we all had to be here for the reading of the will," Hudson whispered as he stared off into the distance. Neither Dorian nor Hudson worked for Cage Enterprises. They had stock with the company, and a few other connections because that's what family did, but they didn't work on the same floors as some of us and hadn't been elbow to elbow with our father before he had retired. Though dear old dad had worked in our small town more often than not in the end. In fact, Hudson didn't even live in Denver anymore. He had moved to the town we owned in the mountains.

Because of course we Cages owned a damned town. Part of me wasn't sure if the concept of having our name on everything within the town had been on purpose or had occurred organically. Though knowing my grandfather, perhaps it had been exactly what he'd wanted. He had bought up a few buildings, built a few more, and now we owned three-quarters of the town, including the major resort which brought in tourists and income.

And that was why we were here.

"You have to be here because you're evidently in the will," I said softly, trying not to get annoyed that we were waiting for our father's lawyer. Again.

"You would think he would be able to just send us a memo. I mean, it should be clear right? We all know what stakes we have in, we should just be able to do things evenly," Theo said, his gaze off into the distance. My younger brother also didn't work for the company, instead he had decided to go to culinary school, something my father had hated. But you couldn't control a Cage, that was sort of our deal.

"Why would you be cut out of the will?" I asked, honestly curious.

"Because I married a man and a woman," he drawled out. "You know he hasn't spoken to me since before the wedding," Ford said, and I saw the hurt in his gaze even though I knew he was probably trying to hide it.

"Well, he was an asshole, what do you expect?" James asked.

I looked behind Ford to see my brother and co-chair of Cage Enterprises standing with his hands in his pockets, staring out the window.

With Flynn, our vice president, standing beside him, they looked like the heads of businesses they were. While they wore suits and so did I, we were the only ones.

Dorian and Hudson were both in jeans, Hudson's having a hole at the knee. And probably not as a fashion statement, most likely because it had torn at some point, and he hadn't bothered to buy another pair. Theo was in slacks, but a Henley with his sleeves pushed up, tapping his finger just like Hudson, clearly wanting to get out of here as well. Ford had on cargo pants, and a tight black T-shirt, and looked like he had just gotten off his shift. He owned a security company with his husband and a few other friends, and did security for the Cages when he could, though I knew he didn't like to work with family often. And I knew it wasn't because of us. No, it was Father—even if he had officially *retired*. It was always Father.

And he was gone.

"Can't believe the asshole's gone," I whispered.

Ford's brows rose. "Look at that, you calling him an asshole. I'm proud."

"You should show him respect," Mother said as she came inside the room, her high heels tapping against the marble floors. I didn't bother standing up like I normally would have, because Melanie Cage looked to be in a *mood*.

She didn't look sad that Dad was gone, more like angry that he would dare go against their plans. What plans? I didn't know, but that was my mother.

She came right up to Dorian and leaned down to

kiss his cheek. She didn't even bother to look at the rest of us. Dorian was Mother's favorite. Which I knew Dorian resented, but I didn't have to deal with mommy issues at this moment.

No, we had to deal with father issues at this point.

"I'm going to go get him," Flynn replied, turning toward the door. "I'm really not in the mood to wait any longer, especially since he's being so secretive about this meeting."

As I had been thinking just the same, I nodded at Flynn though he didn't need my permission. However, just then, the door opened, and I frowned when it wasn't just Mr. Winstone walking into the conference room.

I stared as an older woman walked through the door following Mr. Winstone, and four women and another man with messy hair and tattered cut-up jeans that matched Hudson's walked behind them.

The guy looked familiar, as if I'd seen him somewhere, or maybe it was just his eyes.

Where had I seen those eyes before?

"Phoebe? What are you doing here?" Ford asked as he moved forward and gripped the hands of one of the women.

"I was going to ask the same question," Phoebe asked as she looked at Ford, then around the room.

Those of us sitting stood up, confused about why

this other family—because they were clearly a family—had decided to enter the room.

"We're here to meet the lawyer about my father's death, Ford. Why would you and the Cages be here?" she asked, and I wondered how the hell Mr. Winstone had fucked up so badly? Why the hell was he letting another family that clearly seemed to be in shock come into our room? This wasn't how he normally handled things.

Ford was the one who answered though—thankfully—because I had no idea what the hell was going on.

"Phoebe, we're here for my dad's will reading. What the hell is going on?" he asked. Phoebe looked around, as well as the others.

I stared at them, at the tall willowy one with wide eyes, at the smaller one with tears still in her eyes as if she was the only one truly mourning, and at the woman who seemed to be in charge, not the mother. Instead she had shrewd eyes and was glaring at all of us. The man stood back, hands in pockets, and looked just as shell-shocked as Ford.

But before Mr. Winstone or anyone else could say anything, my mother spoke in such a crisp, icy tone that I froze.

"I don't know why you're acting so dramatic. You

knew your father was an asshole. He just liked creating drama," she snapped.

As I tried to catch up with her words, the older woman answered. "Melanie, stop."

This couldn't be happening. Because things started to click into place. The fact that the man at the other end of this table had our eyes, and that everybody looked so fucking shocked. I didn't know how Ford knew this Phoebe, and I would be getting answers.

"We had a deal," my mother continued, as it seemed that the rest of us were just now catching on. "You would keep your family away from mine. We would share Loren, but I got the name, I got the family. You got whatever else. But now it looks like Loren decided to be an asshole again."

"What are you talking about?" the shrewd sister asked as she came forward, her hands fisted at her side.

"Excuse me," I said, clearing my throat. I was going to be damned if I let anyone else handle this meeting. I was The Cage now. "Will someone please explain?"

"Well, I wasn't quite sure how this was going to work out," Mr. Winstone began, and we all quieted, while I wanted to strangle the man. What did he mean how *the hell this would work out*? What was this?

This seemed like a big fucking mistake.

"Loren Cage had certain provisions in his will for both of his families. And one of the many requirements that I will go over today is that this meeting must take place." He paused and I hoped it wasn't for effect, because I was going to throttle him if it was. "Loren Cage had two families. Seven sons with his wife Melanie, and four daughters and a son with his mistress, Constance."

"We went by partner," the other mother corrected.

I blinked, counting the adults in the room. "Twelve?" I asked, my voice slightly high-pitched.

"Busy fucking man," Dorian whispered.

Hudson snorted, while we just stood and stared at each other.

This could not be happening. A secret family? No, we were not that cliché.

"I can't do this," Phoebe blurted, her eyes wide.

"Oh, stop overreacting," my mother scorned.

"Do not talk to my daughter that way." The other mother glared.

"It was always going to be an issue," Mother continued. "All the secrets and the lies. And now the kids will have to deal with it. Because God forbid Loren ever deal with anything other than his own dick."

"That's enough," I snapped.

"Don't you dare talk to us like that," the shrewd sister snapped right back.

"I will talk however I damn well please. I am going to need to know exactly how this happened," I shouted over everyone else's words.

Out of the corner of my eye I saw Phoebe run through the door. Ford followed and then the tall willowy one joined.

"Shit," I snapped.

"Language," Mother bit out.

I laughed. "Really? You are going to talk to me about language."

I looked over at James, who shrugged, before he put two fingers in his mouth and whistled that high-pitched whistle that only he could do.

Everyone froze as Theo rubbed his ear and glared at me.

"Winstone," I said through gritted teeth. "I take it we all have to be here in order for this to happen?"

He cleared his throat. "At least a majority. But you all had to at least step into the room."

"Excuse me then," I said.

"You're just going to leave? Just like that?" my mother asked.

I whirled on her. "I'm going to go see if my apparent *family* is okay. Then I'm going to come back and we're going to get answers. Because there is no way that I'm going to leave here without them."

I stormed out the door, and thankfully nobody followed me.

Of course, though, I shouldn't have been too swift with that, as the woman who had to be the eldest sister practically ran to my side, her heels tapping against the marble.

"I'm coming with you."

"That's just fine." I paused, knowing that I wasn't angry at these people. No, my father and apparently our mothers were the ones that had to deal with this. I looked over at the woman who Mr. Winstone and the mothers had claimed was my sister and cleared my throat.

"I'm Aston."

"Is this really the time for introductions?" she asked.

"I'm about to go see your sister and my brother to make sure that they're fine, so sure. I would like to know the name of the woman that is running next to me right now."

"I'm running, you're walking quickly because you have such long legs."

I snorted, surprised I could even do that.

"I'm Isabella," she replied after a moment.

"I would say nice to meet you Isabella…" I let my voice trail off.

She let out a sharp laugh before shaking her head.

"I'm going to need a moment to wrap my head around this, but not now."

"Same."

We stormed out of the building, and I lagged behind since Ford was standing in front of Phoebe who was in the arms of another man with dark hair and everybody seemed to be talking all at once.

"I just. I can't deal with this right now," Phoebe said, and I realized that something else must have been going on with her right then. She looked tired, and far more emotional than the rest of us.

I looked over at the man holding her and blinked. "Kane?" I asked.

Kane stared at me and let out a breath. "Wow," he said with a laugh.

"We'll handle it," Isabella put in, completely ignoring us. "And if we need to meet again later, we will." Then she looked over at Ford and I, with such menace in her gaze, I nearly took a step back. "Is that a problem?"

I raised my chin, glaring right back at her. "Not at all. However I want answers, so I'd rather not have the meeting canceled right now. But I'm also not going to force any of my," I paused, realization hitting far too hard, "*family* to stay if they don't want to."

And with that, I turned on my heel and went back into the building, with Isabella and Ford following me.

Everyone was still yelling in the interim, and I cleared my throat. As Isabella had done it at the same time, everyone paused to look at me.

"Read the damn will. Because we need answers," I ordered Winstone, and he shook like a leaf before nodding.

"Okay. We can do that." He cleared his throat, then he began going over trusts and incomes and buildings and things that I would care about soon, but what I wanted to know was what the hell our father had been thinking about.

"Here's the tricky part," Winstone began, as we all leaned forward, eager to hear what the hell he had to say.

"The family money, not of the business, not of each of your inheritance from other family members, but the bulk of Loren Cage's assets will be split between all twelve kids."

"Are you kidding me?" Isabella asked. "What money? We weren't exactly poor, but we were solidly middle class."

"We did just fine," the other mother pleaded.

My mother snorted, clearly not believing the words.

I glared at the woman who raised me, willing her to say *anything*. She would probably be pushed out of the window at that point. Not by me, by someone else, but she probably would've earned it.

The lawyer continued. "However to retain the majority of current assets and to keep Cage Lake and all of its subsidiaries you will have to meet as a family once a month for three years. If this does not happen, Cage Enterprises will be broken into multiple parts and sold." He went on into the legalese that I ignored as I tried to hear over the blood pounding in my ears.

"You own a town?" the other man asked.

I looked over at the one man in the room I didn't know the name of. "Not exactly."

"Kyler," Isabella whispered.

In that moment, I realized that I had a brother named Kyler—if this was all to be believed.

"This can't be legal right?" the tall willowy person said.

"Yes Sophia, it can," their mother put in.

Oh good, another sister named Sophia.

Only one name to go. What the hell was wrong with me?

I forced my jaw to relax. "Are you telling us that we need to have all twelve of us at dinner once a month for three years in order to keep what is rightly inherited to us? To keep people in business and keep their jobs?"

"We don't need the money, but everyone else in our

employ does," James snapped. "As do those we work with."

"Damn straight," Dorian growled.

"How are we supposed to believe this?" I asked, asking the obvious question.

"First, only five must attend, and two must be of a different family." The lawyer continued as if I hadn't spoken. "Of course you are *all* family…"

"Again, how are we supposed to believe this?" I asked.

"Here are the DNA tests already done."

"Are you fucking kidding me?" Isabella asked.

I looked at her, as she had literally taken the words out of my mouth.

"Isn't that sort of like a violation?" Kyler asked, his face pale.

"We need to get our own lawyers on this," James whispered.

I nodded tightly, knowing we had much more to say on this.

"There's no way this is legal," the youngest said, and I looked over at her.

"What's your name?" I asked.

"Emily. Emily Cage Dixon," she said softly, and we all froze.

"Your middle name is Cage?" I asked, biting out the words.

"All of our middle names are Cage," Sophia said, shaking her head. "I hated it but Dad wanted to be cute because our father's name was Cage Dixon, or maybe it wasn't. Is he also a bigamist?" she asked.

Her mother lifted her chin. "We never married. And no, your father's name was not Dixon, that was my maiden name."

"What?" Sophia asked. "All this time…are our grandparents even dead?"

"Yes, my parents are dead. The same with Loren's." The other mother's eyes filled with tears. "I'm sorry we lied."

"We'll get to that later," Isabella put in, and I was grateful.

I let out a breath. "In order to keep our assets, in order to keep the family name intact, we need to have *dinner*. For three years."

The small lawyer nodded, his glasses falling down his nose. "At least five of you. And it can start three months after the funeral, which we can plan after this."

"This is ridiculous," Hudson murmured under his breath, before he got up and walked out.

I watched him go, knowing he had his own demons, and tried to understand what the hell was going on. "Why did he do this?" I asked, more to myself than anyone else.

"I never really knew the man, but apparently none of us did," Isabella said, staring off into the distance.

"Leave the paperwork and go," I ordered Winstone, and he didn't even mutter a peep. Instead, he practically ran out of the room. James and Flynn immediately went to the paperwork, and I knew they were scouring it. But from the way that their jaws tightened, I had a feeling that my father had found a way to make this legal. Because we would always have a choice to lose everything. That was the man.

"It's true," my mother put in. "You all share the same father. That was the deal when we got married, and when he decided to bring this other woman into our lives."

"I'm pretty sure you were the other woman," the other mom said.

I pinched the bridge of my nose.

"Stop. All of you." I stared at the group and realized that I was probably the eldest Cage here, other than the moms. I would deal with this. We didn't have a choice. "Whatever happens, we'll deal with it."

"You're in charge now?" Isabella asked, but Sophia shushed her.

I was grateful for that, because I had a feeling Isabella and I were going to butt heads more often than not.

I shrugged, trying to act as if my world hadn't been

rocked. "I would say welcome to the Cages, because DNA evidence seems to point that way, however perhaps you were already one of us all along."

Kyler muttered something under his breath I couldn't hear before speaking up. "You have my eyes," he said.

I nodded. "Noticed that too."

The other man tilted his head. "So what, we do dinners and we make nice?"

I sighed. "We don't have to be adversaries."

"You say that as if you're the one in charge," Isabella said again.

"Because he is," Theo said, and they all stared at him.

I tried to tamp down the pride swelling at those words—along with the overwhelming pressure.

Theo continued. "He's the eldest. He's the one that takes care of us. And he's the CEO of Cage Enterprises. He's going to be the one that deals with the paperwork fallout."

"Because family is just paperwork?" Emily asked, her voice lost.

I shook my head. "No, family is insane, and apparently, it's been secret all along. And it looks like we have a few introductions to make, and a few tests to redo. But if it turns out it's true, we're Cages, and we don't back down."

"And what does that mean?" Isabella asked, her tone far too careful.

Theo was the one who finally answered. "It means we're going to have to figure shit out."

And for just an instant, the thought of that beautiful woman with that gorgeous smile came to mind, and I pushed those thoughts away. My family was breaking, or perhaps breaking open. And I didn't have time to worry about things like a woman who had made me smile.

The Cages needed me and after today's meeting there would be no going back to sanity.

Ever.

In the mood to read another family saga? Meet the Cage Family in The Forever Rule!

From One Way Back to Me

ELI

When my morning begins with me standing ankle-deep in a basement full of water, I know I probably should have stayed in bed. Only, I was the boss, and I didn't get that choice.

"Hold on. I'm looking for it." East cursed underneath his breath as my younger brother bent down around the pipe, trying his best to turn off the valve. I sighed, waded through the muck in my work boots, and moved to help him. "I said I've got it," East snapped, but I ignored him.

I narrowed my eyes at the evil pipe. "It's old and rusted, and even though it passed an inspection over a year ago, we knew this was going to be a problem."

"And I'm the fucking handyman of this company. I've got this."

"And as a handyman, you need a hand."

"You're hilarious. Seriously. I don't know how I could ever manage without your wit and humor." The dryness in his tone made my lips twitch even as I did my best to ignore the smell of whatever water we stood in.

"Fuck you," I growled.

"No thanks. I'm a little too busy for that."

With a grunt, East shut off the water, and we both stood back, hands on our hips as we stared at the mess of this basement.

East let out a sigh. "I'm not going to have to turn the water off for the whole property, but I'm glad that we don't have tenants in this particular cabin."

I nodded tightly and held back a sigh. "This is probably why there aren't basements in Texas. Because everything seems to go wrong in these things."

"I'm pretty sure this is a storm shelter, or at least a tornado one. Not quite sure as it's one of the only basements in the area."

"It was probably the only one that they had the energy to make back in the day. Considering this whole place is built over clay and limestone."

East nodded, looked around. "I'll start the cleanup with this water, and we'll look to see what we can do with the pipes."

I pinched the bridge of my nose. "I don't want to have to replace the plumbing for this whole place."

"At least it's not the villa itself, or the farmhouse, or the winery. Just a single cabin."

I glared at my younger brother, then reached out and knocked on a wooden pillar. "Shut your mouth. Don't say things like that to me. We are just now getting our feet under us."

East shrugged. "It's the truth, though. However much you weigh it, it could have been worse."

I pinched the bridge of my nose. "Jesus Christ. You were in the military for how long? A Wilder your entire life, and you say things like that? When the hell did you lose that superstition bone?"

"About the time that my Humvee was blown up, and when Evan's was, Everett's too. Hell, about the time that you almost fell out of the sky in your plane. Or when Elliot was nearly shot to death trying to help one of his men. So, yes, I pretty much lost all superstition when trying to toe the line ended up in near death and maiming."

I met my brother's gaze, that familiar pang thinking about all that we had lost and almost lost over the past few years.

East muttered under his breath, shaking his head. "And I sound more and more like Evan these days rather than myself."

I squeezed his shoulder and let out a breath, thinking of our brother who grunted more than spoke these days. "It's okay. We've been through a lot. But we're here."

Somehow, we were here. I wasn't quite sure if we had made the right decision about two years ago when we had formed this plan, or rather *I* had formed this plan, but there was no going back. We were in it, and we were going to have to find a way to make it work, flooded former tornado shelters and all.

East sighed. "I'll work on this now. Then I'll head on over to the main house. I have a few things to work on there."

"You know, we can hire you help. I know we had all the contractors and everything to work with us for some of the rebuilds and rehabs, but we can hire someone else for you on a day-to-day basis."

My brother shook his head. "We may be able to afford it, but I'd rather save that for a rainy day. Because when it rains, it pours here, and flash flooding is a major threat in this part of Texas." He winked as he said it, mixing his metaphors, and I just shook my head.

"You just let me know if you need it."

"You're the CEO, brother of mine, not the CFO. That's Everett."

"True, but we did talk about it so we can work on it." I paused, thinking about what other expenses might show up. "And what do you need to do with the villa?"

The villa was the main house where most things

happened on the property. It contained the lobby, library, and atrium. My apartment was also on the top floor, so I could be there for emergencies. Our innkeeper lived on the other side of the house, but I was in the main loft because this was my project, my baby.

My other brothers, all five of them, lived in cabins on the property. We lived together, worked together, ate together, and fought together. We were the Wilder brothers. It was what we did.

I had left to join the Air Force at seventeen, having graduated early, leaving behind my kid brothers and sister. After nearly twenty years of doing what we needed to in order to survive, we hadn't spent as much time with one another as I would have liked. We hadn't been stationed together, so we hadn't seen one another for longer than holidays or in passing.

But now we were together. At least most of us. So I was going to make this work, even if it killed me.

East finally answered my question. "I just have to fix a door that's a little too squeaky in one of the guestrooms. Not a big deal."

I raised a brow. "That's it?"

"It's one of the many things on my list. Thankfully, this place is big enough that I always have something to do. It's an unending list. And that the winery has its own team to work on all of that shit, because I'm not in the mood to learn to deal with any of the complicated machinery that comes with that world."

I snorted. "Honestly, same. I'm glad there are people that know what the fuck they're doing when it comes to wine making so that didn't have to be the two of us."

I left my brother to this job, knowing he liked time on his own, just like the rest of us did, and went to dry my boots. I was working by myself for most of the day, in interviews and other "boss business," as Elliot called it, so I had to focus and get clean.

I wasn't in the mood to deal with interviews, but it was part of my job. We had to fill positions that hadn't been working out over the past year, some more than others.

Wilder Retreat was a place that hadn't been even a spark in my mind my entire life. No, I had been too busy being a career military man—getting in my twenty, moving up the ranks, and ending up as a Lieutenant Colonel before I got out. I had been a commander of a squadron, and yet, it felt like I didn't know how to command where I was now.

When my sister Eliza had lost her husband when he was on deployment, it had been the last domino to fall in the Wilder brothers' military career. I had been ready to get out with twenty years in, knowing I needed a career outside of being a Lieutenant Colonel.

I wasn't even forty yet, and the term retirement was a misnomer, but that's what happened when it came to my former job.

East had been getting out around that time for reasons of his own, and then Evan had been forced to. I rubbed my hand over my chest, that familiar pain, remembering the phone call from one of Evan's commanders when Evan had been hurt.

I thought I'd lost my baby brother then, and we nearly had. Everett had gotten hurt too, and Elijah and Elliot had needed out for their own reasons. Losing our baby sister's husband had just pushed us forward.

Finding out that Eliza's husband had been a cheating asshole had just cemented the fact that we needed to spend more time together as a family so we could be there for one another.

In retrospect, it would have been nice if Eliza would have been able to come down to Texas with us, to our suburb outside of San Antonio. Only, she had fallen in love again, with a man with a big family and a good heart up in Fort Collins, Colorado. She was still up there and traveled down enough that we actually got to get to know our sister again.

It was weird to think that, after so many years of always seeing each other in passing or through video calls, most of us were here, opening up a business. And all because I had been losing my mind.

Wilder Retreat and Winery was a villa and wedding venue outside of San Antonio. We were in hill country, at least what passed for hill country in South Texas, and the place had been owned by a former Air Force General who had wanted to retire and sell the place, since his kid didn't want it.

It was a large spread that used to be a ranch back in the day, nearly one hundred acres that the original owners had taken from a working ranch, and instead of making it a dude ranch or something similar, like others did around here, they'd added a winery using local help. We were close enough to Fredericksburg that it made sense in terms of the soil and weather. They had been able to add on additions, so it wasn't just the winery. Someone could come for the day for a winery tour or even a retreat tour, but most people came for the weekend or for a whole week. There were cabins and a farmhouse where we held weddings, dances, or other events. We had some chickens and ducks that gave us eggs, and goats that seemed to have a mind of their own and provided milk for cheese. Then there was the main annex, which housed all the equipment for the retreat villa.

The winery had its own section of buildings, and it was far bigger than anything I would have ever thought that we could handle. But, between the six of us, we did.

And the only reason we could even afford it, because one didn't afford something like this on a military salary, even with a decent retirement plan, was because of our uncles.

Our uncles, Edward and Edmond Wilder, had owned Wilder Wines down in Napa, California, for years. They had done well for themselves, and when we had been kids, we had gone out to visit. Evan had been the one that had clung to it and had been interested in wine making before he had changed his mind and gone into the military like the rest of us.

That was why Evan was in charge of the winery itself now. Because he knew what he was doing, even if he'd growled and said he didn't. Either way though, the place was huge, had multiple working parts at all times, and we had a staff that needed us. But when the uncles had died, they had left the money from the sale of the winery to us in equal parts. Eliza had taken hers to invest for her future children, and the rest of us had pooled our money together to buy this place and make it ours. A lot of the staff from the old owner had stayed, but some had left as well. Because they didn't want new owners who had no idea what they were doing, or they just retired. Either way, we were over a year in and doing okay.

Except for two positions that made me want to groan.

I had an interview with who would be our third wedding planner since we started this. The main component of the retreat was to have an actual wedding venue. To be able to host parties, and not just wine tours. Elliot was our major event planner that helped with our yearly and seasonal minute details, but he didn't want anything to do with the actual weddings. That was a whole other skill set, and so we wanted a wedding planner. We had gone through two wedding planners now, and we needed to hire a third. The first one had lied on her résumé, had given references that were her friends who had lied and had even created websites that were all fabrication, all so she could get into the business. Which, I understood, getting into the business is one thing. However, lying was another. Plus, we needed someone with actual experience because we didn't have any ourselves. We were going out on a limb here with this whole retreat business, and it was all because I had the harebrained idea of getting our family to work together, get along, and get to know one another. I wanted us to have a future, to be our own bosses.

And it was so far over my head that I knew that if I didn't get reliable help, we were going to fail.

Later, I had a meeting with that potential wedding planner. But first, I had to see what the fuck that smell was coming from the main kitchen in the villa.

The second wedding planner we hired was a guy with great and *true* references, one who was good at his job but hated everything to do with my brothers and me. He had hated the idea of the retreat and how rustic it was, even though we were in fucking South Texas. Yes, the buildings look slightly European because that was the theme that the original owners had gone for. Still, the guy had hated us, hadn't listened to us, and had called us white trash before he had walked away, jumped into his convertible, and sped off down the road, leaving us without help. He had been rude to our guests, and now Elliot was the one having to plan weddings for the past three weeks. My brother was going to strangle me soon if we didn't hire someone. And this person was going to be our last hope. As soon as she showed up, that was.

I looked down on my watch and tried to plan the rest of my day. I had thirty minutes to figure out what the hell was going on in the kitchen, and then I had to go to the meeting.

I nodded at a few guests who were sipping wine and eating a cheese plate and then at our innkeeper, Naomi. Naomi's honey-brown hair was cut in an angled bob that lit her face, and she grinned at me.

"Hello there, Boss Man," she whispered. "You might need to go to the kitchen."

"Do I want to know?" I asked with a grumble.

"I'm not sure. But I am going to go check in our next guest, and then Elliott needs to meet with the Henderson couple."

"He'll be there." I didn't say that Elliot would rather chew off his own arm rather than deal with this, considering we had a family event coming in, one that Elliot was on target with planning. The wedding for next year was an important one, so we needed to work on it.

Naomi was a fantastic innkeeper, far more organized than any of us—and that was saying something since my brothers and I knew our way around schedules, to-do lists, and spreadsheets. Naomi was personable, smiled, and kept us on our toes.

Without her, I knew we wouldn't be able to do this. Hell, without Amos, our vineyard manager, I knew that Evan and Elijah wouldn't be able to handle the winery as they did. Naomi and Amos had come with the place when we had bought it, and I would be forever grateful that they had decided to stay on.

I gave Naomi another nod, then headed back to the kitchen and nearly walked right back out.

Tony stood there, a scowl on his face and his hands on his hips. "I don't understand what the fuck is wrong with this oven."

"What's going on?" I asked as Everett stood by Tony. Everett was my quiet brother with usually a small smile on his face, only right then it looked like he was ready to scream.

I didn't know why Everett was even there since he was part responsible for the financials side of the company and usually worked with Elliot these days. Maybe he had come to the kitchen after the smell of burning as I had after Naomi's prodding.

Tony threw his hands in the air. "What's going on? This stove is a piece of shit. All of it is a piece of shit. I'm tired of this rustic place. I thought I would be coming to a Michelin star restaurant. To be my own chef. Instead, I have to make English breakfasts and pancakes with bananas. I might as well be at a bed and breakfast."

I pinched the bridge of my nose. "We're an inn, not a bed and breakfast."

"But I serve breakfast. That's all I do these days. That and cheese platters. Nobody comes for dinner. Nobody comes for lunch."

That was a lie. Tony worked for the winery and the retreat itself and served all the meals. But Tony wanted to go crazy with the menu, to try new and fantastical items that just weren't going to work here.

And I had a feeling I was going to throw up if I wasn't careful.

"I quit," Tony snapped, and I knew right then, it was done for. I was done.

"You can't quit," I growled while Everett held back a sigh.

"Yes, I can. I'm done. I'm done with you and this ranch. You're not cowboys. You're not even Texans. You're just people moving in on our territory." And with that, Tony stomped away, throwing his chef's apron on the ground.

I was thankful that the kitchen was on the other side of the library and front area, where most of the guests were if they weren't out on one of the tours of the area and city that Elliott had arranged for them. That was the whole point of this retreat. They could come visit, and could relax, or we could set them up on a tour of downtown San Antonio, or Canyon Lake, or any of the other places that were nearby.

And yet, Tony had just thrown a wrench into all of that. I didn't know what was worse, the smell of burning, Tony leaving, the water in the basement that wasn't truly a basement, or the fact that I was going to smell like charred food and wet jeans when I went to go meet this wedding planner.

"You're going to need to hire a new cook," Everett whispered.

I looked at my brother, at the man who did his best to make sure we didn't go bankrupt, and I wanted to just grumble. "I figured."

"I can help for now, but you know I'm only part-time. I can't stay away from my twins for too long," Sandy said as she came forward to take the pan off the stove. "I wish I could do full time, but this is all I can do for now."

Sandy had come back from maternity leave after we had already opened the retreat. She had been on with the former owners and was brilliant. But she had a right to be a mom and not want to work full time. I understood that, and I knew that Sandy didn't want to handle a whole kitchen by herself. She liked her position as a sous chef.

I was going to have to figure out what to do. Again.

"I'll get it done," I said while rubbing my temples.

"You know what we need to do," Everett whispered, and I shook my head.

"He'll kill us."

"Maybe, but it'll be worth it in the end. And speaking of, don't you have that interview soon? Or do you want me to take it?" His gaze tracked to my jeans.

I shook my head. "No, help Sandy."

Everett winced. "Just because I know how to slice an onion, it doesn't mean I'm good at cooking."

"I'm sorry, did you just say you could slice an onion? Get to it," Sandy put in with a smile, pointing at the sink. "Wash those hands."

"I cannot believe I just said that out loud. I just

stepped right into it," Everett said with a sigh. "Go to the interview. You know what to ask."

"I do. And I hope we don't get screwed this time."

"You know, if we're lucky, we'll get someone as good as Roy's wedding planner, or at least that woman that we met. You know who she is." Everett grinned like a cat with the canary.

I narrowed my eyes. "Don't bring her up."

"Oh, I can't help it. A single dance, and you were drawn to her."

"What dance? You know what? No, I don't have time. We have to work on lunch and dinner. Tell me while you work," Sandy added with a wink.

Everett leaned toward her as he washed his hands. "Well, you see, there was this dance, and he met the perfect woman, and then she got engaged."

Sandy's eyes widened. "Engaged? How did that happen? She was dating someone else?" she asked as she looked at me.

I pinched the bridge of my nose. "It was at Roy's place when we were looking at the venue to see if we wanted to buy the retreat here." I sighed, I knew if I just let it all out, she would move on from this conversation, and I would never have to deal with it again. "Somehow, I ended up at a wedding there, caught the garter. This woman caught the bouquet, and she happened to be the wedding planner. We danced, we laughed, and as she walked away, her boyfriend got down on one knee and proposed."

"No way!" She leaned forward with a fierce look on her face, her eyes bright. "What did she say?"

"I have no clue. I left." I ignored whatever feeling might want to show up at that thought. Everett gave me a glance, and I shook my head. "Enough of that. Yes, the wedding that she did was great, but I honestly have no idea who she is, and she has a job. She doesn't need to work here." And I didn't know what I would do if I saw her again or had to work with her. There had been such an intense connection that I knew it would be awkward as hell. But thankfully, she had her own business and wasn't going to come to the Wilder Retreat for a job.

I left Sandy and Everett on their own, knowing that they were capable, at least for now. And I knew who we would have to hire if she said yes, and if my other brother didn't kill me first.

I washed my hands in the sink on the way out, grateful that at least I looked somewhat decent, if not a little disheveled, and made my way out front, hoping that the wedding planner who came in through the doors would be the one that would stick. Because we needed some good luck. After the day we've had, we needed some good luck.

I turned the corner and nearly tripped over my feet.

Because, of course, fate was this way.

It was her.

Of all the wedding planners from all the wedding venues, it was her.

In the mood to read another family saga? Meet the Wilder Brothers in One Way Back to Me!

Also from Carrie Ann Ryan

The Montgomery Ink Legacy Series:

Book 1: Bittersweet Promises (Leif & Brooke)

Book 2: At First Meet (Nick & Lake)

Book 2.5: Happily Ever Never (May & Leo)

Book 3: Longtime Crush (Sebastian & Raven)

Book 4: Best Friend Temptation (Noah, Ford, and Greer)

Book 4.5: Happily Ever Maybe (Jennifer & Gus)

Book 5: Last First Kiss (Daisy & Hugh)

Book 6: His Second Chance (Kane & Phoebe)

Book 7: One Night with You (Kingston & Claire)

Book 8: Accidentally Forever (Crew & Aria)

Book 9: Last Chance Seduction (Lexington & Mercy)

Book 10: Kiss Me Forever (Brooklyn & Reece)

Book 11: His Guilty Pleasure (Dash & Aly)

Book 12: Maybe it's You (Riley & Gage)

The Cage Family

Book 1: The Forever Rule (Aston & Blakely)

Book 2: An Unexpected Everything (Isabella & Weston)

Book 3: If You Were Mine (Dorian & Harper)

Book 4: One Quick Obsession (Hudson & Scarlett)

Book 5: Pretend it's Forever (Sophia & Carson)

Book 6: Wish it Were You (Flynn & Luna)

Ashford Creek

Book 1: Legacy (Callum & Felicity)

Book 2: Crossroads (Bodhi & Kiera)

Book 3: Westward (Atlas & Elizabeth)

Book 4: Patience (Teagan & Rush)

Clover Lake

Book 1: Always a Fake Bridesmaid (Livvy & Ewan)

Book 2: Accidental Runaway Groom (Jamie & Sharp)

Book 3: His Practically Fake Proposal (Galen & Addy)

The Wilder Brothers Series:

Book 1: One Way Back to Me (Eli & Alexis)

Book 2: Always the One for Me (Evan & Kendall)

Book 3: The Path to You (Everett & Bethany)

Book 4: Coming Home for Us (Elijah & Maddie)

Book 5: Stay Here With Me (East & Lark)

Book 6: Finding the Road to Us (Elliot, Trace, and Sidney)

Book 7: Moments for You (Ridge & Aurora)

Book 7.5: A Wilder Wedding (Amos & Naomi)

Book 8: Forever For Us (Wyatt & Ava)

Book 9: Pieces of Me (Gabriel & Briar)

Book 10: Endlessly Yours (Brooks & Rory)

The Falling for the Cassidy Brothers Series:

(Formerly the First Time Series)

Book 1: Good Time Boyfriend (Heath & Devney)

Book 2: Last Minute Fiancé (Luca & Addison)

Book 3: Second Chance Husband (August & Paisley)

Montgomery Ink Denver:

Book 0.5: Ink Inspired (Shep & Shea)

Book 0.6: Ink Reunited (Sassy, Rare, and Ian)

Book 1: Delicate Ink (Austin & Sierra)

Book 1.5: Forever Ink (Callie & Morgan)

Book 2: Tempting Boundaries (Decker and Miranda)

Book 3: Harder than Words (Meghan & Luc)

Book 3.5: Finally Found You (Mason & Presley)

Book 4: Written in Ink (Griffin & Autumn)

Book 4.5: Hidden Ink (Hailey & Sloane)

Book 5: Ink Enduring (Maya, Jake, and Border)

Book 6: Ink Exposed (Alex & Tabby)

Book 6.5: Adoring Ink (Holly & Brody)

Book 6.6: Love, Honor, & Ink (Arianna & Harper)

Book 7: Inked Expressions (Storm & Everly)

Book 7.3: Dropout (Grayson & Kate)

Book 7.5: Executive Ink (Jax & Ashlynn)

Book 8: Inked Memories (Wes & Jillian)

Book 8.5: Inked Nights (Derek & Olivia)

Book 8.7: Second Chance Ink (Brandon & Lauren)

Book 8.5: Montgomery Midnight Kisses (Alex & Tabby Bonus(

Bonus: Inked Kingdom (Stone & Sarina)

Montgomery Ink: Colorado Springs

Book 1: Fallen Ink (Adrienne & Mace)

Book 2: Restless Ink (Thea & Dimitri)

Book 2.5: Ashes to Ink (Abby & Ryan)

Book 3: Jagged Ink (Roxie & Carter)

Book 3.5: Ink by Numbers (Landon & Kaylee)

The Montgomery Ink: Boulder Series:

Book 1: Wrapped in Ink (Liam & Arden)

Book 2: Sated in Ink (Ethan, Lincoln, and Holland)

Book 3: Embraced in Ink (Bristol & Marcus)

Book 3: Moments in Ink (Zia & Meredith)

Book 4: Seduced in Ink (Aaron & Madison)

Book 4.5: Captured in Ink (Julia, Ronin, & Kincaid)

Book 4.7: Inked Fantasy (Secret ??)

Book 4.8: A Very Montgomery Christmas (The Entire Boulder Family)

The Montgomery Ink: Fort Collins Series:

Book 1: Inked Persuasion (Jacob & Annabelle)

Book 2: Inked Obsession (Beckett & Eliza)

Book 3: Inked Devotion (Benjamin & Brenna)

Book 3.5: Nothing But Ink (Clay & Riggs)

Book 4: Inked Craving (Lee & Paige)

Book 5: Inked Temptation (Archer & Killian)

The Promise Me Series:

Book 1: Forever Only Once (Cross & Hazel)

Book 2: From That Moment (Prior & Paris)

Book 3: Far From Destined (Macon & Dakota)

Book 4: From Our First (Nate & Myra)

The Whiskey and Lies Series:

Book 1: Whiskey Secrets (Dare & Kenzie)

Book 2: Whiskey Reveals (Fox & Melody)

Book 3: Whiskey Undone (Loch & Ainsley)

The Gallagher Brothers Series:

Book 1: Love Restored (Graham & Blake)

Book 2: Passion Restored (Owen & Liz)

Book 3: Hope Restored (Murphy & Tessa)

The Carr Family Series:

(Formerly the Less Than Series)

Book 1: Breathless With Her (Devin & Erin)

Book 2: Reckless With You (Tucker & Amelia)

Book 3: Shameless With Him (Caleb & Zoey)

The Fractured Connections Series:

Book 1: Breaking Without You (Cameron & Violet)

Book 2: Shouldn't Have You (Brendon & Harmony)

Book 3: Falling With You (Aiden & Sienna)

Book 4: Taken With You (Beckham & Meadow)

The Campus Roommates Series:

(Formerly the On My Own Series)

Book 0.5: My First Glance

Book 1: My One Night (Dillon & Elise)

Book 2: My Rebound (Pacey & Mackenzie)

Book 3: My Next Play (Miles & Nessa)

Book 4: My Bad Decisions (Tanner & Natalie)

The Ravenwood Coven Series:

Book 1: Dawn Unearthed

Book 2: Dusk Unveiled

Book 3: Evernight Unleashed

The Aspen Pack Series:

Book 1: Etched in Honor
Book 2: Hunted in Darkness
Book 3: Mated in Chaos
Book 4: Harbored in Silence
Book 5: Marked in Flames

The Talon Pack:

Book 1: Tattered Loyalties
Book 2: An Alpha's Choice
Book 3: Mated in Mist
Book 4: Wolf Betrayed
Book 5: Fractured Silence
Book 6: Destiny Disgraced
Book 7: Eternal Mourning
Book 8: Strength Enduring
Book 9: Forever Broken
Book 10: Mated in Darkness
Book 11: Fated in Winter

Redwood Pack Series:

Book 0.5: An Alpha's Path
Book 1: A Taste for a Mate
Book 2: Trinity Bound
Book 2.5: A Night Away

Book 3: Enforcer's Redemption
Book 3.5: Blurred Expectations
Book 3.7: Forgiveness
Book 4: Shattered Emotions
Book 5: Hidden Destiny
Book 5.5: A Beta's Haven
Book 6: Fighting Fate
Book 6.5: Loving the Omega
Book 6.7: The Hunted Heart
Book 7: Wicked Wolf

The Elements of Five Series:

Book 1: From Breath and Ruin
Book 2: From Flame and Ash
Book 3: From Spirit and Binding
Book 4: From Shadow and Silence

Dante's Circle Series:

Book 1: Dust of My Wings
Book 2: Her Warriors' Three Wishes
Book 3: An Unlucky Moon
Book 3.5: His Choice
Book 4: Tangled Innocence
Book 5: Fierce Enchantment
Book 6: An Immortal's Song
Book 7: Prowled Darkness
Book 8: Dante's Circle Reborn

Holiday, Montana Series:

Book 1: Charmed Spirits

Book 2: Santa's Executive

Book 3: Finding Abigail

Book 4: Her Lucky Love

Book 5: Dreams of Ivory

The Branded Pack Series:

(Written with Alexandra Ivy)

Book 1: Stolen and Forgiven

Book 2: Abandoned and Unseen

Book 3: Buried and Shadowed

About the Author

Carrie Ann Ryan is the New York Times and USA Today bestselling author of contemporary, paranormal, and young adult romance. Her works include the Montgomery Ink, Redwood Pack, Fractured Connections, and Elements of Five series, which have sold over 3.0 million books worldwide. She started writing while in graduate school for her advanced degree in chemistry and hasn't stopped since. Carrie Ann has written over seventy-five novels and novellas with more in the works. When she's not losing herself in her emotional and action-packed worlds, she's reading as much as she can while wrangling her clowder of cats who have more followers than she does.

www.CarrieAnnRyan.com

www.ingramcontent.com/pod-product-compliance
Lightning Source LLC
LaVergne TN
LVHW030606120526
838644LV00054B/1402

* 9 7 8 1 6 3 6 9 5 6 0 1 5 *